PRAISE FOR *A DISGUISE TO DIE FOR*

"Meet Margo Tamblyn, the newest, savviest, smartest heroine to join the cozy mystery world. Her style, creativity, and courage make *A Disguise to Die For*, the first in author Diane Vallere's wonderful new Costume Shop Mystery series, a must-read for sure! Weave in a quirky cast of characters, a fascinating setting, a fast-paced plot, and yummy recipes, and you have a thoroughly appealing whodunit that will keep you guessing all-night long."

—Kate Carlisle, *New York Times* bestselling author

"Margo Tamblyn is in the business of creating new identities in costume—the perfect concept for a mystery series. Both madcap and moving, *A Disguise to Die For* has the right amount of humor, poignancy, and danger for a most irresistible whodunit. Highly recommended!"

—Naomi Hirahara, Edgar® Award–winning author of *Grave on Grand Avenue*

"A fresh, funny voice, irresistible characters—and oh, the costumes! No disguising the fact that Diane Vallere's new cozy is a winner."

—Lucy Burdette, national bestselling author of *Fatal Reservations*

D1012799

continued . . .

Berkley Prime Crime titles by Diane Vallere

Material Witness Mysteries

SUEDE TO REST
CRUSHED VELVET

Costume Shop Mysteries

A DISGUISE TO DIE FOR

A Disguise to Die For

DIANE VALLERE

BERKLEY PRIME CRIME, NEW YORK

An imprint of Penguin Random House LLC
375 Hudson Street, New York, New York 10014

A DISGUISE TO DIE FOR

A Berkley Prime Crime Book / published by arrangement with the author

ISBN: 978-0-425-27828-4

PUBLISHING HISTORY
Berkley Prime Crime mass-market edition / February 2016

PRINTED IN THE UNITED STATES OF AMERICA

10 9 8 7 6 5 4 3 2 1

Cover illustration by Mick McGinty.
Cover design by Sarah Oberrender.
Interior text design by Kelly Lipovich.

This is a work of fiction. Names, characters, places, and incidents either are the product of
the author's imagination or are used fictitiously, and any resemblance to actual persons,
living or dead, business establishments, events, or locales is entirely coincidental.

PUBLISHER'S NOTE: The recipes contained in this book are to be followed exactly as
written. The publisher is not responsible for your specific health or allergy needs that may
require medical supervision. The publisher is not responsible for any adverse reactions to
the recipes contained in this book.

Penguin
Random
House

To Jessica Faust. You know what you did.

Acknowledgments

Many thanks to Yumiko Hoshiyama for the gracious use of her name and to Megumi Higa for being my consultant and helping me understand Japanese-American culture.

Thank you to Josh Hickman, who never questioned my desire to take a vacation in Primm, Nevada, and was adventurous enough to spend a few days wandering around small desert towns in search of a location for Proper City. Also for his help in the fine art of recipe writing, a talent in which I am sorely lacking.

My heartfelt appreciation to Gigi Pandian, whose firm grasp of deadlines helps me achieve my own.

I owe a lifetime of gratitude to Jennifer Schlegel, who reminds me that you can cherish your inner four-year-old self and still be an adult with a cause, and to Kendel Lynn, who inspires me to achieve something new every single day.

Thank you to my editor, Katherine Pelz, whose astute comments made the book even better than I'd hoped, and to my copyeditor Randie Lipkin, cover illustrator Mick McGinty, cover designer Sarah Oberrender, and the rest of the fabulous team at Berkley Prime Crime/Penguin Random House. I am lucky to have them in my corner.

This series would not exist if not for my agent, Jessica Faust. My teddy bear claims credit, but we both know the truth.

Chapter 1

"**GIVE ME THE** knife," demanded the cranky man in the wheelchair.

"I don't think so," I said.

"I'm not playing, Margo. Give me the knife."

"Why? I already told you I could do it. It's just going to take longer than I thought."

"That's because you can't climb the ladder in those silly boots."

"Why are you so worried about my go-go boots? You bought them for me. Besides, you're the one wearing two different shoes."

My dad—the cranky man in the wheelchair—looked down at his feet. He wore one brown wing tip and one black.

"I pay that nurse too much to end up leaving the house wearing two different shoes," he said. "And this stupid chair makes everything worse. If I can get up and down the stairs okay, then I don't need it."

"You're in that chair because you're still weak. The doctors don't want you running all over the place and having a second heart attack. And the nurse didn't mismatch your shoes on purpose. Most of the nurses don't expect to have such colorful patients."

He stuck his feet out in front of him and shook his head at the sight of the mismatched shoes. "I said brown wing tips. How hard is that?"

I was pretty sure my dad wasn't used to relying on a woman to dress him—nurses or otherwise. He'd been a widower since my mother died giving birth to me thirty-two years ago. While growing up, I'd notice the way women who came into the costume shop looked at him in his paisley ascots, tweed blazers, and dress pants. He was a catch, my father. And now that he was recovering from an unexpected heart attack, he was a cranky, stuck-in-his-ways catch that the nurses of Proper City Medical Care had the distinct pleasure of dressing, at least until I'd arrived. I wondered if the mismatched-shoe situation was payback for his attitude.

"You're going to have to let me help you. Got that?" I said, pointing an accusatory finger at his nose. He swatted it away.

"It's not right. I'm your father. I'm supposed to take care of you, not the other way around."

"I'm a grown-up now."

"You're too grown-up, if you ask me." He glared at my outfit a second time.

"What? We have this exact same outfit in the '60s section of the store." I pointed to the back corner of the shop, where a kaleidoscope mural in neon shades covered the walls.

The store in question was Disguise DeLimit, our family's costume shop. The store had been around far longer than I had, starting sometime in the '70s by a couple who had worked in the movie business in Hollywood. My dad had started as a stock boy before he was old enough to work legally, and slowly graduated first to salesperson and then manager.

Eventually, the couple decided their time running the store was over. Turns out Dad had been saving for a rainy day and bought them out, inventory and all. Shortly after he became owner he met my mother and they fell in love. They married and planned to start a family and run the shop together. Two years later, the love of his life was gone and in her place was a newborn baby: me.

"Besides, you always said the fact that my outfits are inspired by costumes in our inventory was good for business. Remember?"

He grunted an answer and rolled back to the boxes.

The outfit that ruffled his feathers was a mod, zip-front minidress colorblocked in red, white, blue, and black. It ended midthigh, which left an expanse of skin between the bottom of the hem and the top of my white patent leather boots.

The summer before I moved out of Proper, I bought a box of patterns from the '60s at a yard sale and made myself this dress. The bandleader at the local high school stopped me one day and asked where I got it. They were planning a Beatles tribute concert and thought dresses like mine would be perfect for the choir. He came to the store and placed an order, and I spent the next two weeks knocking out dresses just like it. One by one the girls came in and bought up our inventory of white patent leather boots, plastic hoop earrings, and colorful fishnet stockings. I didn't always dress like a go-go dancer, but when I got the call from Nurse Number Three that my dad was trying to inventory the costume shop against her direction, there hadn't been time to change. So here I was in the white patent leather go-go boots he'd bought me before I moved to Las Vegas seven years ago—the perfect complement for my mod minidress but not so practical for balancing on a ladder while your father glares at you—reaching for a rubber knife that someone had hung on the Western wall by the fake pistols and plastic holsters. Everybody knows you don't bring a knife to a gunfight.

I extended my reach the way I'd been taught in the ballet class I took last year and nudged the peg until the knife fell. It dropped—the peg, not the knife—and landed by my dad's brown shoe. The knife landed by his black one. I picked up both and set them on the counter.

"Dad, I don't get why this is so important. Inventory can wait until you're better."

"We're heading into spring. Remember what that means? Outdoor birthday parties and the Sagebrush Festival. I have to know what props we already have stocked so I can start planning concepts."

"You can't expect to carry on business as usual while you're recovering. It's too much."

"That's right. I can't, but you can. You grew up here. You know as much about the costume business as I do."

He was right. While other children were playing on backyard jungle gyms, I was playing in the store. My birthday presents had come from costume suppliers and my clothes had come from our inventory. By the time I'd turned sixteen, it was natural for me to work part-time hours after high school.

After graduation, I took the occasional night course but most of my time had been inside these four walls. I'd been responsible for painting the walls around the gangster clothes black with white chalk stripes and also the psychedelic flower-power mural by our '60s section. It was my dad who encouraged me to move away—he wanted to make sure I knew there was a whole world out there before I accepted Proper City as my home base—and kicked me out on my twenty-fifth birthday. I moved to Las Vegas—which was only about forty miles from Proper but might as well have been the moon for how different it was—and experienced independence for the first time. It was far enough to feel as though I was on my own but close enough to come home for major holidays. I'd been in Vegas ever since.

"I can't stay indefinitely. You know that. I think you have to sit this season out."

"Nobody's sitting anything out. You got that, sister?" asked a black woman from the doorway. She held a small, white bichon frise under one arm. His fur was brushed out in the same manner as her natural Afro.

I rushed forward and flung my arms around her. "Ebony!"

The small dog yipped from inside the hug. I backed away and patted his puffy head. "Hello to you too, Ivory," I said.

The woman assessed me from head to toe. "Margo Tamblyn, as I live and breathe. You've grown into a fine young lady. I bet this old man wants to take the credit for that, doesn't he?" She winked at me.

"I think we all know you had a little something to do with it."

Ebony Welles was a fifty-six-year-old woman who had lived in Proper City her whole life. College had been out of her financial reach after high school, so instead she started Shindig, her own party planning business, when she graduated. She'd expanded from birthdays to all of the major holidays and a few minor ones too. She wore her hair in a brushed-out Afro and dressed in a largely '70s vibe. She bragged that she could still fit into the clothes she owned in high school, and four out of five days a week she proved it. Considering my wardrobe came from bits and pieces from the costume shop, I didn't think it was all that strange.

Ebony had become a part of my life when I was five. She'd been hired to plan an anniversary party for the local dachshund society. At a loss for inspiration, she'd headed out to clear her mind. My dad had recently redone the windows of Disguise DeLimit in a *Wizard of Oz* theme. Ebony thought it was brilliant. She reserved the six costumes he had on display and ordered flying-monkey costumes for all seventeen dogs. She asked me to help put the wings on the dachshunds and she even let me dress like a Munchkin. The pictures from the party had circulated far and wide, and I hadn't been the same since.

"How long do we have you for?" Ebony asked.

I cut my eyes to my dad before answering. "My boss gave me through the weekend."

"Where are you working?" she asked, her eyes darting to my outfit.

I tugged at the hem of my skirt. "I'm a magician's assistant. I asked a friend to fill in for me while I came here."

"I have an idea. Tell the magician you can't go back to work because we accidentally made you disappear." She slapped my dad's knee and laughed so loud I suspected they could hear her in the pet shop across the street.

Ebony and my dad sometimes acted like they didn't get along, but deep down I knew they were close friends. My dad had never gotten over the death of my mother, and judging from how often people told me I looked like her, I knew the constant reminder must have been hard for him. He'd done the best he could, even if my school clothes had mostly come from Disguise DeLimit. Some days I dressed like a flapper, others, a cowgirl. My wardrobe was more costume than couture, a fashion quirk I attributed to his influence. By the time I started shopping for myself, I found the latest trends lacking a certain spark of individuality. To this day I accessorized with props from our inventory rather than jewelry or scarves from the local department store: a holster with cap guns when I went

Western, white patent leather go-go boots when I felt mod, a top hat and cane when I wore a tuxedo. Getting a job in Las Vegas had been a natural, because everybody in Vegas was in some kind of a costume.

My job history had been spotty at first: receptionist for a real estate agent, vintage clothing store clerk, concession stand clerk for a theater. The big money was as a showgirl, but the fact that I preferred to wear clothes at work kept me at a certain income level. Hey, a girl's gotta have standards.

Eventually I met a fledgling magician who wanted an assistant. I provided my own costume—a black, cutaway tuxedo jacket over a red-sequined bodysuit, fishnets, and pumps—and we hit the circuit. He paid me 20 percent of the take from the door, which paid for my half of the rent and bills. On a good night, I bought steak from the grocery store. On a bad night, I ate ramen noodles.

Ebony was the closest thing I had to a mother. She taught me about makeup, clothing, and men. When I headed off to Vegas for a job, I caught her crying. She said she had something in her eye and I pretended I believed her.

"Listen up, Jerry," she said. "Margo came here because of you, so don't go getting better too fast. She and I have a lot of catching up to do." She put her arm around me and turned me away from him. "How's your love life? Anybody on the horizon?"

"The quality of men in Vegas isn't what you'd think. How about you?"

"Honey, I like my life just the way it is. Can't imagine turning my world upside down for a man."

"How'd you know I was here?" I asked.

"Elementary, my dear Watson," she said in a poorly affected English accent. "I saw the white scooter out front and took a guess. We don't have many scooter riders around here."

"She's lying!" my dad cried out. We both turned to him. He had pulled on a deerstalker hat and held a pipe in his hands. "She made no such deduction. I told her you were on your way."

Not one to let the fun pass me by, I pulled a tweed cape from a circular rack and draped it over my shoulders. "So the evidence points to a conspiracy," I said, brows furrowed. "Number one: information about my arrival was discussed behind my back. Number two: a suspicious white scooter is parked in front of the store. Number three: I smell sugar cookies, and you know they're my favorite. The mystery isn't how you knew, but what you plan to do about it."

A slow clap filled the air. All three of us turned our heads toward the door. It had been propped open since Ebony arrived, and a young blond man now filled the entrance. He wore a short-sleeved green polo shirt, madras plaid shorts, and navy blue canvas deck shoes. His glowing tan set off blue eyes and white teeth. I got the feeling he spent a lot of time on a golf course or a boat—or both.

"Cheesy, but charming," he said. "Not what I had in mind, though." He entered the store and ran his hand over a rack of colorful feather boas that hung inside the entrance. When the orange boa fell through his fingertips, he turned his attention back to us.

My dad rolled his wheelchair out from behind the counter. "Hello, Blitz," he said. "Octavius Roman says you rented out his facility space for your birthday party. You must be busy with all of the last-minute details. What brings you to Disguise DeLimit?"

"Octavius can't accommodate me. Roman Gardens had a flood in its kitchen and canceled. My birthday is this weekend and the entire plan is out the window."

"That's too bad," Ebony said. Her fingers rubbed the gold of the medallion pendant she always wore. She let go of the necklace and leaned back against the counter on one elbow, holding her other hand in front of her as if she was inspecting her manicure. "This town has come to expect an extravaganza from you. It's going to be hard to find someone to plan a full-blown party in less than a week."

The blond man scowled. "Why do you think I tracked you down here? Nobody else will even consider it."

"Who says I will?" Ebony said.

"I have money. Lots of it."

"I don't want your money," Ebony said.

"You were more than happy to take my dad's money twenty years ago. Are you going to pretend things are all that different now?"

Ebony stiffened. Ivory bared his teeth and growled at Blitz. I moved my eyes back and forth between Ebony and Blitz, gauging the number from one to ten that would best correspond with Ebony's reaction. I didn't know who this guy was, but I didn't like what he was implying about her past.

"We haven't met yet," I said. I stepped forward and held out my hand. "I'm Margo Tamblyn."

"Blitz Manners," he replied. He clamped his hand onto mine pretty hard, squishing my fingertips together. I squeezed back a second too late to block the pain, but soon enough to make it look like everything was fine.

"If I understand the situation correctly, you were planning to have a party at Roman Gardens but they're no longer available because of a flood in their kitchen. You'd like Ebony to put together a new party plan on short notice. Is that correct?" I asked. I used the voice Magic Maynard had taught me to use to divert the crowd's attention from his act. Soft and steady, and pay no attention to the man behind the curtain. Blitz took a couple of extra seconds to reply, but when he did, I nodded and stepped him away from Ebony.

I picked up the pad of paper my dad had been taking inventory on and flipped to a blank page.

"How many guests?"

"Forty."

"That's a pretty big party."

"I'm known for my parties, sweetheart. Are you new around here? Better make it forty-one."

I bit back a laugh at the expense of his come-on and stayed professional. "Do you have a caterer? Music? Theme?"

"Roman Gardens was going to supply everything."

"They must still have the music and theme arranged, even if their location is out. So really, you need a location. That shouldn't be so hard—"

"I canceled everything Octavius had planned and took back my deposit. He's not getting a dime out of me. I need a new plan and I need it fast. The works."

It had been a while since I'd worked at the store, but I knew what he was asking for was borderline impossible. "I'm sorry, but I don't think that's doable."

"Sure it is. That's your business, isn't it?"

"Our business is costumes." I held a hand up and made a sweeping gesture toward the rows of clothing hanging on racks over our heads. "If you have a theme, we can suggest costumes, and you can either rent them or buy them. We do custom costumes too, but that takes time. There's a considerable price break if you rent instead of buy, but the deposit is nonrefundable. If you don't have a theme, we can show you around the store and maybe something will inspire you."

"That skit you were doing when I walked in. What was that for?"

"Skit? We weren't performing a skit." I turned around and looked at my dad. He still wore the deerstalker, but had set the pipe on the counter. "Sherlock Holmes?" I said.

"He's a mystery guy, right? That could be cool. Intellectual. Nobody's done anything like that around here. It'll be highbrow, literary. Yep, I like it. Everybody comes as their favorite detective. Bring out all the famous ones. Perry Mason, Sherlock Holmes, the works. Just remember, keep it young. I'm turning twenty-six, not eighty-six."

"I don't think you understood me. We do costumes, not party planning—"

"But I do," Ebony interjected. She stepped between Blitz and me. "Give me the night to secure the location, entertainment, and catering. Come to my shop tomorrow and we'll work out details."

"There aren't any details to work out." He pulled an envelope out from inside his jacket and tossed it on a table. "Twenty thou should get you started. I'll pay the rest when it's done."

Chapter 2

WE ALL STARED at the thick envelope on the table, but none of us made a move to pick it up.

Blitz turned to me. "You work with the costumes?"

"Yes."

"You're going to turn me into the hottest detective Proper City has ever seen. I'll come back tomorrow to pick up my costume. Better have the rest done by then too, so I can figure out who'll wear what."

"Tomorrow? I can't have forty custom costumes ready in twenty-four hours!"

"Sure you can, toots. Your store's reputation depends on it." He pulled a brown leather billfold out of the back pocket of his shorts and extracted a piece of paper. "My measurements. Make sure it fits in all the right places." He winked.

I didn't take the paper. "I'm sorry. Like I said, I can't hit that deadline."

"I don't think you understand. I just paid you twenty

grand for this gig, and that means I own you. So if I want to pick up costumes tomorrow, then you'll have them ready. Got it, babe?"

He put on a pair of black Ray-Ban sunglasses and flashed teeth that were whiter than my boots. He shut the door behind him, and Ebony threw a pair of fuzzy dice at the door after it closed. I shook my arms to get rid of the heebie-jeebies. Blitz Manners might be used to flashing his smile and getting what he wanted, but I didn't care how much money he threw at us. As far as clientele went, he left much to be desired.

"Who was that guy again?" I asked.

"That guy was trouble," Ebony answered.

I waited for more. My dad wheeled himself to the front of the store and scooped the fuzzy dice from the floor. He wheeled back to the counter and set them on top of the case. "Blitz Manners. Local trust fund baby. His family lives in the mansion at the end of Winnie Lane."

"Winnie Lane. Isn't that part of the new big development? Christopher Robin Crossing?" I asked.

"Yes. When the money moved into Proper, that's where they built."

Ebony spoke up. "There's all sorts of mansions out that direction, like they're afraid to let their property get too close to the rest of us. Pretty silly, all those rich people living in a development named after Winnie-the-Pooh." My dad shot her a look. "Well, it is. Ten years ago one of 'em tried to petition the city council to rename the streets. I guess Piglet Lane doesn't look so fancy even when it's engraved on an invitation."

My dad shook his head at Ebony's insights.

"Those houses were there when I lived here. Why don't I know the name?"

"Those kids went to private schools and then out-of-state colleges. Most of the families that live out that way have their own social circles." He rolled his wheelchair back a few inches and then forward, trying—and failing—to change direction. He rolled the chair back into the same position where he'd been. "As far as I can tell, nobody's said no to Blitz since his father died. He started collecting his inheritance when he turned eighteen. His mother remarried Jack Cannon, but he never had any luck controlling the boy either. Blitz was too far along as a spoiled rich kid. His solution to everything is to throw money at it."

I glanced at the bulging envelope. "What's with the party?"

Ebony spoke up. "There's a competition between the rich kids to outdo each other with their birthday parties. It's been going on for about five years now, I think. Blitz and his friends are currently controlling the game. Grady O'Toole had a hustle party a few months ago. He hired me to provide the catering. I would have loved to design the entire thing, but he gave the job to Candy Girls."

Candy Girls was an operation of women who organized events in Proper. They were started as a postcollege nonprofit by a group of sorority sisters, but when the founders realized the income potential, they were quick to turn their backs on their initial charitable impulses. You could hire Candy Girls to cater, decorate, or simply show up to guarantee a crowd and a decent girl-to-boy ratio at your event.

Even though Candy Girls employed a lot of the women who chose to stay in Proper City, I had never considered working there. Candy Girls were blond, giggly, and popular. They were the kind of women who kept the local salons in business with their highlights and blowouts. I kept my hair in a dark-brown-from-a-box '60s flip with bangs that I trimmed with sewing scissors. It was the way my mom wore her hair for her yearbook photo in 1968. That was my favorite way to remember her. The style worked with just about any costume-inspired outfit I wore. Especially the ones with the go-go boots.

"Why do you think Blitz didn't go to Candy Girls for his party problem?" I asked.

"Rumor is that Blitz's current girlfriend is Grady's ex," Ebony said. "That makes things messy. Besides, Blitz is the kind of person who wants to outdo everybody. If Grady O'Toole's party was the talk of the town and it was done by Candy Girls, then Blitz isn't going to go with Candy Girls. He once threw a casbah party and flew in ten guys from Morocco to put it together."

"Sounds like the competition to outdo each other is pretty steep. What about the kids who don't have trust funds?"

"These parties are a big deal. Most are happy just to get invited." Ebony pulled her sunglasses from a hip pocket and slid them into place. "What am I standing around here talking to you two for? I have a party to plan." She picked up the envelope and thumbed through the bills inside. "Twenty thousand dollars to throw a party in Proper City. Who'da thunk." She set the envelope down, picked up Ivory, and left.

Ebony walked down the sidewalk to a coffee-colored Cadillac Coupe de Ville. She hopped in and drove away, leaving a parking space big enough for three smart cars. I turned back to my dad and asked the question I couldn't shake.

"Dad, what do you think Blitz meant by that comment about Ebony and his dad's money?"

"People like to start rumors. Ignore him."

"But if he's so eager to throw the party of the century, why go with Ebony? Why come to us? Aren't we a little too small-town for him?"

"Just because we live in a small town doesn't mean we *are*

small-town," he said. There was a proud determination to the set of his jaw. "We have five thousand costumes in our inventory, acquired or created over the past forty years. In that time we've gotten bigger than the local costume party circuit. We're known all over Nevada. Some people even tack an extra day onto their Vegas vacations so they can come and see us."

"You know what I meant. Ebony said Blitz flew people in from Morocco last year. You're kind of talking apples and oranges."

"We've been providing costumes for the parties in Proper City for a very long time now and we do it better than anybody. This wheelchair is only temporary and it's not going to change the way we run the store."

He pulled the deerstalker off his head and set it on the glass case. He wheeled over to a circular rack of capes and trench coats. "Blitz wants forty detective costumes. Let's make a list. We can do Sherlock Holmes, Perry Mason, Mike Hammer." He paused. "Who else?"

"What about Trixie Belden, Nancy Drew, and Miss Marple?" I added. "Shaft. Veronica Mars. And Encyclopedia Brown!"

The pencil flew across the paper as he wrote the names down. His expression had changed from determination to enthusiasm. "What do you think? Are you up for this?" he asked.

"Sure am. It'll be like one of those murder mystery parties, only times a hundred. But what about you?"

"I can't do it by myself. It's going to be a lot of work and because of this chair, the brunt of it is going to fall on you."

I pulled on a tweed cape, pulled the deerstalker down over my hair, and caught my reflection. My flip curled up just above my shoulders. My eyes were wide and brown and framed with fake eyelashes. I'd gotten so used to wearing them in Vegas that I felt naked without them. I pulled the hat off and set it next to the register.

"Margo, this is a big opportunity for the store. Candy Girls has expanded from catering to party planning, and I heard they're starting to sell prepackaged costumes. This party would give us a chance to show off what makes us special. Custom costumes. And the money is good. It'll help cover some of my medical bills."

"Don't you have insurance?"

He looked away. "Yes, but there are deductibles to meet."

"Is the shop in trouble?" I lowered myself onto an orange beanbag chair and looked up at him. He spun his wedding ring with the fingers on his right hand like I'd watched him do my whole life.

"If you weren't here, I wouldn't even consider taking this job," he said.

"Then it's settled," I said. I stood up and straightened my dress. "We'd better get to work if we're going to have costumes to show Blitz Manners by tomorrow."

WE spent the next two hours sorting through the inventory for mystery-themed costumes and related accessories. Since my dad was temporarily confined to the wheelchair, he was in charge of props and concepts. I moved around the shop and collected elements that we could modify: trench coats, plaid wool suits, capes, deerstalkers, and fedoras. I assembled Columbo from the suit and tie that went with our traveling salesman costume, a beat-up trench coat that went with our hobo, and a plastic cigar. Rockford was also easy: jeans, plaid shirt, and stick-on sideburns. I designed two Nancy Drews: a '30s one with cloche hat, capelet, and below-the-knee-length skirt, and a '50s one with an argyle sweater, plaid kilt, knee socks, and loafers. I had to flip through most of the skirts in our schoolgirl section to find one that was long enough to be appropriate for a girl detective—not that I believed the woman who wore it would have chosen the modest length. Tom Swift came from our steampunk section, and Cherry Ames, school nurse, came from the medical corner.

I checked in with my dad after the first hour and found him sorting hats, monocles, pipes, and magnifying glasses into piles. "Do you think it's okay to have more than one Sherlock?"

"Why not? Who's to say if he wants to be BBC Sherlock or CBS Sherlock or Robert Downey Jr. Sherlock?"

"What about regular old Sherlock? Tweed cape, tweed hat, gloves, ascot. You know, the classic image of him."

"You heard what Blitz said about keeping things modern."

"That's too bad. If he wants to be Sherlock Holmes, there's pretty much only one way to go so everybody knows who he's supposed to be. I mean, what's he going to do, dress like that guy on the TV show? His Watson isn't even a man!"

"You convinced me." He stroked an imaginary beard and looked up at the ceiling. "Go to the back room and bring me the houndstooth fabric that we used for the *My Fair Lady* costume. The taupe one with the navy, burgundy, and forest green pattern. Better yet, wheel me back there. The sewing shop is set up and I can knock out a cape and trousers while you're working in here."

I stood behind the wheelchair and rolled him backward and then forward, past the cases of colorful makeup, paste jewelry, and other accessories that we didn't hang on the shelves. I stopped next to the bald caps and pulled one out. "Kojak," I said. He nodded, and we continued until we reached the back room.

Behind the interior of the shop was a long, narrow room

set up with various sewing machines and a table for cutting out fabric. Two forms stood like sentries at the end of the room: a male and a female. Large, round metal trash bins held bolts of fabric that protruded out like giant flower stems without blooms.

I didn't know when my dad had first taught himself to sew. I imagined that my mother had been the one to make most of the costumes while he watched the shop and fabricated what needed to be made from wood or sheet metal, but as far as I remembered, our costume assortment had been limited only by what he could create. At an early age I learned how to adapt already-made clothing into costumes by shortening hems, narrowing pants, and hand-sewing patches on second-hand castoffs. We shopped the local thrift stores for items that we could use and, with dye and imagination, created wizards, princesses, hobos, animals, and a whole lot more. By the time I'd graduated high school, I was a pro at turning flea market finds into high-ticket costumes. My *Chicago* collection had been rented by seventeen different groups by the time I moved to Vegas.

It was close to eight when we finished our list. I'd collected items from throughout the shop and had a list of the few remaining props we needed.

"Dad, you look exhausted. Let me wrap things up here and we can finish tomorrow."

"Fine. I'll start dinner. Spaghetti and meatballs sound okay to you?"

"Sounds perfect. Give me fifteen minutes to get things organized and I'll be up to set the table."

The doctors had recommended the wheelchair, and I knew my dad hated it. I watched him wheel himself to the back stairs, lift himself out of the chair, and slowly ascend the staircase. It wouldn't have mattered if we did have a ramp or an elevator. In his mind, the chair was temporary, and he wouldn't allow himself to get used to it.

I found a large plastic bin of hangers and clear garment bags on a shelf behind the cash register and assembled each costume in a bag. Because of the short window of time, we'd expected each person to wear their own footwear, but I made a note with suggestions on index cards and taped them to the front of the hanger with the name of the costume.

Behind me, the door rattled. Blitz Manners was on the sidewalk, surrounded by a gaggle of men around the same age as he was. He stumbled inside. He wore a crooked smile and reeked of beer and cigarettes. He reached out and put a finger under my chin and grinned. A tall man with hair the color of freshly minted pennies and the blue eyes and freckles to go with followed him into the store. The rest of his entourage stayed on the sidewalk out front.

"Let's see what you got for me, babe," Blitz slurred.

"Our store is closed for the night. You can come back tomorrow to see what we've put together."

"I wanted to keep you on your toes." He swayed forward and back, but I didn't think he knew he did it. I looked at the redhead. He grinned and shrugged, like he was used to Blitz doing whatever Blitz wanted to do. I smiled back, and he winked at me.

"The costumes that we finished are over here." I walked him to the ballet barre that held the numbered garment bags. "I think we came up with a nice assortment for you. We have Hercule Poirot, Columbo, Kojak, and Jim Rockford. I assume you'll be inviting women to your party too, right? There's Miss Marple, two Nancy Drews, Cherry Ames, and Veronica Mars. And four different Sherlock costumes: BBC, steampunk, CBS, and a custom classic Sherlock that my father made this afternoon." I bent backward at the waist to put distance between the scent of happy hour and my nose. "Personally, I think it's a standout." I picked up the hanger with the tweed cape and deerstalker.

"Is this some kind of joke?" he asked. He grabbed the hanger from me and threw the costume on the ground. "I thought I told you to keep it hip. These are costumes for an old person's party," he said.

"This is exactly what you asked us for," I said defensively, and bent to scoop the clothes from the ground. "This very costume is the one you saw when you came into the store."

He looked over his shoulder at the guys standing on the sidewalk out front, and stepped back and gave me a full-body scan from my face to my boots, and back up to my face. "Things don't look like they did when I was here earlier. Maybe I didn't communicate clearly enough what I wanted."

He overenunciated his words. I didn't doubt that he was well on his way to passing out, but I also didn't doubt that this was a regular occurrence. It wasn't my problem if Blitz was blitzed. I just wanted him out of the store.

The cowbell over the door clanged and another man entered. He was tall and had broad shoulders. Longish straight black hair was pushed away from his face. There were traces of a beard and mustache that looked more like the product of a couple of days without shaving than a conscious decision to wear facial hair. His features were Asian with a mix of Roman. Black-brown eyes studied me from under strong eyebrows. Aquiline nose. Naturally red lips. I smiled a cautious greeting—cautious because I was alone and didn't want to encourage the rest of the group to enter too—and turned my attention back to Blitz.

"I'm sorry to disappoint you, but this is the best we can do on short notice." I put my hands on the rolling rack and moved it away from him. I picked up the envelope of money from the counter where Ebony had left it and held it out. "Here's your deposit back," I said.

The redhead snickered. "You were right, Blitz, she's not like the rest of them. All the girls we know would have kept the money."

"Shut up, Grady," Blitz said. He kept his eyes on me. The solicitous drunk who had come into the store had turned into a sullen one. He shot a nasty look at the third man who had entered, snatched the envelope of cash from my hand, and turned around and stormed out the door.

Grady leaned forward. "Don't admit defeat yet. He'll change his mind. He always does." He stared at me for a few seconds and then turned and followed Blitz outside.

The third man was gone too. I gave the crowd a couple of seconds to start down the street, and then popped my head out and looked left and right. Blitz's crowd had gone one way, the Asian man was by himself, walking in the other direction. He turned around and caught me watching him. I froze. He pulled a hand out of his jacket pocket and waved tentatively. I waved back in like fashion.

I locked the door, pulled the shades down, and turned out the lights. After moving the rack of costumes to the back of the store by the register, I headed upstairs. Dad was in the kitchen, stirring a pot of marinara sauce.

"What kept you? It sounded like I heard voices," he said.

"Blitz Manners showed up after you left. I told him the store was closed but he didn't seem to care."

"Customers like Blitz don't pay attention to store hours. So how'd it go?" he asked. "Was he impressed with our work?"

"Not really." I dropped into a red vinyl kitchen chair, part of a '50s diner set my dad had scored on one of his flea market trips. "He had a bunch of his friends with him. He said he didn't like what we pulled together. Is this normal?

People throw money at you to spend your day working for them and then they insult your work?"

"No, it's not normal. Last week Molly Cunningham came in and bought five princess costumes for her nieces to wear to her wedding. And the week before that, Black Jack Cannon had a *Maverick*-themed poker party and rented our best Western garb. It's not all bad, Margo. At least Blitz paid in advance."

"When he said he wasn't happy with what we'd pulled together, I gave him back his money."

My dad studied my face. I knew it had been the right thing to do and I knew he knew it too. But I remembered what he'd said about medical bills and I wondered again if there was more—or less—to the store's financial situation than he was letting on.

Chapter 3

A SMOKE-GRAY CAT sauntered up from under the table and ran his head against my dad's pant legs. My dad set down the spoon and sat in a diner chair.

"Is this Soot?" he asked.

"Yep."

"He was just a kitten when I last saw him."

Soot jumped into my dad's lap, turned three circles, and settled into a curled-up position. I ran my hand over the top of Soot's head and he started to purr. The cat, not my dad.

When I moved away from Proper, I'd experienced homesickness in a big way. No family, no friends, nobody to talk to. I adopted a gray kitten from the owner of a candy store next to my apartment building and named him Soot. He had grown from a playful kitten into an ornery cat, but had a sixth sense when it came to sharing his affection with those who needed it. Turns out he was a whiz at catching mice too, which was less than thrilling when I found his catch of the day in one of my shoes. When I left Vegas for Proper City, I packed a suitcase and strapped it to the back of my scooter. And then I hired a taxi to follow me with Soot—in his carrier, of course—in the backseat.

THE next day I dressed in a yellow sweater, khaki skirt, and cowboy boots. I pulled my hair into two low ponytails and put a yellow cowboy hat on my head. I wrapped a belt with two holsters on it around my hips and filled the holsters with plastic pistols. Nobody would think twice about my outfit as long as I was working in the costume shop. When I wore this same outfit to the Whole Foods store last week, I got a couple of stares.

There was a note from my dad on the kitchen table that said he and his buddy Don Digby had taken off for Area 51. What was he thinking? He was recovering from a heart attack. He had no business taking off for parts unknown with Don.

I grabbed my phone and called him. "Where are you?"

"Somewhere on Route 66. Hard to tell."

"I want you to turn around and come back here. I don't think it's a good idea for you to be out and about. You need to rest."

"I talked to my doctor last night and he saw nothing wrong with this trip as long as I took it easy. Don's here, and he was a registered nurse for thirty years before he retired."

"But why now? Why today?"

"I've been in touch with a sci-fi fan who lives in Area 51. He has a collection of costumes that he's been wanting me to appraise. With you there to run the store, the timing was perfect."

"I came back to Proper City to take care of you while you get better. Magic Maynard only gave me through the weekend. When are you coming back? I can't take care of you if you're not here."

"If you take care of the store, it's like you're taking care of me. I'll be back tomorrow, or maybe the next day. If things get busy, call Kirby Grizwitz. His number is taped to the wall to the left of the register. He's in high school now, and he's been working part-time."

"Dad, I don't know about this. I don't want anything to happen to you."

"I can't let this stuff end up on eBay, Margo. Besides, what's going to happen? We're driving five hundred miles through the desert. There's not another car in sight."

"Just be careful," I said.

He left the address and phone number of the hotel where he was planning to stay. We briefly discussed what I needed to know to run the store and made arrangements to talk the following day. We had talked every day since I moved to Las Vegas, even if our conversations sometimes were shorter than the length of time it took one of us to answer the phone.

Scouting out costumes had always been my dad's favorite part of running the store: meeting with people who owned costumes and learning the history of the garments. We had a few collectibles in our inventory and they rented for top dollar. Sometimes the items were in too sad of a state to be worn, but he'd either repair them—people called it "the Jerry Touch"— or use them as templates to make copies. He taught me to sew using a damaged clown costume as a template, which explains why we had a surplus of clowns in our inventory.

I started the day the way I always did, with a smoothie for breakfast. I dumped almond milk, yogurt, a banana, and a few glugs of orange juice into the blender. After adding a scoop of protein powder, I hit liquefy. The resulting product was healthy, plus it matched my outfit.

I poured the smoothie into a glass and carried it downstairs and outside. The thing about Proper City weather was that it was always hot and always dry. The thermometer hit the eighties in April and climbed to over a hundred in the summer. One hundred degrees in a dry climate wasn't the same as one hundred degrees in a humid climate. Sunscreen was essential, as was water, but a constant breeze kept it comfortable. We rarely had to use the air conditioner, and most days I could shape my thick hair into a flip with my fingers and let it air-dry. Today was a typical hot, dry August day.

Before I had a chance to finish my smoothie, Blitz's friend Grady walked into the store. The bright sun illuminated his copper hair. He flashed a megawatt smile, much like the one Blitz had used on me yesterday. I didn't trust men with megawatt smiles. They were a dime a dozen at the casinos and it usually meant they were about to ask you for something not defined in the employee handbook.

"I hope you didn't lose too much sleep over Blitz," Grady said. "He really tied one on last night. Pretty sure he's still sleeping it off."

"Is that a regular habit?"

"Sometimes the guy likes to blow off steam. Besides, he's still jealous because he can't outdo my party." Things were beginning to make sense. "We weren't formally introduced yesterday. Grady O'Toole," he said, extending his hand. "Sherlock Holmes enthusiast, hustle expert, and best friend to the spoiled rich guy."

I raised an eyebrow. "That's quite a combo."

"I'm quite a guy."

Where did these guys get their self-assurance? I needed an Annie Oakley outfit to make me feel like I was somebody special.

"You look different than you did yesterday," he said.

"Yesterday I went mod. Today I went Western."

"Is that a regular habit?"

"Sometimes a girl likes to change things up," I said, more playfully than I'd intended.

"I bet you always get your man too."

Heat climbed up my face. "Did you have any luck convincing Blitz about the party?"

Grady looked disappointed at my change of subject. "That's why I'm here. Blitz was embarrassed about how he treated you after you did so much work."

Blitz Manners hadn't impressed me as the type to get embarrassed about the way he treated people, but I saw no benefit to accusing Grady of lying on his friend's behalf.

"So you're here to smooth things over?" I asked.

"I'm here because Blitz asked me to buy the whole lot."

I glanced at the rack of costumes and did some quick math in my head. Costumes usually rented for $150 each, with $50 of the deposit being refunded when the costume was returned in good shape. That left $100 a costume for us. Forty costumes at $100 rentals would be $4,000, with a possible two grand more if the costumes came back damaged—which I suspected they might. Not bad for a day's work.

But to buy them? I didn't know what to quote. Our income came with repeat rentals. One costume could be rented over and over and earn us thousands of dollars minus the cost of cleaning. Blitz's had said that the $20,000 was supposed to get us started, but $500 a costume would take up the whole amount. Ebony would have nothing left to offset the costs of the party execution. If I cut the price by much less than $500, I'd be giving away potential long-term profits, not only of the costumes we'd assembled, but also the ones we'd pillaged to come up with these so quickly.

"Once costumes are sold, they're nonreturnable. Rentals are for five days, which would get you through the weekend. They'd have to come back on Sunday. Would you rather do that? Blitz won't be out as much if he doesn't have the party."

"Nope." He pulled a black Amex out of his billfold and handed it to me.

"Don't you want to know the price first?"

"Not necessary. I'll square it with Blitz's stepdad. Present for Blitz."

"It's going to take me a while to tally up the contents of the costumes."

"Take your time. I'll look around." Grady wandered into the front of the store. A round silver rack held double-breasted suits for men and fringed flapper dresses for women. Low bookshelves painted to match the wall held tommy guns, headbands, long strands of pearls, cigarette holders, and fake cigars. We rotated the inventory every few months according to popularity, but the 1930s Mafia section stayed in the front. The old-school mob look remained consistently popular regardless of the season.

Grady disappeared behind the rack of pinstriped suits to the shelves where we kept the colored hair spray and face paint. I wrote up a description of each costume on a receipt pad. The last costume was the classic Sherlock. I added the hat, the pipe, a magnifying glass, and a pair of gloves, zipped it all into a clear garment bag, and set about determining a price for everything.

There was a price list in a binder behind the register. The binder was divided into costumes for men, women, children, and pets. The system wasn't much more organized than that. Names of costumes had been written on each line, with a price for rental and a price for purchase. In this day and age, it surprised me that my dad still relied on handwritten price lists and a calculator instead of a website and database. I backtracked through the pages until I had a feel for the pricing, kept a running tally on the calculator, and finally named a figure for the whole lot. Grady didn't blink. I punched it into our credit machine, swiped his card twice before remembering the black Amex had to be keyed by hand, and asked for his signature.

"I think I'll keep the Sherlock outfit for myself. My fee for handling the small detail of the costumes. That'll burn up Blitz pretty good, don't you think?"

"You're going to wear one of our costumes?"

"Any reason I shouldn't?"

"I heard your girlfriend worked for Candy Girls. I assumed you'd get something from them."

"See, this is how rumors get started. Blitz is the one with a girlfriend at Candy Girls, not me." He grinned. "In fact, I could use a date for the party. You wouldn't want to be my Watson, would you?"

"That would make it look like I was in on the plan to burn up Blitz."

"Nothing wrong with playing opposite Blitz's team. Get him back for the way he acted last night." Grady flashed a third megawatt smile, and I was starting to feel blindsided.

"You can pick the costumes up tomorrow," I said, switching the subject.

Again, his face fell. "You're going to have to deliver them," he said. He pulled a folded piece of paper from his wallet and held it between his first two fingers. When I reached for it, he pulled his fingers in toward his palm so the paper was out of my reach. I held my hand open and waited for him to give it to me. After a few seconds, he pressed the slip of paper into my palm and folded my fingers over it.

"You will be at the party, won't you?"

"I'll probably be there to help Ebony."

"Good. I'm looking forward to seeing which costume you kept for yourself."

I put the paper into my pocket and thanked him for his purchase. After he left, I returned to the register and put the signature slip in a clear pouch. The store had been open for twenty minutes and already things were looking good.

I propped the front door open with a concrete block and rolled a rack of discount clown outfits outside. They were bright and colorful and cheap, the trifecta of what makes a perfect sidewalk sale item. After adding a handwritten sign that said TODAY'S SPECIAL: CLOWN COSTUMES, $20, I picked a blue and pink polka-dotted costume off the end of the rack and carried it inside. A little modification and it would make a nice jumpsuit.

It was a good day for sales. By six o'clock I'd sold four clown costumes from the rack out front, a half-dozen fairy wings from our princess section, and ten cowboy hats. I'd stopped only once, to dispose of a mouse that Soot had caught in the stockroom and delivered to the register area. I was hungry and I was pooped.

After pulling the rack of clown costumes inside and locking the door, I cashed out the register and went upstairs. I ate a bowl of Fruity Pebbles for dinner, changed into cotton pj's, and took a pair of scissors to the clown costume.

*   *   *

FRIDAY morning I was up early to open the store. I dressed in what I'd renovated last night. After removing the collar, sleeves, and elastic by the ankles of the costume, I'd been left with a wide-legged jumpsuit that had colorful polka dots on it. I cinched the waist with a pink obi belt from a box of uniforms we'd inherited when the Las Vegas Benihana changed its dress code, and slipped on a pair of bright pink suede flats. I put a white plastic hair band on my head to keep my hair from falling into my face and added a sheer pink lip gloss to my lips.

After blending up a smoothie with blueberries and raspberries that made a nice complement to the polka dots, I rolled the same rack of clown costumes out front and, based on my own outfit, sold five more plus two obi belts. If things kept up, I was going to have to find another sidewalk sale item! My dad checked in at closing time; he and Don were spending another night with the collector. He—the collector, not my dad—wanted to treat him and Don to a tour of Area 51, and I knew my dad well enough to know he couldn't pass that up. After a heavy grilling of Don about my dad's pulse and then a lecture with my dad about medication and taking it easy, I told him that business was under control.

BY the time Saturday rolled around, talk of Blitz's party was all over town. Everyone was excited to see what Ebony had planned on short notice. Even though both Blitz and Grady had extended invites to me, I chose to remain a member of the staff and volunteered to help Ebony behind the scenes.

I dressed as Honey West and assembled my outfit from a black, V-neck dress with a high slit cut up one leg, a garter from the mob section, and a plastic pistol tucked into the garter. I pinched a stuffed ocelot from the jungle section of the store and hooked a leash to a studded collar from the '80s section. Since my hair was far from her golden blond, I tucked it under a tight cap and pulled on a wig. This girl for hire, indeed.

I strapped the stuffed ocelot onto the back of my white Vespa scooter and slowly fitted my helmet over the wig. It was a couple miles drive to the fire hall that Ebony had rented for the party, and I arrived in about fifteen minutes. Parking was limited, but a small spot on a side street called my name. Thankful for the compact size of the scooter, I backed it into the space. The blond wig came off when I removed my helmet, leaving my head—in a black stocking cap!—exposed. I tugged the wig on quickly and glanced around, hoping nobody had seen.

Ebony met me and the ocelot at the fire hall doors. She whistled when she saw my outfit. "Only you could turn out forty costumes in twenty-four hours and still have the best-looking one for yourself."

"I never turn down an opportunity to wear a wig. You know that."

"You're practically the same age as Blitz and his crowd. You should be here as a guest, not an employee. Who knows, you might even meet Mr. Right."

"Mr. Right? Let's see, I made a Mr. Moto, but I don't remember making a costume for Mr. Right." I looked at her sideways. "Besides, I'm six years older than Blitz. Maybe six years is nothing to you, but that would be practically cradle robbing to me. And you don't want me to become part of Blitz's scene any more than I want you to move to the moon. What's up?"

"It wouldn't kill you to meet a nice guy and settle down."

For a self-proclaimed independent-for-life woman, Ebony had an odd obsession with me meeting "a nice guy." I rolled my eyes, the standard response for when she brought "him" up, and went inside.

The interior of the fire hall had been converted. Tables and chairs were arranged to one side, leaving ample space for a band and a dance floor. There were four portable bars manned by bartenders in plaid capes and deerstalker hats. Servers circled with heavy, leather-bound encyclopedias in place of serving trays, each covered in clear trays of crudités and hors d'oeuvres. Guests were given large magnifying glasses instead of plates, and they selected items from the servers and set them on the surface of the glass. The handles made them easy to carry.

Ebony handed me a magnifying glass that held a rolled piece of roast beef with a dab of horseradish on the top. "What's he doing here?" she asked.

I followed her stare. An older gentleman, dressed nattily in a fitted black suit and narrow trousers, stood off near the side entrance. He wasn't so much dressed as a detective as he was dressed from the pages of *GQ*. He looked across the hall at her and crossed his arms over his chest.

"Who's he?"

"Octavius Roman. Otherwise known as He with the Broken Pipes."

"Otherwise known as Blitz's First Choice."

She shook her head. "Takes a lot of nerve to show up here after his services were terminated. I can't see Blitz sending him an invite."

"Where is Blitz, anyway?" I asked.

"I don't know. He said he was playing a joke on his friend Grady and we might not see him until after the party was in swing. You're lucky Grady already paid you for the costumes. Blitz said he'd pay me tonight. I know the boy's got money but I put this whole thing together on his promises."

Again, I felt bad for giving back Blitz's money. Whatever point I'd tried to make had gone unnoticed, and Ebony was now on the hook for the entire expense of the party. Sure, Blitz had the money to pay her, but would he? Especially after his dig to Ebony's past.

"What did Blitz mean when he mentioned you and his dad? Do you know his father?"

"Girl, don't you start with that gossip too. Bad enough I had to take it from him. He was talking about his real dad, Brody Manners. Important lawyer. Now there was a man with character."

"But why did Blitz say his father hired you?"

A cloud of darkness passed over Ebony's features. "I better go check on the goose and the coffee." She walked away.

I rested against the wall with my arm around my stuffed ocelot. I never liked the idea of working the room or approaching strangers to make conversation at a cocktail party, but the fact that everyone here was in costume took away that anxiety. Costumes gave people the confidence to be someone else and leave their insecurities behind—me included.

Columbo was talking to Veronica Mars by the side of the stage. A small group of men and women stood by the bar, wearing red windbreakers with B.W.G. embroidered on the back like the Bob-Whites of the Glen from Trixie Belden. Mr. Moto looked like he was trying to start something up with '30s Nancy Drew, but she seemed more interested in Kojak, who stood a few feet away. Tom Swift stood off to the side, comparing notes with Miss Marple. The whole scene was fantastic!

Three women dressed like Charlie's Angels were poised by the door. We hadn't provided Charlie's Angels costumes. I walked across the room to get a better look and recognized them as Candy Girls. Farrah Fawcett wore a bikini top and hip-huggers, Kate Jackson wore plaid pants and matching sweater vest over a snug polyester printed shirt, and Jaclyn Smith wore a white pantsuit and platform shoes. They each had identification tags clipped on that said TOWNSEND DETECTIVE AGENCY.

Charlie Chan stood behind them, in a black suit, white shirt, and narrow black necktie. I hadn't made a Charlie Chan costume and wondered if he'd put it together himself. His hair was slicked back away from his face. His mustache was perfectly styled across his upper lip, turning down by each of the sides, with a small triangular patch under his bottom lip. You never knew what a person would bring to a costume, if they would research the proper hair and makeup to pull it off. This man had. Our eyes connected for a moment, and then he turned and walked away.

Ebony had decorated the fire hall with blown-up images of question marks, fingerprints, and oversized envelopes marked CLUE. Tom Swift had pulled himself away from Miss Marple and inspected a clue from the closest envelope.

My role at the party was as Ebony's helper, but as long as she was in the kitchen, I felt like a wallflower. I wove through servers to see if she needed my assistance with the food. When I pushed through the doors, I saw her standing behind the kitchen island with a large knife in her hand. On the island was a black roasting pan that held a cooked goose. She looked terrified—Ebony, not the goose.

"Do you need help carving that?" I asked. I stepped around the side of the island and instantly understood that the cooked goose was not the reason for her terror.

No, her terror was due to the body of Blitz Manners, dressed in our classic Sherlock costume, that lay by her feet in a pool of blood.

Chapter 4

I DROPPED TO the floor and put my hands on the side of Blitz's neck. There was no pulse. The puddle of blood seeped across the uneven floor, collecting on a series of tiles between us and the wall-mounted phone. I stood up and put my hands on Ebony's arms.

"What happened here?" I asked. I shook her slightly to snap her out of her paralytic stance.

"Is he dead?" she asked. She stared at him, oblivious to my question.

The swinging doors to the kitchen opened up and one of the servers walked in. She took one look at the blood on the floor and raced back outside. "She killed Blitz!" she screamed. I moved my hands from Ebony's upper arms down to her wrists. She dropped the knife and it landed on the floor next to his body.

"Ebony, we have to call the police."

She tore her gaze from Blitz's body to my face. "He's dead," she said. There was no emotion behind her voice. "What's going to happen now?"

I heard the doors swing open a second time, this time drawing a crowd of partygoers. The first women in, two of Charlie's Angels, Kojak, and '30s Nancy Drew skidded to a halt when they saw the body. Nancy spun around and buried her head into Kojak's lapel.

Charlie Chan pushed Charlie's Angels aside and stepped farther into the room than anyone else had been so far. He looked at the body, then at me. "Did you touch him?" he asked.

"I felt his neck for a pulse. I couldn't find one."

"Don't go anywhere." He turned to the growing crowd. "Don't anybody go anywhere," he said to them. He picked up the phone on the wall and called the police.

They arrived quickly. Charlie Chan moved everybody but Ebony and me back out front. He poked his head back into the kitchen after the last of the partygoers had left and asked if we'd be okay.

"I don't know if *okay* is the right word," I said.

"The police are going to want to talk to both of you."

"I'll wait here until they arrive."

He nodded, as if that was an appropriate answer, and left.

Ebony hadn't said anything since dropping the knife. I turned her away from the view of Blitz's body and guided her to the opposite side of the kitchen island. We stopped in front of the large Sub-Zero freezer. I opened the door and a whoosh of frigid air enveloped us. I propped the door open with an empty ice bucket from a shelf on the wall. The cool air would do wonders for Ebony by the time the police came back to us. I hoped.

The third swinging of the doors brought uniformed officers and emergency technicians. The lead officer, an athletic blond woman with girl-next-door features, dressed in a black pantsuit over a white shirt, snapped photos of Blitz's body from every angle. She spoke to the techs. Charlie Chan came in and said something in her ear and then pointed to us. The officer shook Charlie Chan's hand, nodded to the technicians, and approached us.

She introduced herself as Detective Nichols and asked for our names, which she jotted down in a small notebook. "Which one of you ladies found the body?" she asked.

Though it had been pretty clear that Ebony saw the body before me, I spoke first. "I came back to see if Ebony needed help with the goose. When I came into the kitchen, Blitz was on the floor in a pool of blood."

"Where were you, Ms. Welles?" she asked Ebony.

"Goose," Ebony said.

"Excuse me?"

"She was tending to the goose," I translated. "Detective, Ebony is clearly shaken up by what happened here. Can we sit down somewhere?" She looked around for chairs. "Out front, maybe?" I added. My hope was that once Ebony was away from the body and the crime scene, she'd snap out of it.

"Sure," Nichols said.

We followed her, walking past the kitchen island a second time. I diverted my eyes to the wall of silver pots and pans to the left of the swinging doors and pretended nothing was amiss, like a person walking a tightrope might avoid looking at the ground. If my shrink was right and I had a tendency to avoid reality, now was the perfect time to use that skill as a crutch.

The ballroom was empty, save for the decorations and discarded plates and glasses. Charlie Chan stood along the back wall with his arms folded over his chest. When he saw us, he relaxed his arms. The detective waved him forward and then turned to me.

"I'd like to talk to Ms. Welles alone," she said. "Why don't you talk to Mr. Hoshiyama?"

"Who's Mr. Hoshiyama?" I asked.

"He's me," Charlie Chan answered.

"Who are you?" I asked.

He looked at me as if I were nuts. I looked at Ebony.

"You go with the Asian. I'll take the American," she said.

I followed Charlie Chan out a fire exit along the side wall of the banquet hall. He turned to me. "Takenouchi Hoshiyama," he said. "Call me Tak." He held out his hand.

I shook it. "Margo Tamblyn," I said back. "Call me Margo." His handshake was gentle and comforting. I held on for too long, and then dropped it as if I were shaking off water from freshly washed hands. After a few awkward seconds of me wishing I knew the appropriate thing to say at a time like this, I defaulted to what I knew, and I complimented his costume.

"You make a good Charlie Chan."

"You did a good job with the rest of the costume. With all of them. When Blitz hired you to make forty costumes in a day, I had my doubts."

"Blitz told you he hired me to make the costumes?" I asked.

"I was at your shop," he said.

I thought back to the day Blitz had been at the store. "He was alone," I said.

"After happy hour."

It wasn't until then that I remembered the man who had come in when Blitz and Grady were talking and had walked off in a different direction. "That was you?" I scanned him from top to toes and back again. "I didn't recognize you."

"Isn't that the point of a costume?"

Under different circumstances, I could have spent the next half hour extolling the virtues of costumes as shield, confidence booster, identity badge, and creative outlet, but now hardly seemed the time. Besides, I was too worried about Ebony to have a superficial conversation with one of Blitz's friends. And considering Charlie Chan—Tak—was one of Blitz's friends, he was taking the murder much differently than the other party guests. Involuntarily, I stepped backward to put distance between us.

"Why are you here?" I asked.

"Detective Nichols wanted to talk to your friend alone," he said.

"I mean here at the party. Here with me. Why aren't you out front with the rest of Blitz's friends? Why are you so calm? Your friend was just killed and you're talking to me about costumes." My voice rose.

"It's okay," he said. He stepped toward me and I stepped back and threw my hands up in front of me as if I were warding off an attack. He stopped where he was. "I'll go see if the detective is ready to talk to you." He turned away and went back inside.

MY conversation with Detective Nichols was of the tell-me-what-happened variety. My experience giving statements to the police was limited but not nonexistent thanks to a couple of scares in Vegas. Let's just say the kind of apartment a magician's assistant can afford isn't in the best part of town. The detective thanked me and handed me her business card in case I remembered anything else. The Proper City shield was printed on the card along with the name Nancy Nichols, PCPD, and contact info for cell, precinct, and e-mail.

The banquet hall was secured, keeping everything from Ebony's kitchen supplies and leftover decorations to my stuffed ocelot inside. I didn't want to leave her alone—Ebony, not the ocelot, though I wouldn't have minded having the ocelot with me too—so I wandered the perimeter of the build-ing until I found her sitting in the passenger side of her Coupe de Ville. The door was open and particles of dust floated in the hot, dry air.

"Let me drive you home," I said.

"Girl, you drive that little Vespa. You don't know how to drive my Caddy."

"You let my prom date borrow your Caddy in high school. Are you saying you trust a teenager in a tuxedo more than you trust me?"

"The boy had ruffles on his shirt. If he looked more like Isaac Hayes, *I* would have gone to the prom with him." She pulled the keys out of her handbag and held them out. "Take the corners wide and don't get bent out of shape over yellow lights. This baby needs some warning time before coming to a stop." She pulled her medallion to her lips and kissed it as if trusting me to drive her car was an act that required a boost from her good luck charm.

I climbed into the car and cranked the windows down. As I adjusted the rearview mirror, I saw Tak talking to the detective. Ebony noticed.

"What was up with you and Dr. Fu Manchu?"

"Charlie Chan," I corrected. "His name is Tak Hoshi-yama. He's part of Blitz's crowd."

"Hoshiyama?" she repeated. "Like the restaurant?" I must have looked confused, because she continued. "Hoshi-yama Steak House. It's a family-owned teppanyaki grill. Like Benihana except local." She closed her eyes and settled back against the vinyl seat of her car. "Good fried rice. We should go there sometime."

I started the engine and pulled away from the curb. Ebony kept her eyes closed. She was right—driving the Caddy was miles outside of my comfort zone—but I managed.

Despite multiple offers for her to spend the night at Disguise DeLimit, Ebony insisted that she wanted to go home. I didn't tell her that my offers were somewhat rooted in selfishness; after what had happened at the banquet hall, I wouldn't have minded the company myself.

She also insisted that I drop her off first. I'd parked my scooter in a narrow spot on a side street next to the banquet hall, and as much as I didn't want to leave it there, I doubted I'd find a space for Ebony's boat in that neighborhood. After leaving her place, I drove to the costume shop, parked along the curb out front, and went inside.

The house was disturbingly quiet. Soot followed me from room to room as if he sensed my need for companionship. I caught my reflection. I'd forgotten that I was wearing a wig. It added to the feeling that the party, the police, the strange man, and the murder had all been a different person's experience. I took off the wig and sprayed it with fabric spray to freshen it up, then set it on a wig stand on the dresser. I hopped in the shower and then dressed in pj's with cupcakes printed on them. Lonely and alone were two different things, and tonight I felt both. I turned the TV on, moved the pillows from the bed to the sofa, and burrowed underneath them. Soot joined me and we fell asleep somewhere between the second and third commercial breaks to a rerun of *Friends*.

THE next morning I tossed on a beige linen, Indian-inspired tank top and matching bell-bottoms from the '70s. Both pieces were trimmed with a band of turquoise, coral, and white beads. I parted my hair down the center and braided both sides, and then pulled a turquoise and black beaded headband around my head under my bangs. After stepping into suede booties trimmed with fringe and tossing my keys, wallet, and phone into a fringed pouch that I wore cross-body, I made a kale, peanut, and banana smoothie and poured it into a to-go cup. Despite my best intentions, I didn't get far.

Ebony's Cadillac was still parked along the curb in front of my house, but even the most skilled driver would have had trouble with it today. The two tires facing me were flat. The driver's side windows had been smashed out.

And the word *Murderer* had been spray-painted across the hood.

Chapter 5

I DROPPED THE smoothie. The lid to the cup popped off on contact with the sidewalk and the murky green concoction oozed out. I bent down to pick it up and saw a scrap of plaid fabric caught on the metal trim by the car's window. I crept closer to the Caddy, feeling broken shards of glass crunch under the thin soles of my moccasins. As I bent forward to get a better look at the fabric, a dark gray RAV4 pulled up behind the car. Tak Hoshiyama hopped out.

Today he wore a blue oxford shirt and khaki pants. The Charlie Chan facial hair was gone, as was the slicked-back hairstyle. His shirt was rolled up a few times at the cuffs, exposing what looked to be an expensive watch on his wrist. His longish hair was pushed away from his face, but a few strands had fallen down and waved loosely by his cheekbone. His strong brows were drawn together in a look of concern.

"Greetings, Pocahontas, I come in peace," he said.

I stared at him, having forgotten my outfit, braids, and beaded headband. When I didn't answer, he continued. "That was supposed to be a joke. Is everything okay?"

"I don't think so."

He came around the side of the car and took in the broken windows and the flat tires. "Is this your car too?" he asked.

"No, it's Ebony's. What do you mean, 'too'?"

"I knew you drove the scooter—that's why I'm here." He gestured toward the SUV with a hitchhiker-like thumb jerk. "You were about to get a ticket. I loaded it into my truck and brought it here."

"How did you know it was mine?"

"I saw you arrive at the party yesterday."

Translation: he saw my wig come off when I took off the helmet and then watched me wrestle a stuffed ocelot from where it had been bungeed to the back of the scooter. My hairline grew damp.

As if he could read my thoughts, he continued, "If I hadn't seen the wig come off, I might not have known it was you in the costume." I didn't say anything, and an awkward silence grew. "Let me get it now." He walked around to the back of his truck.

While he was gone, I picked the piece of plaid fabric from the door. It looked familiar, as if it had come from one of the costumes at the party yesterday. But more than one costume had been plaid, so which one? And what was it doing stuck on Ebony's car?

A few seconds later, Tak returned with my scooter. I shoved the scrap of fabric into my fringed suede pouch while he rolled it—my scooter, not the pouch—up the sidewalk, right through the puddle of dumped smoothie. He made a face.

"Sorry about that," he said.

"It's just a smoothie," I said. "I dropped it when I saw the car."

"What's in it?"

"Banana, kale, peanuts, almond milk . . ."

"That's what you eat?"

"For breakfast."

I took the handlebars from him and rolled the scooter to the front of the shop. He opened the door and I steered it inside and parked it next to the rack of colorful boas that Blitz had fingered earlier that week. A trail of green sludge followed along, growing gradually more faint the farther I went.

"I need to call Ebony." I looked at the phone on the counter and then back at Tak. "Can you give me some privacy?"

Tak stepped back. "Sure."

He stepped outside. I pulled the shop door shut and flipped the dead bolt. Even though he said he'd wait, I wanted to ensure privacy.

I could tell from the sound of Ebony's voice that I woke her up. "Margo, girl, I thought that Vegas lifestyle would have made you a night owl. And after yesterday, I'd just as soon stay in bed till noon. What's so urgent?"

"It's your car," I said.

"I'm not ready to get up and face the day yet. You can drive my car over here this afternoon and I'll drive you back."

"No, that's not it. I left it parked in front of the shop and someone vandalized it. I was about to call the police, but I wanted to tell you first."

"Somebody messed with my Brown Sugar?" she asked, instantly alert. "The universe is sending me some kind of

message. What'd they do? Did they key the doors? Don't *tell*
me they keyed the doors. I hate that."

"They didn't key your doors."

"Thank the man upstairs for that."

"They punctured your tires, smashed your windows, and
spray-painted a nasty word on the hood."

"Oh," she said. "What's the word?"

"Murderer."

She cursed and then immediately apologized for her language, like she'd been doing since I was five. Considering
I worked in Vegas, I'd heard much worse. "What did Jerry
say?" she asked.

"Dad's not back from his road trip. He doesn't know
about this."

"That's probably good. No use upsetting him in his condition. But I don't want you calling the cops neither," she
said. "I'll come to the store this afternoon. Can you throw
something over the car until I get there? No need to advertise
somebody's opinion of me."

"Sure. Are you sure you don't want me to call the police?
We should report this."

"It's not a matter for the police. It's a matter for the insurance company, and my rates are high enough already. I'll
handle it."

I turned around and looked outside. Tak was squatted on
the sidewalk, taking pictures of the glass next to the side of
the car.

"Ebony, what can you tell me about Tak Hoshiyama?" I
asked.

"Why do you want to know about him?"

"He brought my scooter here from the banquet hall this
morning. Now he's outside looking at the car."

"Don't know much about him, only his parents. They're good people. Go talk to him. I'll be there as soon as I can."

After hanging up, I went to the storage area to find a tarp. The best I could do was a set of water-damaged Twister mats. I grabbed a roll of duct tape and met Tak on the sidewalk.

"Can you help me make a tarp out of these?" I asked. "Ebony can't get here right away and she asked if I could cover the car."

His eyes cut to the Twister mats and he looked as if he was fighting off a smile. I braced myself for a snide comment, but none came. He took the Twister mats and the duct tape from me.

"I can handle the tarp," he said.

"Thanks." I turned back to the store.

"Where are you going?"

"To get a broom to sweep up the glass."

"We should probably leave everything the way it is for the police."

"I didn't call the police."

"Why not?"

"Ebony asked me not to."

"You shouldn't listen to her," he said.

"Why not? She's the second-most important person in my life. If it wasn't for her and my dad, I wouldn't have anybody."

I was as shocked by my admission as Tak appeared to be. I regretted the outburst. Tak took the Twister tarps and turned away. I went inside for a broom and dustpan. When I returned, he was surrounded by unfolded Twister tarps laid out in a grid. He secured the edges with strips of the durable silver tape while I swept the sidewalk.

"Do you think it's weird that the glass is on the outside of the car and not the inside?" I asked.

He stared at me. The dark brown intensity of his eyes made me uncomfortable, but I couldn't stop myself from talking. "Someone would have had to break the window from inside the car." I put my hand on my suede pouch, thinking about the torn fabric. For the moment, I kept it to myself.

"Did you look inside the car?" he asked.

"No. You arrived right when I first saw the damage. Why? Did you look?"

He hesitated. "No," he finally said. I remembered seeing him crouched by the side of the car taking pictures with his phone, and immediately knew he was lying. I just didn't know why.

"I'll finish this up out here if you want to get your store opened," he said.

"That's okay. I'll stay and help you." I moved to the far end of the Twister-mat tarp and waited for him to finish taping the last ends together. When he was done, we each picked up a corner and carried the patchworked plastic to the Cadillac. I went behind the car and he went to the front.

The makeshift tarp barely covered the enormous vehicle. I peeled off two short strips of tape and secured the back corners to the undercarriage next to the wheel wells and then did the same for the front. I didn't want anybody—Tak included—poking around Ebony's car before she arrived.

"Thanks for your help," I said with a small wave. I opened the shop door, but Tak called out behind me.

"Margo—hold up." He caught the door with his hand. "Were you here last night? All night?"

"Of course I was," I said. And then added, more tentatively, "Why?"

"I was wondering why you didn't hear this."

In the section of Vegas where I lived, I'd learned to hear the questions that people often wouldn't ask out loud. My self-protection walls went up. It didn't seem like a good idea to tell Tak or anybody that I was staying at the shop alone. It also seemed as though I needed to convince Ebony that maybe there was a very good reason for reporting the vandalism to the police.

"My dad's a heavy sleeper," I said, which was true. I was sure wherever he was sleeping in the middle of the desert, he hadn't woken up once. "And I fell asleep in front of the TV."

"I guess that explains it," he said. "But still, you should be careful. Whoever did this might come back, and the next time they might do more than vandalize a car."

Tak drove off. I propped the front door open, wheeled a rack of fringed ponchos onto the sidewalk, and went back inside to open the register. A petite woman in tennis clothes followed me. A canvas tote, weighed down by something bulky, hung over her shoulder.

"Are you open yet?" she asked.

I glanced at the clock. "Close enough," I said.

"Oh good. I wanted to get here before I hit the courts." She went to the counter and pulled a bunched-up garment bag from the tote. "I want to have this appraised."

I stepped around the back of the counter. "What is it?"

"It's a costume," she said. She studied me out of the corner of her eyes. "You do buy costumes, don't you? You don't make everything yourself, right?"

"Right." I hung the garment bag on an empty hook that was mounted to the wall. I'd watched my dad inspect potential costumes hundreds of times, and I'd learned how to back into an offer based on how much we could rent the costume for. I unzipped the garment bag and looked inside.

It was the sweater vest, shirt, and pants from one of the Charlie's Angels costumes at Blitz's party. Judging from the shoulder-length brown wig that was clipped to the hanger and the large pinkish glasses, I guessed it was Kate Jackson.

"You and your friends did a great job with the Charlie's Angels costumes," I said. "Do the other women plan to bring theirs in too?"

"We didn't talk about it. After what happened, we haven't talked about much." She pulled her bobbed brown hair off her face. A sparkling diamond on her left hand caught the light and glittered. It was bigger than any engagement ring I'd ever seen.

"That's a beautiful ring," I said. "Looks heirloom."

She dropped her left hand and closed her right hand over it. "It was Blitz's mom's ring. I—I can't bring myself to take it off, even though"—she tucked her head, and fat droplets of tears fell onto the front of her tennis whites—"even though we can't go through with our plans anymore."

"I didn't know Blitz was engaged," I said. I studied the woman in front of me. She clearly knew what had happened to Blitz. So why was she trying to pawn her costume the day after he was killed? The timing—if nothing else—was strange, at best. "I'm sorry for your loss," I added. It was an expression that I'd heard my whole life, from the earliest memories I had of people expressing their condolences to my dad over the passing of my mother. The words felt empty, because I knew they couldn't change what had happened.

The woman wiped her eyes and kept her head down. I waited for her to say more, but she didn't.

I turned my attention back to the costume. The wig was a standard, store-bought brown. The glasses were vintage '70s and had their share of scratches. The long-sleeved blouse was made from stretchy polyester. I took the shirt off the hanger and studied the plaid pants. Aside from the style, they could have passed for brand-new. There were no pills, no stains, no missing buttons. They were in just about perfect condition.

Except for the tear on the back of the leg that roughly matched the size of the fabric I'd pulled from the window of Ebony's car.

Chapter 6

"I'LL TAKE IT," I said. I made her an offer, low enough that I'd have wiggle room, but high enough that it sounded respectable. She agreed to it. "How would you like me to pay you? Store credit?"

"Can you do cash?"

I knew I could. But I also knew the cash was locked up in the safe, and besides, if I gave her cash, I'd have no way of knowing her identity.

"How about a check?"

She seemed less happy with this option. "Sure, okay. Can you make it out to 'Cash'?"

"I'm sorry, I need a name. I have to have a record of the sale, and part of that record is getting your name and contact information. It's our regular policy."

"I didn't realize that," she said.

"It'll only take a second."

She reached up for the outfit on the hook. "I changed my mind. I think I'll keep it anyway." She threw the clothes and garment bag over her arm and left.

The only explanation I had for her behavior was that she was guilty of something. Could that something be murder? Lover's quarrel or jealous rage? Add in that she was planning on a morning of tennis the day after her fiancé had been murdered, and something was definitely rotten in the state of Denmark—or Nevada, as the case may be.

I regretted not trying to match the square of torn fabric from Ebony's car with the pants when I had them all in front of me. I pulled the fabric from my fringed pouch and looked at it. It was a nondescript plaid in shades of khaki, plum, navy blue, and brown, the same shades of her pants.

In her haste to leave, she'd left the wig and glasses to the costume on the counter. I grabbed them and raced to the front door. A red Prius pulled away from the curb just as I reached the sidewalk. If she saw me waving the props at her, she ignored them. Her little red car turned right at the intersection on the corner, passing the bus that was letting off passengers.

Proper City had established a public transportation route called the Zip. There were four buses in total, going by the simple names of the One, the Two, the Three, and the Four. They circled around the city between the hours of seven a.m. and seven p.m. and were driven by a group of retirees who liked having something to do with their time. The vehicles themselves were repurposed school buses, large and yellow.

Ebony was one of the passengers who got off the Zip-Four. Today she wore a caftan and gold sandals. Her Afro was brushed out to its full dimensions, adding four inches of height to her already tall stature. By the time she crossed the street, I was on the corner. I threw my arms around her and she hugged me back.

"What's this about Jerry going out of town?" she asked.

"He's with Don Digby. They're scoping out a sci-fi collection somewhere in the desert."

"You let him go just like that?"

"They left while I was asleep."

"Those two are trouble when they're together. They turn into thirteen-year-old boys." She put her arm around me and we walked back to the shop. "Next question: what was Amy Bradshaw doing at Disguise DeLimit? Scoping out the competition?" she asked.

"That woman in tennis clothes? You know her?"

"Sure looked like Amy. Brown hair, button nose, about yay tall." She held her hand up to approximate the customer's height. "She works for Candy Girls."

"She wanted to sell her costume from yesterday." I chewed my bottom lip. "She was wearing a giant heirloom diamond ring and she said it was from Blitz. She made it sound like they were engaged."

"If they were, it was a secret."

"Don't you think it's strange that she was in here trying to sell me her costume the day after Blitz was killed?"

Ebony waved her hand back and forth. "I don't spend time trying to understand half the people in this town. All I know is that Amy was the point person for Grady's hustle party, if you can believe it. She can't be more than twenty-two. What would a young thing like that know about the hustle era?"

"I think you're going to have to let that go." I stared down the street in the direction that Amy's little red car had gone. There was something off about her story, but I couldn't put my finger on it. "Do you want to go inside for something to drink?"

"No, I want to take care of this car situation. This is your idea of a tarp?"

I nodded.

Ebony inspected the taped joints of the Twister mats. "You didn't do this," she said. "This is precision work."

"That guy Tak stayed and helped me after I talked to you."

"That was nice of him."

"Not really. I told him to leave but he wouldn't. And he wanted me to call the police. And he took pictures of the glass before I swept it up. I think he was up to something."

"Or maybe he wanted to see you again," she said. She reached under the wheel well and freed the duct tape. "Let's see the damage."

Reluctantly, I helped her fold the Twister mats up so she could see the extent of the vandalism. The word *Murderer* had smudged under the tarp and was less legible than it had been when I first saw it. She reached inside the broken window and unlocked the door. Inside the car were a couple of empty cans of paint. More shards of glass were inside between the seat and the door.

"Maybe Tak was right. Maybe we should call the police," I said. "If this was random, they wouldn't have sprayed that word on. This is related to what happened to Blitz."

"Margo, this attack connects me to that murder, just like being in the kitchen with a knife connects me. Three strikes and I'm gonna be out."

"That's not how it works," I said. "I know you didn't kill Blitz, and that means someone else did. And someone else did this. Maybe *those* two things are connected. Did you think of that?"

"Trust me, Margo. There are things that I don't want to come out in public, and the only way to keep that from happening is to keep my mouth shut." She pulled out her phone and scrolled through her contacts until finding the one she wanted. "Yo, Dig? This is Ebony. I need a tow. Uh-huh. Uh-huh. Uh-huh." She gave the address to the costume shop and said thanks.

"Dig Allen is on his way. How about you go make me one of those smoothies you're always drinking." She pulled a brown vial out of her purse. "Put this in it. Lemon balm oil drops. Helps calm the nerves."

I left Ebony on the sidewalk and went inside and upstairs. Since my smoothie had landed on the sidewalk, I blended up enough for two people. By the time I made it back downstairs, Dig and his tow truck had arrived.

Dig Allen was a bald black man who favored bowling shirts with the sleeves torn off, boxy black work pants, and a wallet on a chain that was hooked to his belt. He had a tattoo of Tweety Bird on one muscular biceps and an anchor on the other. He was half a head shorter than Ebony even if you didn't count her Afro. Even though she was ten years older than he was, he asked her out every chance he got.

Today Dig looked like he'd stumbled onto the mother lode of rescue fantasies. Not only had Ebony called him, but she needed him. He had a hand on the small of her back and was in the middle of offering to replace and balance all four of her tires—though only two were flat—when I returned.

"Margo Tamblyn! Long time no see. You come here to tell Jerry to take it easy after his heart attack?"

"Something like that."

"Is he listening?"

"He's somewhere along Route 66 chasing down government conspiracies and alien costumes."

Dig laughed. "That sounds like Jerry. How long do we have you for?"

When I asked my boss, Magic Maynard, how many days I could take, he grumbled about finding a replacement before he could make a decision. My roommate, a former employee at one of the older casinos, had volunteered to step in for me while I was gone so my job wouldn't go to someone else permanently. I hoped she was doing a good enough job to keep me employed when I didn't return to work on Tuesday.

"I have to go back soon," I said, "but not yet. Not until I feel like Ebony and my dad are both going to be okay."

Dig looked at Ebony with concern. "Margo's got a point. You might need a man to look after you for a few days."

"Ain't no man who can take care of me like I can take care of myself," she said. "But I tell you what. You help me out with those tires and the removal of the paint and I'll take you out to dinner to the restaurant of your choice. Within reason."

"What are we waiting for?" Dig said. He fumbled with something by the dashboard, and after a series of loud noises, the back of the truck tipped down. He freed a large hook and secured it under Ebony's Caddy and then went back to the dash and did something else that made the hook retract. The Caddy resisted, but with enough force, finally lifted from the ground. By the time Dig was done with the process, the front two wheels of the Caddy were resting on the tilted bed of the truck. Sadly, this made it even easier to read the word that was painted on the car.

"Will it be hard to get the paint off?" Ebony asked.

"Nah, little bit of turpentine'll do the trick. Besides, it's still fresh. See?" Dig dragged his finger over the paint and left a streak through the *M*.

"That doesn't make any sense," I said. "I found the car like this around ten o'clock this morning. Spray paint dries in half an hour. Hour, tops." I stepped closer to the car and looked in the window. The cans of paint had rolled to the far side of the car. I walked around and reached in and picked one up.

It wasn't a can of spray paint at all. It was a can of temporary hair color, like the kind we stocked in the costume shop.

Chapter 7

I TURNED THE can over in my hands. A small white price sticker on the bottom read CANDY GIRLS. I shook the can a few times and the ball inside clinked back and forth, the same way an empty can of spray paint might sound.

"Ebony, didn't you say Amy Bradshaw works for Candy Girls?" I asked.

"Yep. Why?"

I held the empty can up. "This isn't paint, it's hair spray. It'll come off with a bucket of warm soap and water." I pointed to the price tag. "It came from Candy Girls."

"What does that tell you?" Ebony asked.

"Not much. We sell this stuff by the truckload. It's one of the most popular everyday items. I bet they do too."

Ebony took the can from me and read the label. I had enough experience with the colored hair spray to know that you needed to spray it in short bursts, otherwise the nozzle would drip and the spray would get on your hands. The user of this can didn't know that. The black spray had run down the label and spidered around it. Ebony looked inside her car. There was a black splotch on the middle of the camel-colored vinyl interior.

She held the can up in front of her like Hamlet about to address a skull and said, "I'm gonna git you, sucka!" and then handed me the empty can. As long as she was quoting blaxploitation movies, I knew she was taking the vandalism in stride. Better than I was, all things considered.

"I have to get back inside and open the store. Dig, do you have this under control?" I asked.

"Yes, ma'am," he said. He guided Ebony to the passenger side of his truck and opened the door for her. She looked back at me and rolled her eyes.

I waited until after they'd driven off before digging out my phone. Maybe Ebony was okay with the vandalism in front of the store, but I wasn't. I needed to talk to somebody I could trust, somebody who could tell me if the growing sense of fear was normal.

Soot came out from the stockroom. He skulked across the floor and brushed up against my ankles. I sat down and stroked his fur.

"Hey, Soot. Got a minute to talk?" I dangled my hand back down and he circled around and made another pass at my ankles. He lowered himself and stuck his paws out in front of himself like a sphinx, and then looked up at me and meowed, as if saying, *The psychiatrist is in.*

"I thought it would be fun to help Dad and Ebony out with the party. I don't even know if the two of them could have pulled it off without my help. But now the client is dead and the police think Ebony did it."

Soot licked his front paw a few times and then tucked it underneath him. I ran my hand over his dark gray fur several times and he started to purr. "I know I have a tendency to think that the worst will happen to the people around me. I think it's because I'm so scared of losing my dad." I stopped petting Soot for a moment and he looked up at me. "I think his heart attack shook me up more than I want to admit, but he needs me to hold myself together. So does Ebony."

Soot stood up and put his front paws on my knee. I bent down and butted heads with him.

"This is a good opportunity for self-growth. Remember how scared I was when Magic Maynard first tried to saw me in half?"

Soot meowed.

"And that turned out mostly okay. This will too. I have to be strong for both of them. But do you mind if, every once in a while, we have a talk like this?"

Soot bumped heads with me again and let out a small mew. I scooped him up and held him close for a second until he wriggled free. He dropped down to the floor and took off for the stockroom.

I guess my time was up.

But what really *had* happened to Blitz? Someone had killed him at his own birthday party. Who? And why? Sure, he'd been obnoxious, but that was hardly a reason to murder someone.

There was a connection between Ebony and Blitz, or more accurately, between Ebony and his father. Blitz had alluded to it the day he hired us to put together his party. When I asked her about it, she hadn't denied it. And when Blitz had used knowledge of that connection to get Ebony to do what he wanted, it had worked. He'd shown her that he had a power over her, a power he wouldn't hesitate to use in order to get her to do what he wanted. I couldn't help her until I knew what those secrets were and how damaging they would be.

Sunday hours at the store were twelve to five. When no customers had entered by twelve thirty, I started a list of as many items as I could remember using in the detective costumes. Blitz's short timetable had forced me to swipe parts of our existing costumes, and I'd need to get them back in order before being able to rent them out. First I listed the characters, and next to them, the items I'd used in each costume and where those items had come from.

Kojak: man's suit from '70s, bald cap (general accessories), lollipop from candy store

Columbo: trench coat from hobo, man's suit from salesman, cigar (general accessories)

Tom Swift: jetpack and goggles from steampunk, suspenders and knickers from chimney sweep

Miss Marple: sweater and plaid skirt from '50s sorority girl, glasses from '80s accessories, sensible shoes from church lady

And so it continued. It would have been nice to know who wore which costume, but I didn't know many of the people who were invited. I'd spent more time appreciating the way the characters had mixed and mingled, and no time noticing the individual people under the costumes.

It all went back to the way I felt about myself. I learned early on that there was something special about wearing a costume in public. People in costumes were friendlier, happier, less stressed. It wasn't just something that I noticed with kids, but adults too.

Growing up in the store, I'd had ample opportunity to play

dress-up. Even after my dad stopped providing my school wardrobe from Disguise DeLimit's inventory, I turned to our shelves for my accessories. When I was a teenager searching for my own identity, I found it in the characters who I dressed up as: cowgirl, tomboy, artist, mechanic. There was a costume to suit my every mood, and dressing up in character helped me identify myself and got me through the day.

Maybe that's why I hadn't paid attention to the people in the costumes at Blitz's party. What I remembered were clusters of people talking among themselves. Columbo talking to Veronica Mars. The Bob-Whites talking to Cherry Ames. Rockford flirting with Nancy Drew, who kept her eyes on Kojak. Tom Swift and Miss Marple. Too bad I hadn't paid more attention to the people under each disguise. The only person I remembered was Octavius Roman, who hadn't bothered with a costume. I wondered briefly if that was significant.

By twelve forty-five, I couldn't stand the idea that I was trapped behind the counter for the next five hours. I found Kirby Grizwitz's number where my dad said it was and called.

"Kirby, this is Margo Tamblyn," I said.

"Hey, Margo. How's Jerry?"

"He's recovering faster than anybody expected."

"Did he take off to go see those alien costumes?" he asked.

"How'd you know about them?"

"He's been wanting to go check them out for months. He keeps asking me to take on full-time hours so he could get away."

"He and his friend Don took off Thursday morning. I don't know when they're coming back."

"That sounds like Jerry," he said.

"Are you calling with my schedule for the week?" Kirby asked.

"Sort of. I know this is short notice, but can you work today?"

"Sure."

"Great. Come over as soon as you're ready. I'll be waiting for you."

KIRBY arrived at the store a little after one. He went straight to the register and signed in on a time card.

Kirby Grizwitz was a freckle-faced teenager who worked part-time at the shop. He was captain of the Proper City Prawns, the local high school swim team. He maintained a year-round tan from early-morning practices and lived in T-shirts from swim meets around the country. He had a typical male swimmer's build: broad shoulders and lean muscles, which made him popular with the girls in his class, despite his obvious prioritizing of sports over dating.

"Sure is crazy what happened to Blitz Manners yesterday," he said.

"How did you hear?" Kirby wasn't known for being up on current events since he spent most of his time in a swimming pool.

"After practice this morning, I went to the gym. Grady O'Toole was bench-pressing without a spotter. He was struggling with the barbell and I jumped into place just in time."

"That's unusual, right? Isn't it standard to bench with a partner?"

"Yeah. I don't think Grady was too happy to hear me say that, but he could have hurt himself. He stormed off afterward. I said something at the registration desk, and they told me what happened to Blitz. Guess Grady was working off some steam."

I thought about the turmoil of emotions that Grady must be feeling in the wake of his friend's murder and wondered if the steam he was working off had come from residual anger or frustration.

I took the empty hair spray can I'd rescued from the back of Ebony's car and went upstairs, where I set the can on the dining room table next to the torn square of plaid fabric. My own little evidence collection. Evidence of what, I still wasn't sure.

I sat down at the table and stared at the two items. I might never have connected the vandalism to Blitz's murder if not for the word *Murderer* that had been sprayed on the hood of Ebony's Caddy. Someone was either convinced that she was guilty, or was trying to influence the tide of public opinion against her.

I set the hair spray can and the torn fabric on two separate sheets of paper and labeled each individually: HAIR SPRAY, CANDY GIRLS and CHARLIE'S ANGELS COSTUME? I turned the piece of fabric over in my fingers. Maybe it hadn't come from the Charlie's Angels costume. There had been a lot of plaid at the party: Nancy Drew's skirt, Sherlock's cape, the deerstalker worn by Roquefort, the mouse from *The Aristocats*. I had a list of all of the costumes downstairs by the register. Again, I wished I'd paid more attention to who wore what.

But there was one thing I did know that, until now, I'd overlooked: Grady O'Toole had said he was keeping the classic Sherlock costume for himself. So why had Blitz been wearing it when he was found murdered? Had Blitz been the intended victim, or had this been a case of mistaken identity gone horribly wrong?

Downstairs, I found Kirby at ease behind the register, reading a copy of *Dune Buggies and Hot VWs* magazine. Ever since I'd known him, he'd talked about getting a dune buggy, and it appeared that the fantasy remained unfulfilled.

"Are you any closer to getting one?" I asked, gesturing toward the magazine.

"Not allowed until after Nationals," he said. "Can't risk injury this late in the season. If I'm lucky, I'll have enough money by graduation."

"You better be sure there's enough undeveloped land around here to make it worth your while."

"Shoot, there's twenty miles of desert past the edge of Proper," he said. "Nobody's going to develop that. Not when they can keep putting money into Primm and Las Vegas."

Kirby was right. Our small town was the last that had benefited from a developer's imagination, and, despite the money he'd poured into it, the population growth remained constant. For every family that moved in, another moved out. We were the even steven of real estate.

Proper City was named after Pete Proper. Legend had it that Pete vowed to give up all of his vices if only he'd strike gold. Sure enough, he did. Overnight, he swore off drinking, women, and gambling—a big deal in a state where most of it was legal. He built a house in the desert in the late 1800s and encouraged like-minded folks to join his new community. And thus, Proper City was born.

After his death in 1930, the town fell into decline. Its one feature—location, location, location—worked to its disadvantage. Proper City was close enough to the California state line to attract vagrants and scofflaws looking to escape California jurisdiction. Soon enough, the only people looking to develop in Proper were the very bootleggers and gamblers Pete Proper had renounced. Families left and Proper City all but imploded.

In the '50s, the Clark County Council announced plans to reinvent Proper City as a census-designed town. Small, square, pastel-colored tract houses popped up along street names picked out of children's books. The town was approved for a library and post office, and retailers were offered tax incentives to move in. These days you can still see the remnants of the early layout of Proper City in the same small houses and the old movie theater downtown. New restaurants came and went and a few old ones stuck around.

I'd been away from Proper for seven years except for holidays when I came home, and it seemed each time I returned, a fresh crop of coffee shops and cupcake stores had moved in along with a batch of theme restaurants that played with the fairy-tale aspects of town. But drive to the town's edge and you'd be met with miles upon miles of desert, bisected only by a narrow two-lane road. Prairie dogs and rattlesnakes were the residents out that way.

"Have you chosen a college yet?" I asked Kirby.

"Nope. If I don't get a swimming scholarship, I'm going to the Proper City Community College. In my spare time, I'll have to work to make the money for tuition."

I could tell from the look on Kirby's face that he knew college was more important than the dune buggy he'd been saving for. I wasn't in a position to offer him anything more than the limited part-time hours my dad already had him working, and twenty hours a week in a costume shop wasn't going to buy much in the way of higher education.

FOR the next two hours, Kirby and I sorted through bins of costume accessories that had been amassed into a large pile in the back corner of the shop. We were two months away from Halloween, which was to us what tax season was to accountants, but our shop didn't exist by Halloween alone.

Going hand in hand with Proper being census designed was the fact that, aside from what Pete Proper—or Proper Pete as he'd been nicknamed after giving up all of his vices—had established back in 1892, there was no history of important battles being fought here or of celebrities having once dined here—although Clark Gable had been waiting for Carole Lombard at a bar in nearby Goodsprings when her plane went down—so what we were left with was a void. We weren't known for gambling or shopping or drinking or prospecting. We were a town without an identity.

Nobody really knew who to credit with the costume party craze, but the oldest of the photos that were now featured on the Proper City website were from the early '60s. Once the parties started, the identity stuck. Backyard barbecues, sweet sixteen parties, promotions, and holidays all became an opportunity to pick a theme and dress accordingly. The Proper City Chamber of Commerce accepted photos from anybody who submitted them, and our quirky love of costume parties became what we were known for in our small corner of the state. Newcomers to our town must have wondered about our sanity.

Disguise DeLimit was born out of that trend. The store became the go-to destination for the clothes to match whatever someone dreamed up. Some towns have a Macy's. Our town didn't need one. We had five thousand costumes in our inventory, and if you didn't like them, we could make you what you wanted. Assuming you weren't looking for long-term quality. It wasn't about the clothes themselves, it was about the character you could be for a couple of hours.

Kirby and I organized pieces of costumes that had been cast into go-back boxes behind the register. Somewhere between the fourth box and the fifth, it became clear that he could handle the shop on his own. He practically knew the layout better than I did. Besides, my mind was still caught in a loop about Blitz in the costume Grady had said he was going to wear, and though I knew there could be a simple explanation—like Grady letting Blitz wear what he wanted since it was his party—I couldn't shake off my questions without getting the facts.

"Kirby, can you watch the store while I go out and run a few errands?"

"Sure. Do your errands have to do with what happened yesterday?"

I sighed. "I can't help think about how Grady must be feeling today. He and Blitz were best friends, but they ribbed each other constantly. Today, his best friend is gone. I know I just met him, but I need to offer my condolences."

"That whole friendship is funny, considering what Blitz did to Grady in high school." While he spoke, Kirby sorted a wad of neckties into piles by color. "I don't know if I'd be so quick to look the other way if I were Grady."

I picked up a tie and smoothed out the wrinkled silk. "What happened?"

"Somebody snuck booze into Grady's eighteenth birthday party. Probably Blitz. But then he thought it would be funny to call the cops. Grady spent the night in prison and was suspended from high school."

"I guess that would be pretty hard to forgive." I set the ties down on the counter.

"That's not all. Because of the suspension, Grady didn't graduate that year."

I thought back to being eighteen. Graduating high school was just about the biggest thing to happen at that age. "I can see why you say their friendship is funny."

"Yeah, and it actually gets worse. Blitz's prank cost Grady admission into the college he wanted. Plus, the whole incident is on his permanent record."

Chapter 8

"HOW LONG AGO was this?" I asked Kirby.

He stopped sorting ties for a moment and rolled his eyes up while he thought. "Must have been eight years ago, I think. For a while, it was all anybody talked about. Our coach made everybody over fourteen sit out of practice so a drug and alcohol counselor could talk to them about the dangers of drinking. Coach never let anybody out of practice, so even though I was only ten, I knew it was a big deal. Blitz graduated but Grady didn't get his diploma until the following year."

"If something like that happened to you, how would you feel?"

He misunderstood. "Something like that wouldn't happen to me. I'm an athlete." He puffed himself up and tapped his chest. "I keep poisons out of my body."

"I don't mean that. I mean, how would you feel if your best friend did something that destructive to you?"

"My best friend wouldn't do that. But Blitz and Grady and all those guys, they're in a whole different league. When Blitz turned eighteen, he inherited twenty-five million dollars and his new dad *gave* him a dune buggy. Not that he even appreciated it. There's not a lot you can't buy with that kind of money," he said, looking wistfully at his magazine.

"Kirby, you'll appreciate your dune buggy a thousand times more than if it had been handed to you," I said.

"I know," he said. His dejected body language suggested that I was not the first person to point this out.

I pushed myself up until I was standing and adjusted the beaded Indian headband on my forehead. "I'll be back later to close up."

"Don't worry about the store. Jerry lets me work by myself all the time."

My Vespa was still inside where I'd rolled it after Tak had unpacked it from his SUV. I unlocked the steering and walked it out the front door, pulled my helmet on, and took off.

The city planners of Proper City had zoned out areas for residencies, businesses, and entertainment, and I liked to think that an aerial view of our town was a little like a series of crop circles on our western and eastern sides connected by a long straight line. Creative planners that they were, they'd actually named the street that ran end to end "Line Road." Since then, more roads that connected the various end-to-end businesses had been put in, so, as a nod to the original planners, the name of the main road became that: Main Line Road.

Today I drove down Main Line Road, past Baby Cakes, the local cupcake store, and Packin' Pistils, the local florist. A stretch of car dealerships lit up like casinos filled the last quarter mile, and after that the road dead-ended. A right turn would have led me to the highway access and eventually to the heart of Las Vegas. A left turn took me to Christopher Robin Crossing.

My dad had said that Blitz Manners lived in the mansion at the end of Winnie Lane, but it turned out he was slightly mistaken. The large white mansion sat at the intersection of Winnie Lane and Pooh Bear Drive, making it the house at Pooh Corner. I wondered how *that* looked on an engraved invitation!

I pulled over to the side of the road and flipped my visor up. The house stood majestically on its plot. Although it was surrounded by equally impressive architecture, it was by far the most grand of the development. A shiny black town car sat in the driveway. I could tell from the way the tall blades of grass behind the car bent backward that the engine was running and the exhaust, though invisible, was present. A well-appointed blond woman in a lightweight black suit came out of the house and gingerly descended the stairs that led to the driveway. She looked as though a team of professionals had been tasked with her hair and makeup. The driver stepped out of the car, came around to the side, and held the door open for the woman. I guessed her to be Blitz's mom.

"Thanks for coming on such short notice, Claude," she said. "I thought my husband was going to be able to drive me, but he had to go to the dealership."

"It's no trouble, Mrs. Manners," the driver said. "I'm awfully sorry about your son."

"Please," she said, holding her hand up. "I have to hold it together for a town council meeting and it's taking all of my energy not to break down."

"Of course," the driver said.

Blitz's mom sat in the back of the shiny car and the driver closed the door. He walked around the front and backed it out of the driveway.

I flipped my visor back into place and pulled away from the curb. The town car passed me just before I reached the stop sign at Tigger Trail. I turned right and circled around the rest of the streets of the development until I realized I'd gotten myself lost somewhere in the Hundred Acre Woods. I parked along a curb and climbed off the scooter, taking to foot so I wouldn't burn up more gas. The thin suede soles of my moccasins provided little in the way of support, and after only a few blocks, my arches were tired and I was no closer to finding the way out. In the distance, a street sign announced Winnie Lane. Sure enough, when I turned at the intersection, I was back at Pooh Corner. Now the only trick would be to figure out where I'd left my scooter.

"Hey!" a voice called out. I looked to my left and right, finally spotting Grady hanging out the window of a silver sports car. He pulled up alongside of me. "Margo, right? What are you doing in my neck of the woods?"

"Truth?" I said, knowing I was about to deliver a lie. "I took my scooter out for a ride and got a little turned around. My tank is low so I started walking to find the way out of this development."

"Is your scooter that little white thing with the red seat?"

"Yes. Do you know where it is?"

"You don't?"

"Directions aren't my strongest suit."

"Hop in, m'lady, or should I say, hop in, Indian princess?"

The lock popped open and Grady reached across from the driver's side and pushed the door open. I climbed in.

"Thank you. I don't think these boots were made for walking," I said. I rubbed at the ball of my foot through the suede.

"You're something of a mystery aren't you?" he asked. "Mod, Western, Indian. How do I know which is the real Margo Tamblyn?"

"As soon as I figure it out, I'll let you know."

"Are you saying this is the result of an identity crisis?"

"This"—I gestured to my outfit—"is the result of growing up in a costume shop. How about you?"

"Me? No identity crisis here. This"—he tapped the dash of his car—"is the result of growing up in a casino. I like to gamble, and I like to win."

"You won your car gambling?" I asked, feeling my eyes grow wide.

"Nah, my dad owns a casino." He laughed. "Gotcha, though. You should have seen your face."

Grady pulled the car away from the curb and drove to the end of the road. He turned left—I would have put money on the fact that we needed to go right, which explained both why I didn't gamble and how I'd gotten so absolutely lost—and drove a couple of blocks before turning right and then right again.

"So how does your dad owning a casino get you a car like this?" I asked.

"Dad's got favors all over town," he said. "The car came from Black Jack's place. Black Jack Cannon gave dad the car in exchange for a seat at his penthouse poker game."

"Black Jack Cannon," I repeated. "He's Blitz's dad, isn't he?"

Grady made two more rights and pulled his car up behind my scooter. "New dad. He married Blitz's mom after his real dad died."

The mood in the car went from light to sober in a snap. I regretted the playfulness that I'd exhibited and searched for the right words to convey my condolences. Grady beat me to the punch.

"I can't believe he's gone," he said. He stared straight ahead as though focusing on a dead bug on the windshield. "We've been friends for as long as I can remember."

I bit back the rumors that Kirby had told me. Grady didn't seem like he held a grudge against Blitz for sabotaging his high school graduation and plans for college. Even if he had, asking him about it felt too awkward.

"Grady, I'm sorry for your loss." The more I repeated the line, the more impersonal it sounded.

"Yeah, well, you win some, you lose some." His whole demeanor changed, like he remembered he was late for an appointment and I was holding him up. He hit the unlock button on the door and released the emergency break. "See you around sometime," he said.

"Sure. Thanks for helping me find my ride," I said. I got out of his car and he pulled away before I had a chance to close the door.

AFTER riding along with Grady, I had a better understanding of how the roads of his development were laid out, and I ended up back on Main Line Road in a matter of minutes. It was getting close to five and I wanted to get back to the shop before Kirby left. I pulled into a gas station and started filling the small tank. Across the street, a giant playing card rotated on a pole in front of an auto dealer. The name BLACK JACK was below the playing card in large black letters that were illuminated by little round bulbs. The entire thing had a Vegas quality about it—out of place in our otherwise local, costume party–themed community.

As I watched, a dark gray RAV4 pulled into the parking lot. Tak Hoshiyama got out and went inside the dealership. I became so distracted by the scene that I forgot about the gasoline. It splashed out of the tank and onto the hem of my pants and my suede shoes. I jumped back, too late.

"Shi-oot," I said, changing the instinctive curse word into

something more PG-13. I'd been trying to convince Magic Maynard to drop his curse words when he was practicing his routine, and now my knee-jerk reaction was to self-edit.

"Shi-oot?" asked a tall man in a cowboy hat.

"I splashed gasoline on myself," I said, "and I was trying not to swear."

"Well, then shi-oot is right. Your costume is all messed up now. You are going to a costume party, aren'tcha?" He tore a length of brown paper towel off a roll that sat by the windshield wiper station and handed it to me. I blotted my hands dry and dabbed at the smelly liquid on my pants and shoes.

I could have asked him the same thing. He had on mirrored sunglasses that kept his eyes hidden. His shirt had mother-of-pearl snaps as buttons and was secured at the neck with a bolo tie shaped like a cow skull. A camel blazer, jeans, and lizard-skin boots finished off the outfit. If it wasn't a hundred degrees, it was close. How he'd managed to not sweat through a few of his layers, I didn't know.

"I always dress like this," I said. "How about you?"

He laughed. "Me too. Cowboys and Indians. We should have somebody take our picture." He held out a hand. "I'm Black Jack Cannon. Couldn't help notice you staring at my dealership over there. See something you like?"

"You're Black Jack?" I stammered. "What are you doing over here?"

"This here gas station is mine too. Buy a car, get a year's worth of free gas. Nice incentive, don'tcha think?" He pulled a business card from his wallet and handed it to me. The back of his card was the same image as the playing card that was rotating on the pole.

"You're Blitz's dad, aren't you?" I blurted out. Immediately, I backpedaled. "I mean, I'm so sorry for your loss," I tacked on.

"Blitz was my wife's son," he said. "Tragedy, what happened yesterday. I hope they catch the killer soon or people are going to start thinking Proper City is like all those other desert towns around here."

"We are a desert town," I said.

"Not like the others. The people who pay the taxes around here make sure our money goes back into our own community. We pay the salary of the police who are supposed to keep us safe at night. We don't need outside elements coming in here trying to change the way we live."

For a moment, I saw a ray of light in Black Jack Cannon's point of view. If he suspected that an opportunistic vagrant had killed Blitz—and he put public pressure on the police force to find said vagrant—then the police couldn't spend time chasing Ebony for a crime she didn't commit. It wasn't much, but as far as theories went, I was willing to accept it.

"So you think somebody was passing through Proper City and saw the party? Maybe saw an opportunity to get something to eat or even rob a bunch of people, and was able to get in because everybody was in costume? Nobody would have noticed that there was a stranger among the rest of the partygoers."

"Could be. We love our costume parties around here, but it sure does make it easy for a stranger to infiltrate our world."

"I hadn't thought about that before, but I guess it does." I threw the wadded-up paper towel into the trash and screwed the gas cap back onto my scooter.

"You're Jerry Tamblyn's girl, aren't you?" he asked.

I nodded. "I'm Margo."

"So I guess that makes you part of the problem, doesn't it?"

"Excuse me?"

He turned to the side and jabbed his elbow at my arm.

"I'm just joshin' ya. Your dad designed the costumes for my *Maverick* party a few months back."

"I heard about that," I said.

"Gonna be hard for Sol Girard to top that for next month's poker game." He laughed. "You tell Jerry to keep up the good work and don't pay any attention to my theories." He put his hand on my shoulder and nodded toward the gas pump. "Sorry about the gasoline on your shoes. Next time you need a fill-up, you come see me first. It'll be on the house."

"Thanks, Mr. Cannon," I said.

"Call me Black Jack. Everybody else does. And this little scooter is mighty cute, but if you ever decide you want a real car, you come see me about that too."

"Maybe I will." I climbed back on, buckled my helmet under my chin, and glanced at Black Jack's parking lot. Tak's RAV4 was still there. I took off before he came back and spotted me.

I returned to Disguise DeLimit as Kirby was closing out the register drawer. He held up an index finger while he counted the change. I straightened the wall of fringed flapper dresses and put the bin of cigarette holders back on the shelf where they belonged. The peg next to the dresses that usually held an assortment of sequined headbands was empty except for one pink, one red, and one blue.

"Okay, I'm done counting," Kirby said. "We had a good day. The Proper City Cheerleaders were looking for something special for their halftime routine, and they flipped when they saw the flapper dresses. They took dresses, headbands, and fishnet stockings." At the word *stockings* he turned red under his freckles.

"Sounds like it's going to be quite a halftime routine," I said. "I noticed that we were low on headbands. Are you saying they bought all but the three we have left?"

"Yes."

"I guess I know what I'll be working on tonight," I said.

Accessories were easy to order from our suppliers, but we'd always known that it was the merchandise that we could make ourselves that would separate us from more commercial costume shops. It wasn't hard to make a headband of bright, sequined elastic and add on a feather or a paste gem, but by making the headbands in-house, we could experiment with different types of feathers and stretchy supplies and come up with combinations that regular costume shops couldn't stock. One of our most popular items was the black beaded headband with the peacock feather. It was the perfect unique accessory to set off a little black dress, even for an event that didn't require a costume.

"I put the money in the safe and tallied up the sales slips. I can stay behind and help you fill in the shelves for tomorrow, if you want," Kirby said.

"No, you should go home. It's after five. Enjoy the rest of your night." I apologized for not being able to give him a schedule for the week, since I didn't know when my dad and Don would be back. We agreed to play it by ear. I walked Kirby to the front door and threw the lock after he left.

Eager to shed the residue of gasoline that clung to my hands and clothing, I headed upstairs for a shower. I changed into a pair of loose cotton pajamas that had pictures of little green aliens on them. They were silly and completely inappropriate for a thirty-two-year-old woman but they made me feel closer to my dad, who was on his own alien adventure. I pulled on fluffy alien-head slippers and called him—my dad, not the alien-head slipper—to see how his trip was going.

"Hi, Dad. Are you okay?" I asked.

"Yup. Are you?"

"Yup."

Over the past seven years that I'd been in Las Vegas, there had been times when this had been the extent of our daily phone call. After spending a lifetime in Proper City with him and Ebony, moving away had been hard. Part of me had wanted to cling to the people and place that I knew and never leave. The people who knew my mother used to tell me that I was a miracle, that the doctors didn't expect me to survive childbirth. That's a heck of a thing to carry with you when your mom was the one who sacrificed her own life so you could live.

My dad had been the one to encourage me to move. "Margo," he'd said, "I've never been able to show you the world because I've had to be here minding the store. But I promised myself when the time came, I wouldn't push the shop onto you. You need to see what else is out there in the world before you decide where you want to be and what you want to do."

He gave me fifty thousand American Airlines miles and encouraged me to go anywhere I wanted. It was an amazing gift that allowed me to spend a week in Europe, but it might as well have been Oz, because as I traveled along the European rails by myself, the one thought that I couldn't shake was that there was no place like home.

I moved to Las Vegas—close enough to home to feel connected but wacky enough to stretch my boundaries—and bounced around a series of low-paying jobs. Eventually I took the job with Magic Maynard. It wasn't the best job in the world, but it was fun—except for the nights he sawed me in half. I'd never get used to that trick.

"How's Area 51?" I asked.

"It's amazing. This guy papier-mâchéd a series of gray alien heads that are out of this world." He laughed at his own joke. "After dinner he took us to his garage. He has the whole crew of the starship *Enterprise*. Even the red shirts who get killed in the first five minutes of the show."

My stomach turned at the mention of the word *killed*.

"There's too much to fit in the back of Don's car so we're going to rent a trailer in the morning. What about you? How are things in Proper?"

Judging from his tone, he hadn't heard the news about Blitz. I didn't want to tell him anything that would upset him—not while he was still recovering from his heart attack—but I couldn't pretend it hadn't happened.

"Blitz Manners is dead," I said. "He was killed at his birthday party." The phone was silent for a few seconds. "Dad? Are you still there?"

"I'm here."

"The police think Ebony was involved because she was standing over his body with the goose knife in her hand when I walked in on them, but she couldn't have done it."

"Margo, slow down. Tell me what happened."

I closed my eyes. The image of Blitz's body lying facedown in the puddle of blood slipped into place like a slide show. Slowly, I felt myself rock back and forth. "Ebony was in the kitchen. It was time to carve the goose. I wanted to be helpful so I went back to see if there was something I could do. When I walked in, his body was facedown in a puddle of blood and Ebony was standing over him with the carving knife in her hand."

"Did the police question her?"

"They questioned everybody. We all had to wait until they took our statements. I think Ebony and I were the last two people to talk to them."

"Where's she now?" he asked.

I flopped back on the bed and stared at the ceiling. "At

her store, probably. The last time I saw her was this morning. Someone vandalized her car and Dig towed it for her."

"Margo, listen carefully. If the police go digging into Ebony's past, they're going to find some things out that she'd rather not have become public. You need to do something for her."

"Sure, Dad, what?"

"You need to contact Takenouchi Hoshiyama and ask him for his help."

Chapter 9

"**WHAT DOES TAK** Hoshiyama have to do with anything?" I asked.

"You know him?"

"He was at the party. He's a friend of Blitz's."

"Tak is friendly with most people, I'd imagine. He worked for the district attorney's office in Clark County until a few months ago."

"He's a lawyer?" I asked.

"No, city planner, I think. I don't know why he moved to Proper, but when Don had trouble with his neighbor encroaching on his property line, Tak was a big help."

"We're talking about murder here, not property lines," I said.

"Margo, Tak is a smart man and he comes from a good family. Everything's going to be okay, but Ebony is going to need some help. Do you want me to come home? I can."

"No, you haven't had a chance to get out of Proper for years. Stay with Don."

"Only if you'll promise to call Tak. Think about everything Ebony's done for you. She's our family. Do this for her."

"You don't have to ask twice."

The tone of the conversation shifted from the joy of discovering the sci-fi costumes to the seriousness of Ebony's situation. My dad had promised to head back the following day. I told him to take it easy and promised to call Tak in the morning. Though sincere, both promises felt empty. Usually a talk with my dad left me feeling warm and cozy. Today, not so much.

EBONY didn't answer any of her phones. I left messages to call me back and hung up. My next call was to my roommate in Vegas. Maynard expected me to show up for work on Tuesday, and it wasn't looking as though I was going to make it.

"Margo? Is this Margo? The phone says it's you but I can't hear you. Hold on, let me get to the hallway, where I get better reception. Can you hear me? Can you hear me? Hello? Margo?"

"Hi, Crystal, I can hear you. Can you hear me?"

"Of course I can hear you. Maynard's been asking when you're coming back. I don't think he likes me as much as you. He keeps telling me to dress the part. What exactly do you wear for this performance?"

"Think *Desperately Seeking Susan*," I said. "Vintage '80s dance class with a tux jacket over top."

"It doesn't matter. You're coming back tomorrow, right?"

"That's why I called. I'm going to be here longer than I thought. Do you think Maynard will hold my job for me?"

"Girl, I'm doing what I can, but those doves freak me out."

"Thanks, Crystal."

"Vintage '80s with a tux jacket, huh? Where am I supposed to find that?"

I sighed. "The bottom two drawers on the right-hand side of my dresser."

"You have two drawers filled with costumes for Magic Maynard's act? You are one weird woman."

IT was close to eight o'clock when I finished my phone calls. I prepared an unfulfilling dinner of Fruity Pebbles doused with milk and carried the bowl downstairs. Halfway through, I abandoned it on the counter and walked around the store, determining what needed to get done for the week.

First item: restock the flapper section. Headbands, I already knew, but we were low on garters and fishnets too. There were a few dresses left on the rack, but when I checked the sizes, I saw that they were mostly small and extra small. Fringe wasn't the easiest thing to work with, so I made a note to check our suppliers to see what colors and styles were available for immediate delivery.

Next to the flapper section of the store was a rack of poodle skirts and cashmere twinsets from the '50s. We were in the middle of the hottest six months in Proper City, and even if somebody was heading to a sock hop or a '50s-themed party, they'd request a custom costume instead of the heavy wool on these. I made a note to rotate the store's inventory and replace the winter-weight costumes with something lightweight like hula girls and surfers.

When I finished my tour of the store, my to-do list was four pages long. There was a chance I was creating work so I wouldn't have to think about my dad's health or Blitz's murder or Ebony's predicament, but I couldn't help myself. Outside the store, the sky grew dark with night. Even during the hot days from April to October, it was worth going outside at night. The sun took a break from scorching the town and a cool breeze danced around buildings, cars, gardens, and residences.

I set my notebook on a chair. Air would feel good. I flipped the dead bolt and opened the door just as a truck screeched to a halt in front of the store.

I jumped back inside and pushed the door shut. The hydraulic arm kept it from slamming. When it fell into place, I flipped the lock and backed away into a shadow. The silhouette of a person approached. I felt his presence even though I couldn't see. Why hadn't I drawn the shade on the door? What was I thinking?

I flattened myself against the wall between the entrance and the display window. The person moved away from the storefront. I didn't move. In a few seconds, I heard a thud on the sidewalk, and then another. The sound repeated twice, and then the truck drove away.

My heart thumped in my chest. Was someone out there still? I didn't think so. *Come on, Margo*, I told myself. *Grow a pair. Nobody's waiting on the sidewalk to get you.*

I pulled the shade down and dropped to my knees. When I peeked out of the corner of the window I spotted four bulging black trash bags in front of the shop. Creepy thoughts flooded my brain and I shuddered. I could call the police, I thought. They could come and investigate the bags. Or I could wait until tomorrow when it was light out. Or I could call the city trash collector and ask him to pick up the bags and take them away.

As options played out in my head, Soot approached the door. He pushed his nose into the small space below the door.

I stroked his fur and started to calm down. I grabbed the doorknob, stood up, and pulled the shade down. The pull tab from the window shade caught on the button of my pajama top and I yanked at it to free myself. The shade retracted all the way and I found myself face-to-face with Tak.

I screamed. He might have screamed too. Soot jumped a foot in the air. When he landed he scrambled his feet against the linoleum tile floor, searching for traction. Seconds later his nails caught and he took off for the stairs.

Tak tried to open the door but it was locked. I stumbled backward a few times. My heart did a jive in my chest. Tak stepped out of view. The phone rang and I kept my eyes on the door while I felt around the counter for it.

"H-h-hello?" I said.

"This is Tak. I'm sorry I scared you. Your dad called. He said you were going to call me, but when you didn't, I thought I'd come over and see if you wanted to talk in person."

"I don't believe you," I said.

"I admit it might have been a bad idea to come over here tonight. How about we meet tomorrow?"

Soot's curiosity apparently had replaced his fear. He crept back into the store, his tail fat and his walk low. He approached the front door and stood on his hind legs with his paws on the glass. Tak reappeared and dropped down to a squat. He held his hand up to the door and Soot ran his head against the glass like he wanted Tak to pet him.

My cat was a lot of things, but he wasn't known for being particularly friendly. His behavior was downright odd. "What did you do to my cat?" I asked.

"What could I possibly do to your cat? I'm on the other side of your door."

"He's never this friendly unless somebody has food for him."

"He probably smells the fish."

"What fish?"

He stood up and looked at the bags. "The fish in your garbage. That's what all these bags are, right?"

"Our garbage goes out back. Somebody drove up and dumped those bags in front of the store."

"I don't want to tell you how to run your business, but if you don't do something with these bags soon you're going to have a whole lot more cats by morning."

All of a sudden it struck me as very, very silly that Tak and I were talking on the phone to each other when we stood less than ten feet apart. I got the giggles.

"What's so funny?"

"You. Us. We're acting like I'm in a containment unit."

He cracked a smile. "There's one way to change that," he said. "You could unlock the door and invite me in."

It wasn't until I caught my reflection in the glass of the door—alien pajamas and fluffy green slippers—that I realized just how silly the situation was. I grabbed a men's topcoat from a rack and shrugged into it. The itchy wool scratched my neck and the sleeves fell far past my hands.

I unlocked the dead bolt and held the door open. Tak grabbed the knot of two of the black garbage bags and carried them in. I scooted to the sidewalk and grabbed the other two. They bulged with soft contents. Tak was right; they smelled of fish.

Soot eagerly followed the bags into the store. He chewed on the bottom corner of the first one Tak had set down. I nudged him away with one of my alien-slippered feet. He jumped when he saw the fluffy green head and ran in the other direction. I looked at Tak. He tried to hide a smile. I secured the topcoat around my body.

"I'm going to run upstairs and change," I said.

"Don't do it on my account," he said. "I hear the alien look is big on the Paris runways."

I pulled a slipper off and threw it at him. He caught it and tucked it under his arm.

"Be right back," I said. I scooped up Soot and ran upstairs, my bare foot cold against the floor. My Indian outfit was still on the bed where I'd left it, but gasoline-scented beige linen probably wasn't the best thing to wear when going through garbage bags that smelled of fish. I pulled on a navy blue polyester tracksuit with white stripes down the arms and legs and knotted on a pair of sneakers. Within seconds, I was back in the shop.

"Okay, I'm ready," I said.

Tak stood by one of the bags with a white envelope in his hand. "This was taped to the outside of one of the bags and it has your name on it." He held the envelope out. I recognized the handwriting before the envelope was in my hand, and suddenly everything made sense.

Chapter 10

A SMILE BROKE across my face and I eagerly tore into the envelope.

> *Margo,*
>
> *These came in during our last clothing drive, but I thought maybe you or Jerry could do something with them. If yes, I'll accept a donation in exchange. Just like old times!*
>
> *—Bobbie K.*
> *P.S. Sorry about the smell.*

The letterhead read: MONEY CHANGES EVERYTHING.

"I'm guessing you know the donor," Tak said. Absorbed in Bobbie's letter as I was, I'd forgotten that he was standing there.

"My high school best friend. She runs a nonprofit." I said. "She must have heard I was back in town." I set the letter on the counter and unknotted the first bag. The scent of fish grew stronger. I waved my hand back and forth in front of my nose.

Tak located a fan in the corner of the store and turned it on, and then propped the front door open and positioned the fan to blow the scent outside. I reached into the bag and pulled out a white sailor top. Underneath it was another. And another. And another. What the heck?

"Open that one," I instructed Tak. His bag held a stack of black sailor pants. The rest of the bags held more of the same: sailor tops and pants. Either the smell faded or I was becoming immune to the scent of fish, because by the time we had all four bags unpacked, I barely noticed it.

"Do you know what we're looking at?" Tak asked.

"Bobbie Kay volunteers at a local women's shelter. They do a clothing drive in the fall and in the spring. It looks like someone dropped these off during the last one. I can't imagine who would have all these sailor outfits and why they'd smell like tuna, though." I picked up one of the tops from the pile. A tag from the sleeve read ARMY NAVY STORE. I picked up a pair of pants and found the same thing. Tak caught on and checked the stack nearest him. "These too," he said.

"Looks like the Army Navy store donated them to the women's shelter and your friend gave them to you," Tak said.

"In exchange for a donation," I clarified. Which I was happy to give. "But what's with the fish smell?"

"They *are* sailor suits," he said. "Adds a note of authenticity. I bet Candy Girls doesn't have pre-scented costumes."

The idea of promoting that the costumes at Disguise DeLimit came with thematic scents brought on another fit of giggles. It was late, and after the adrenaline crash of having been scared by Bobbie's covert costume drop-off and then

Tak's subsequent arrival, I was left in a state of silly. It took longer than I would have liked to get the giggling under control. Tak stood by, patient, with a smile on his face.

"You never told me why you were here," I said when I was able to talk again.

"Yes I did. Your dad called me. He said you were going to call me to talk about Ebony's situation. I couldn't sleep, so I went out for a drive. I guess I ended up here because I was already thinking about you. I didn't expect you to be working, but when I saw the trash bags out front and the lights on inside, I thought maybe you were up too."

"I was full of energy a couple of hours ago, but I'm starting to wind down. Can you help me carry these to the steamer in the back?"

"Sure."

We lugged the sailor costumes past the sewing area to a small room that housed a steel steamer box, about eight feet high by ten feet deep. I turned the dial on the outside to generate pressure, and then unfolded several dryer sheets and clipped them to empty plastic pants hangers.

"What are those for?" Tak asked.

"The heat from the steamer activates the scent in the dryer sheet and neutralizes odors. I usually only use one per rolling rod, but I'm pretty sure this fish smell is unprecedented."

After placing the dryer sheets on the rod, we hung the tops and pants between them. We had approximately fifty items, spaced an inch or so apart from one another. I opened the steamer cage and rolled the chrome rod inside. After clamping the door shut with a *ka-chung,* I checked the pressure gauge and then pushed the green button. It turned red, and the sound of steam filling the metal box came like a *whoosh* next to us. In sixty seconds, the light clicked back to green. I yanked on the handle and a cloud of steam washed over me.

"Your own private steamer. I'm impressed."

"It's a lot easier to keep the costumes fresh this way. Plus, dry cleaning is too harsh on most fabrics. Some of our costumes are twenty and thirty years old. A couple are older than that." I pulled the rolling rod out of the steamer cage. Droplets of condensation speckled the metal rod between hangers. The scent of fish had been replaced with the freshness of the dryer sheets.

"These are still damp, but they'll dry by tomorrow morning," I said. "What time is it?"

He checked his watch. "Ten thirty," he said. "I didn't realize it was so late. You probably want to get to bed."

I turned the pressure switch from the steamer to the off position and walked Tak back out to the front of the store. When I'd first moved to Vegas, I'd had to adjust to the fact that most jobs didn't have nine-to-five hours. Working shows that closed at twelve thirty and not getting home until after one had gradually taken its toll on my internal sense of time. These days I was more of a night owl than a morning person. After falling asleep in front of the television last night and waking to find that I'd slept through the vandalism of Ebony's car, maybe it would be good to give in to my night owl tendencies and keep watch.

"I'm still on Vegas time," I said. "I'll probably be up for the next couple of hours."

"Vegas time? Is that where you live?"

I nodded.

"I lived in Las Vegas for a few years. What part?"

"No place special."

"Everybody's home is special," he said.

"I live in an apartment on top of a Chinese restaurant."

"See, now that sounds special. Do you like it?"

"Actually, yes. Some nights I get home so late I don't

have the energy to cook. I'll get an egg roll or fried rice and eat it at two o'clock in the morning."

We stood in the front of the store next to the counter. I watched his eyes cut to the half-empty bowl of cereal behind me, and I blushed. What must he think of me? My father called him and told him to check on me. When he showed up, I was in alien pj's. And now he'd discovered that I ate Fruity Pebbles for dinner!

"I'd like to keep talking with you. If you're game, I know where to get the best fried rice in Proper."

"They're open at ten thirty on a Sunday?"

"I have connections."

Truth was, I wanted to keep talking with Tak too. He was at the party where Blitz was murdered, so he was connected to the whole thing. My dad's and Ebony's reassurances that he was a good guy from a good family helped, as did the need to talk to an impartial person about what had happened since I'd arrived back in town. I ran upstairs for my wallet and keys and then returned to the store. Tak waited out front while I locked up. I hopped into his SUV and we left.

THE Proper City streets were mostly quiet at this hour on a Sunday. Retailers and businesses that thrived in the first half of the day, like florists, coffee shops, and bakeries, had long since closed, leaving only the illumination from the occasional nightclub or restaurant. Tak drove us down Main Line Road in the same direction I'd driven earlier that day. The rotating playing card in front of Black Jack's car dealership was lit up like a party favor. We passed that too, and then turned into the parking lot of a small Japanese-style building.

Across the front wooden roofline that curved up slightly on both sides were the words HOSHIYAMA KOBE STEAK

HOUSE. The lack of cars in the lot and lights around the building confirmed my suspicion that we were past regular operating hours. Tak parked around the side of the building and turned off the engine.

"Ebony told me your parents owned a restaurant," I said. "But I think we're a little late for happy hour."

"I have special privileges," he said. "Come with me."

I followed him to the side door. He unlocked three locks with three different keys and then looked at me. "You're in for a treat." Once inside, he flipped a light switch that provided a low-level glow throughout the interior.

The restaurant was made up of six individual islands. Each one had a steel cooktop built into a table. Eight chairs surrounded the islands on three of the four sides; the remaining side, I knew, was for the chef to prepare a teppanyaki feast with twirling knives, flying shrimp tails, and volcanoes built from onions. I'd long been a fan of teppanyaki. Ever since my first meal at Mori's when I graduated from sixth grade, I was hooked.

Tak guided me to a nearby island and pulled out a chair in the middle of the long side of the table. I sat. He walked around to the back and flipped a switch. "The grill is going to get hot in a minute or two. Be careful. I'll be right back."

He disappeared behind a long, green curtain that hid the kitchen and returned with a pushcart. On top were two medium-sized bowls of white rice, a small bowl of minced carrots, onion, and celery, a plate with a blob of what I knew to be garlic butter, and a bottle of soy sauce. Two eggs rested next to the bottle of soy, and a boneless chicken breast sat on a separate plate.

He held his open hand over the grill to check the temperature and then squirted sesame oil onto the surface. With the flat side of a silver spatula, he spread the oil around in circles that grew wider and wider. He added the chicken and then dumped the rice bowls upside down onto the empty surface of the grill next to it.

"My father tells me you work in the Clark County district attorney's office," I said. "I can't imagine this is a necessary skill."

"No, but it keeps me popular at parties." He moved the rice around over the surface and then added the bowl of diced vegetables. Next, the blob of garlic butter went on top. He used two large paddlelike utensils to mix everything together, and then he pushed it all to the side. He cracked both eggs into a silver mixing bowl, scrambled them with a fork, and poured them onto the grill, then set the shells inside the empty bowl, which went back on the cart.

"I feel cheated. Shouldn't you be tossing stuff in the air and catching it in your hat?"

He looked surprised. "You know about the hat tricks?"

"This isn't my first rodeo," I said.

"Well, then I guess I must confess. There's a reason I'm a city planner and not a teppanyaki chef. I never got the hang of the hat part."

I sat back and let him finish making the fried rice in silence. He diced the chicken and blended it in with the rice and veggie mix, added soy sauce and sesame seeds, and scooped it up into two separate bowls. He held out a fork and I waved him off.

"Are you eating with chopsticks?" I asked.

"Yes, but I figured—"

"You figured wrong. I'll take chopsticks too."

He brought me a set of chopsticks from the hostess station and then sat next to me. Small talk became a secondary concern after tasting the first mouthful of fried rice. I'd tried to make it at home—even went so far as to find a clone recipe online—but had never quite replicated the flavor. Maybe it had something to do with the indulgence of watching someone else prepare it for me.

"How is it?" he asked.

"Mmmmmm." I swallowed. "Best fried rice ever."

He grinned.

I hadn't realized how hungry I was until I was scraping the bottom of the rice bowl with my chopsticks. Tak was halfway done with his. He set the bowl and chopsticks on the table and turned to me.

"I don't want to ruin your fried rice experience with a difficult conversation, but Jerry tells me Ebony might be in some trouble."

I set my near-empty bowl down. "Tak, before I tell you what's going on, I need you to understand. Ebony and my dad are the two most important people in my life, and I'd do anything for them. I came back to Proper City because of my dad's heart attack. That scared me more than anything in my life. Now this thing with Blitz is affecting Ebony. She's as much a part of my family as my dad. I want to help her, but I think she's scared too—scared that something from her past, something she doesn't want anybody to know—is going to come out and it's going change the way people view her. I'm afraid of what the investigation is going to do to her."

"Hey," Tak said. He sandwiched his hands around mine. "Family is important. I know that more than most people. But sometimes you have turn your back on what they want in order to do what you think is right."

I couldn't imagine a situation when I'd need to turn my back on the people I loved. From my earliest memories, of my dad tending to my skinned knee when I was five, or dressing me in a *Sound of Music* costume for my first recital when I was fourteen, to the pots of coffee he brewed when I had to stay up all night studying for exams when I was in community college. I remembered how Ebony used her resources at Shindig to throw me the best tenth birthday party in Proper City, how she let me borrow her first bichon frise when I dressed as Little Bo Peep when I was twelve, and how she did my hair and makeup for my senior prom because she knew that's what my own mother would have done if she hadn't died.

Tears welled up in my eyes and I blinked them back so Tak wouldn't notice. The air around us hung heavy with the scent of fried rice and the weight of his words. The silence was punctured by the sound of something falling to the ground by the hostess table.

Tak dropped my hands and stood up. "Who's there?" he asked the darkness.

There was no reply. A shadow moved along the far wall of the restaurant, distorted by the low light that emanated from paper lanterns swaying in the entranceway. I reached out for Tak's hand.

"The lanterns," I whispered and pointed at the entrance. "The front door must be open."

"Wait here." He moved through the empty interior and out the front door. Seconds later, the door slammed shut and I was alone.

Chapter 11

AS SAFE AS I'd tricked myself into thinking I was when we arrived, now I felt a hundred times more scared. It was after midnight. I was alone in a restaurant where I had no business being. I didn't know who had been inside with us or what they'd wanted. I was rooted to my chair as if I weighed a thousand pounds.

I crept toward the exit. Voices outside argued. Then silence. And then—*bam!* I ran outside and found Tak alone in the parking lot. His fists were balled up and he stood facing the Dumpster as if it were his opponent in a street brawl.

"Tak?" I asked. He was so focused on the trash bin that he didn't hear me. "Tak," I said again. In the distance, red and blue lights flashed. A police car approached and turned into the Hoshiyama parking lot. Its arrival snapped Tak's concentration and he turned to look first at the police car and then at me.

"Wait here," he said.

A door opened above me and I looked up. An older Japanese man stood on a small balcony above a narrow flight of stairs. He crossed his arms over his chest and watched Tak. I didn't know if he saw me or not.

A police officer got out of her car. It took me a couple of seconds to recognize Detective Nichols from Blitz Manners's party. She wore a dark blazer over a white shirt and black pants. She and Tak exchanged a few words. Their voices weren't audible, but judging from their body language, they were exchanging more than a polite greeting. They turned in my direction and Tak pointed to me. I glanced up at the man on the balcony. He was watching me too. Tak called out my name. He waved me forward, and I joined him and the detective by the police car.

"Margo, this is Detective Nichols," he said.

"I know. We met at Blitz's party," I said.

"Ms. Tamblyn," she said, nodding my direction. "I received a call that there was a break-in at the restaurant."

"We didn't break in," I said. "Tak had a key."

The detective studied my expression, and I got the feeling she was gauging more than my words. "In any event, it's late and you two should call it a night."

"Sure," I said.

The detective walked around the restaurant, presumably to make sure everything was okay. Tak stood next to me, silent and guarded. I looked over his head to the balcony, but the old man was gone.

"Tak, why did Detective Nichols say someone called about a break-in?"

He watched her taillights fade away into the distance. When he spoke, it wasn't to answer my question. "She's right. It's late. How about I take you home?"

"There's a mess inside. Let me help you clean up first."

"I'll take care of it when I get back." He put his hand on the small of my back and guided me to his car. We didn't talk on the way back to Disguise DeLimit. Tak's mind appeared to be far away.

"Tak, who was the man on the balcony?"

He stared ahead at the road. "My father."

"Was he the one who called the police?"

Tak parked in front of the shop and nodded. "The problems I'm having with my father have nothing to do with you. I'm sorry about tonight. It was a bad idea to go. That's not what I had in mind when I invited you."

I shrugged. "You delivered exactly what you promised. The best fried rice in Proper City."

For the first time since we'd left, he smiled. "Good night, Margo," he said. His car didn't pull away from the curb until after I was upstairs in my bedroom with Soot.

EVEN though I hadn't gone to bed until close to two—after soaking my gasoline-saturated linens and treating my suede moccasins with baking soda to absorb the stain and the odor—I was up by seven. Inspired by the uniforms that Bobbie had dropped off the night before, I dressed in my own sleeveless white sailor's top and black flare-bottom pants. I pulled a cheap black, white, and yellow naval captain's hat over my flipped hair and blended up a pineapple and banana smoothie.

While Soot buried his nose in a bowl of organic fish parts, I sat at the dining room table staring at the hair spray cans and the torn piece of fabric that I'd found on Ebony's car. I'd wanted to talk to Tak about it, but our conversation had been interrupted before I had the chance.

I finished my smoothie and filled the glass and the blender

with water and left them sitting in the sink. The store wasn't due to open for a few hours, and with Kirby in school, I wouldn't be able to leave once we were open like I had yesterday. I stuffed my wallet into a hidden pocket inside the waistband of the sailor pants, grabbed my keys, and left.

SHINDIG was located inside of the house where Ebony had lived since I'd met her. It was a small split-level building. Ebony had opened up the first floor by knocking out walls to make a showroom. The upstairs was modest—a bedroom, bathroom, and a small landing filled with Ivory's toys—but it was all she needed to make do.

Her massive Coupe de Ville was parked in a space in the corner of the lot behind the store. The flat tires had been repaired and all traces of the hair spray had been removed from the hood. Even the windows appeared to be in working order. Dig must have bumped his other business in order to handle Ebony's crisis. No big surprise there.

I locked my helmet to the scooter and pulled the captain's hat onto my head. After letting myself in through the back door, I started a pot of coffee. Ebony had never been a morning person, and she'd long ago given me a set of rules for entering her house before ten a.m. They included starting the coffee, not attempting to clean up any messes that she might have left out the night before, and staying downstairs. As usual, I adhered to the first and third rules and completely ignored the second by moving the dirty dishes in the sink to the dishwasher. I texted her to let her know I was there, and wandered into the showroom out front.

Shindig had been Ebony's party planning business since she'd graduated high school in the '70s. Photos of her early parties lined the walls behind the counter next to the first dollar she'd ever made. In the front of the store were small round tables surrounded by three to four chairs, and on each table was a stack of photo albums that showcased what she'd done for clients in the past. She stocked very little in the way of merchandise, preferring to be hired to coordinate a party rather than to let people come to her for supplies to create their own backdrop. This was the fundamental difference between the way Shindig and Candy Girls approached party planning.

As I wandered the store, I heard the sound of footsteps over my head. Seconds later, Ebony called down the stairs. "I'll be down in a second. Did you start the coffee?"

"Rule number one," I called back.

"Leave those dirty dishes in the sink," she said.

"Too late." I headed to the kitchen to fix her a cup, when I heard something dragging across the floor over my head. "What are you doing up there?"

The dragging traveled to the stairs. Ebony appeared at the top of them, dressed in a tank top, long patchwork vest that hung to her knees, and bell-bottoms over platform sandals. Her gold medallion necklace was tucked inside the tank top. She descended the stairs backward. Ivory scampered down the staircase to greet me—or to get out of the way of the giant brown suitcase Ebony bumped down the stairs—I couldn't tell which. The suitcase, a hard brown plastic with brass trim, slammed against each wooden step. When she reached the bottom of the stairs, she leaned back against the wall and dabbed at her hairline with an orange bandanna.

"This sucker is heavy."

"What's in there?"

"Everything I could fit. Help me get it to the car, wouldya?"

"Have your coffee first."

"No time. In fact, pour that into a travel mug for me and I'll deal with the suitcase."

She struggled to lift the suitcase and carry it out to her Caddy. I dumped her coffee into a travel mug that said GROOVY! and met her outside.

"Where are you going?"

She opened the trunk of the car and heaved the suitcase inside. "Ebony needs a vacation," she said, referring to herself in the third person as she did on occasion. "Ivory too. No business happenin' here since the Blitz thing. Now's as good a time as any to get out of town."

"Ebony, you can't just leave."

"Baby girl," she said. She put her hand alongside my face. "I tried to teach you that every situation was an opportunity to learn something about yourself, right? Maybe that's what I'm supposed to learn from this. That it's time for me to leave the past behind and move on."

"No," I said.

She picked up Ivory and set him inside the car, then turned to me. She gave me a trademark Ebony hug—the kind where she holds so tight the breath is squeezed out of you—and I squeezed back. As soon as we parted, she pulled a pair of sunglasses from her pocket and put them on, rendering her expression unreadable.

"Take care of your old man, now, you hear?" she said. She climbed into the car and started the engine. I stood directly behind the rear bumper. If I didn't move, she couldn't leave. It was selfish, I knew, but as I stood there, watching her adjust her rearview mirror, I felt more alone than I had in years. If Ebony pulled out of that parking space, I felt as though I'd never see her again.

She rolled down the window and propped her elbow on the door. "Margo, fish gotta swim and birds gotta fly." Ivory climbed over her lap and poked his head out the window. Ebony ran her hand over his head and moved him back to the passenger side.

I stepped out of her way. She threw the Caddy into gear. I reached a hand out to her. She touched my fingers and squeezed them, and then pulled out of the parking lot, leaving me alone in a cloud of gravel, dust, and isolation.

The car had disappeared down the long stretch of Main Line Road that led to the highway. When the dust cleared, I spotted a white envelope on the ground next to where her car had been parked. I picked it up and looked inside.

The envelope was filled with a thick stash of hundreds. It looked like roughly the same amount that Blitz Manners had given us to throw him a party. The same money I'd given back when I'd told him we couldn't take the job. But Ebony hadn't been paid at the start of the party. So how did she end up with this envelope of Blitz's cash?

And what was it doing in the parking lot outside of Shindig the day she decided to leave town?

Chapter 12

I RAN TO the corner where Ebony had driven and looked for her car, but I already knew she was long gone. I shoved the envelope of money into the small storage compartment under the seat of the scooter. Ebony was my rock. Ebony was the one who stood up to anybody who got into her path. The fact that she'd left told me more than any words could have said.

Ebony was scared. Of what, I didn't know. But I wasn't going to let her face this alone.

I left Shindig and drove to Money Changes Everything. Bobbie's office was at the end of a modest strip mall that included a used paperback bookstore, a pet groomer, and three fast-food restaurants. I parked the scooter in front of the office and headed inside.

The interior was neat. A single desk, white metal base with

wood laminate top, faced the front door. Colorful sour balls wrapped in clear plastic were nestled in a glass bowl on the corner of the desk next to an old, white phone and a couple of frames. A computer monitor sat to the right. Behind the desk, shelves lined with teddy bears made from scraps of colorful fabric ran from floor to ceiling, covering every inch of the wall save for a small hallway that led to a restroom.

"Mitty!" I heard behind me.

I turned around and saw an older and happier version of the friend I remembered.

"Bobbie Kay!"

Bobbie Kay—birth name Barbara Kennedy—had been my first friend. We met when I was six and she was five. On the surface, Bobbie was straight out of the pages of an East Coast prep school. She dressed in white, pink, or blue polo shirts, pleated khaki pants that she bought in bulk from the Gap, and Tretorn Nylite sneakers, and her trademark bob was trimmed every six weeks like the hairdresser suggested.

Bobbie had joined the entrepreneur's club in high school and while her classmates worked up moneymaking schemes that involved day trading and the occasional gambling trip to maximize their investments, she'd devised a plan to make and sell teddy bears around town. She blew the doors off the next-highest-grossing project and surprised everybody in school when she donated her profits to charity. "Teddy bears should be used for good and not evil," she'd said in a press release.

What most people didn't know about Bobbie was that the pressures of staying at the head of her class had led her to the unhealthy regimen of over-the-counter diet pills, a habit that escalated to dangerously addictive levels. She developed a dependency her senior year and spent the summer after graduation in a treatment program. Not willing to test her newly healthy body with the unknown stresses of the Ivy League college she'd been planning to attend, she declined the scholarship that awaited her and instead accepted an internship with a local business. Now she ran her own non-profit. Both her stress and her figure were maintained through early-morning yoga sessions. She was happy, healthy, and making a difference in the world, one teddy bear at a time.

Bobbie rushed across the office and threw her arms around me. I hugged her back. Even though the more recent years of our friendship had dissolved into birthday text messages, Facebook post "likes," and the occasional e-mail, I felt as if I'd seen her yesterday. Some friendships are like that.

"Does anybody call you Mitty anymore?" she asked.

"Anymore? Nobody ever called me Mitty except for you, and if you stop now, I'll never speak to you again."

Ever since I'd known her, Bobbie had made a point to ignore her given name. Maybe Barbara was too feminine for a six-year-old tomboy who wanted to explore old barns and adopt stray kittens. Or maybe her parents, activists in their own right, nicknamed her Bobbie as a tribute to the presidential hopeful who was assassinated in 1968.

But sometime around her twelfth birthday she'd decided it was time for another identity, and Bobbie Kay was born. She hung a portrait of Mary Kay in her locker as a symbol of what could be accomplished by a woman with a vision and a tube of lipstick.

She'd decided that I needed a nickname too, and cleverly pulled the *M* and the *T* of my names to get Mitty. She claimed it worked because the way I dressed showed that I was partially living in a fantasy world. Come to think of it, her five-cent diagnosis wasn't all that different from my sometimes thera-pist. Today Bobbie was in a pink polo, pleated khakis, and white Tretorns. Her straight brown hair was in her signature bob, parted in the middle, and both sides were tucked behind her ears. Even though she shirked makeup and still dressed like she had decades ago, she now wore a layer of maturity that she'd earned by confronting her personal demons and winning.

"I see you got my donation," she said, standing back and checking out my outfit.

"I'll have you know this came from my own closet, thank you very much," I said. "But yes, the sailor suits are fantastic. We steamed the fishy smell out of them last night and I'm going to put them in the windows later today."

"So Jerry's doing better? I heard about his heart attack."

"You'd barely know he had a heart attack. He's in the desert with Don Digby, chasing alien costumes."

"I bet he wouldn't have considered going if it weren't for you coming here."

"Maybe," I said.

"There's no 'maybe' about it. When the local ice cream shop closed, they donated their backup uniforms to me. I stopped by to see if Jerry was interested in them and he kept me there for an hour showing me photos of a collection of costumes from some German-themed restaurant in Wisconsin. He couldn't get over the lederhosen. I could tell he wanted to go, just to meet the guy and find out the backstory on the costumes, but he couldn't."

"He kept you there for an hour?"

"Yeah, he'll talk to anybody who wants to talk about costumes."

"Since when do you want to talk about costumes?"

"Don't let the outer package fool you. I appreciate a costume as much as the next girl."

"Uh-huh," I said, unconvinced. "What happened to the

ice cream parlor costumes? There's nothing like that in our inventory."

"I don't know. He took the lot and made a nice donation to the cause. They're probably in storage."

I hadn't spent a lot of time thinking about how my dad had been stuck behind the counter of the store all these years. Sure, he had Kirby to keep him company, and he always enjoyed finding new and different ways to satisfy the clients who came into Disguise DeLimit, but he hadn't taken an actual vacation since I was a kid. Moreover, he never told me that he'd wanted to. But after only a few days back in Proper, more than one person had mentioned how much he talked about getting away and exploring the country. Maybe this road trip with Don was the best medicine after all.

"If your dad's in the desert, who helped you steam out the costumes?"

Heat climbed up my face. Bobbie clapped her hands and half sat on the corner of her desk. "There's a guy. It's a guy, right? You went totally red. It must be a guy."

There was something about hanging out with Bobbie that turned us into giggling girls in no time, and even though we'd been in her office for only mere minutes, we'd already time-traveled back to our childhood selves. I leaned against the wall and told her about Tak showing up at the store while I was dressed in alien pj's and slippers.

"Tak Hoshiyama?" She whistled. "That one's a mystery. I thought he was dating Nancy Nichols. Did they break up?"

"Nancy Nichols—do I know her?"

"I don't know why you would. She's Proper City's new police detective."

Oh crap. Crappety crappety crap. "You mean Detective Nichols? The one who looks like a professional volleyball player?"

Bobbie studied me. "Mitty, you look like you just heard the stock market crashed. Are you okay?"

"The detective and Tak Hoshiyama are a couple?"

"That's what I heard but I don't keep up with these things. Why is it such a big deal to you?" she asked.

I buried my face in my hands. "Detective Nichols caught Tak and me at Hoshiyama Steak House after hours last night," I said. "Oh gosh, Bobbie, this is bad."

"How bad can it be? His parents own the place, so it's not like you broke in, right? Besides, maybe they're on a break. You're consenting adults, and whatever she caught you doing is nobody's business but your own."

"She caught us eating fried rice."

"Oh. Sounds innocent to me."

"That's not the problem. It's Detective Nichols and Tak. I bet that's why he keeps showing up and talking to me about what happened. He's helping her. Oh man, I am so stupid. Do you know what I did? I trusted him. I don't know what she's going to do but it can't be good."

"Work with me, Mits. What's going on?"

I looked up at Bobbie. The desire to confide in Tak last night had gone unfulfilled and I desperately needed to talk to somebody. "Do you think you can spare an hour for breakfast?"

MINUTES later we were seated at a booth in the back of Eggcetera, a breakfast restaurant in the corner of the strip mall. I faced down a Belgian waffle covered in quickly melting whipped butter—the stress of Ebony's situation required something stronger than a smoothie—while Bobbie layered lox and cream cheese onto her bagel.

"You heard about Blitz Manners, right?" I asked.

She nodded. "What a horrible situation. Murdered at his own party."

"I was there," I said. At her surprised expression, I continued, "Not as a guest. Blitz hired Disguise DeLimit to provide costumes for the party and hired Shindig to coordinate everything."

"I thought he was going to have his party at Roman Gardens."

"A pipe burst in the kitchen a week before the party and flooded the place. The owner gave back the deposit and that's when Blitz came to us."

"Twenty-four hours to plan a Blitz-sized party? That couldn't have been easy."

"It wasn't. We weren't even going to take the job except—" I stopped midsentence. The twenty grand in cash that I'd found in Ebony's parking lot was locked inside my scooter, now sitting in front of the offices of Money Changes Everything. Anxiety crept up my skin like an army of tiny spiders. I looked out the window to see if my scooter was still there. It was. I sipped water and remembered that nobody knew the money was in the scooter except for me.

"Except that Blitz threw enough money at you to make it worth your while," Bobbie finished.

"How did you know?"

"You don't live in Proper City and not know about Blitz and his money. The day his inheritance came through was the first day of the rest of his life. And it wasn't the fantasy people might think." She took a big bite of her bagel and held her hand up over her mouth while she chewed.

I studied Bobbie. "You sound like maybe you know more about Blitz than you're saying."

She held up her index finger until she swallowed and

followed with a gulp of her green tea. "This stays between us, okay?"

"Sure," I said.

"Blitz's dad died when he was thirteen, but he didn't get his inheritance until he was eighteen. By then, he was already popular. Captain of the football team, homecoming king, you know the type. But when he got that money, his life changed overnight. Suddenly he had an entourage. His family was always rich, so it wasn't like he didn't know what money would do, but he still went a little crazy. When his mom remarried, he waited until their honeymoon and threw a massive party at the house. It lasted three days and somebody called the cops. It was the first of many parties like that. They were legendary."

"How do you know all this?" I asked. Bobbie and I were six years older than Blitz's crowd. Not an insurmountable age difference, but more likely an insurmountable difference in priorities. I couldn't see Bobbie hanging with Blitz's crowd, legendary parties or not.

Bobbie looked down at her green tea, picked up the mug, and then set it down again without taking a sip. "Blitz had the same problems with substance abuse that I had. The difference was, he didn't want to get better. That's how he coped. After one party too many, he was arrested for disturbing the peace. His parents sent him to the rehab clinic."

"The same one where you went?"

She nodded. "I was there when he checked in."

"You didn't need to—"

She held up her hand. "I haven't taken anything stronger than aspirin since I left. Once a year I go back and visit. I can't explain why I do it except that I feel like I owe it to them and to myself to check in and prove that I'm still okay, and to acknowledge the role they played in me getting my life on track."

"So you were there when Blitz checked in."

"And I was there when he bought his way out too. But he still had to serve two hundred hours of community service. I was planning a city fund-raiser and he fulfilled his community service by working with me."

"Doing what?"

"Whatever I needed him to do. Twenty hours a week for ten weeks. When you spend that kind of time together, you start to know each other. And knowing what I knew, I wanted to help him. Blitz started those two hundred hours as a spoiled rich kid who was barely legal, but by the time his sentence was up, I'd gotten to know a whole different person. He was just like every other kid who is a big shot in high school and realizes that life isn't what he thought it would be. He acted out for attention. He kept throwing the parties because people expected him to throw the parties but he knew his popularity had nothing to do with who he was. People weren't coming to his house because they were his friends. He resented being popular for his money, and he never got over his dad's death."

I thought back to the day Blitz had been at Disguise DeLimit. My first impression had been spoiled rich kid who gets whatever he wants, but he'd changed when I gave back his money. When Grady came back, he'd said that Blitz felt bad for the way he'd treated me, and I hadn't believed it. Now I was left wondering if that was the case, if Blitz had gotten so used to people wanting nothing more from him than an envelope filled with cash that he didn't know how to handle my rejection.

"What happened after his sentence was over?" I asked. "Did he ever come back to help you?"

"He helped the only way he knew how," she said. "He donated money."

Nothing I'd learned about Blitz Manners had prepared

me to discover he had an altruistic side. If it hadn't been Bobbie talking, I don't know that I would have believed the information.

"Do you have proof of this? Donation receipts or thank-you letters?"

"No. He didn't want any kind of credit other than knowing he was doing something good. But every couple of months he showed up with an envelope of twenty thousand dollars in cash."

Chapter 13

INVOLUNTARILY, I GLANCED out the window at my scooter again. It stood out by being kitschy in its mod appearance, an anachronism among the rest of the everyday vehicles parked around the area. It was the first time I wished I drove a dirty old car like everybody else.

"Margo, your scooter is safe. There's a special place in hell for the kind of person who would steal a scooter from outside a nonprofit that sells teddy bears for charity. Everybody knows that."

"Sorry, I got distracted," I said. "What did you do with the rest of the donations that Blitz made?"

"I put them in the bank. Why?"

"Did you tell anybody about them? After what happened?"

"Who was I going to tell? Blitz wanted to remain anonymous. He knew what he did, and I knew what he did. And no matter how hard I tried to talk him into it, he wouldn't even take a tax deduction on the money. You're not going to tell anybody about this, are you?"

"No. It's hard to think that I met this person and he's so much different than I thought," I said. "I shouldn't be asking you so many things. I got carried away."

She reached across the table and patted my hand. "I can understand that," she said. "It breaks my heart that none of those kids who showed up at his party ever took the time to know the real Blitz Manners."

I didn't check the seat of the scooter for the money until I was back at Disguise DeLimit. I didn't want to draw attention to it. I wasn't used to driving around with $20,000 in cash, especially the cash of a recent murder victim.

Bobbie had said that Blitz was due to give her his donation on the exact same day he'd shown up at the store and given us the incentive of an envelope of cash. It was curious that he'd had that much money on him in the first place. Was that why? Because he was on his way to Money Changes Everything? And if that was the case, what had happened to make him decide to give us the money instead?

I thought back to later that same night, when he and his tipsy friends had stopped back at the store. Even Grady had made a comment about my actions. *"You were right, Blitz, she's not like the rest of them. All the girls we know would have kept the money."* Had the envelope of twenty grand been some kind of a test?

Upstairs in the kitchen, I wrote *Blitz's deposit, returned by me Wednesday night* on a blank sheet of white paper and set the envelope with the $20,000 on top of it. Now I had three things to investigate: the money, the empty hair spray can that had been in the backseat of the car, and the torn piece of fabric. Two had come from Ebony's vandalized car. The third had come from her parking lot. Which meant all three were connected to her.

One thing might have been easy to dismiss. Two, even. But three things—plus the fact that for the first time since I'd known Ebony, she'd decided to leave town—were too many to ignore. I didn't know what she was afraid of. But Ebony had been there for me when I'd been scared—of going to junior high school, of taking my driver's test, and of moving to Las Vegas—and now that she needed me I wasn't going to let her down.

I knew, beyond the shadow of a doubt, that Ebony wouldn't hurt a fly unless that fly was threatening someone or something she loved. Which meant somebody else had murdered Blitz. Somebody at the birthday party. But who? The guest list of a party was supposed to be made up of people who were your friends. So which of Blitz's friends would have viewed the party as an opportunity to get back at him instead of a chance to celebrate with him? Who would have had a motive to murder the very person who had been included on his special day?

My mind swam with images of costumed detectives at the party, each one running into the next. I'd made forty costumes as requested, but some of the costumes at the party had come from Candy Girls or even somewhere else. The police knew who was in attendance; they spoke to each person at the party before anybody was allowed to leave. That included guests, entertainment, Ebony's serving staff, the kitchen crew, and the valet parking attendants. It was highly possible that this was the biggest locked-room mystery ever, and it was most probable that too many detectives had spoiled the stew.

I carried the swatch of fabric downstairs and checked it against the roll that my dad had used on the Sherlock costumes. The pattern was similar, but not a perfect match. That told me something, but not much. I thought again about the tear in the costume that Amy Bradshaw had wanted to sell. Why had she changed her mind? What was she trying to hide?

The store hours listed on the Candy Girls website were nine to seven. I called the store and asked to speak to Amy. A few minutes later, she took the call.

"Amy, this is Margo Tamblyn from Disguise DeLimit. I wanted to talk to you about the Charlie's Angels costume you brought in on Sunday." I charged ahead before she could hang up. "I've had a chance to look at our inventory, and I'd be interested in acquiring all three costumes if you can convince the other two women to sell."

"How did you know I worked here?" she asked.

"I asked around," I said. "After I saw your costume, I wanted to find out who made them. I thought if they came from Candy Girls, you would have returned them there, so you must have made them yourself."

"It's too late for you to buy that costume. I threw it out."

"That's a shame. I'm sure the tear in the pants could be fixed."

"What tear?"

"In the back of the leg. I saw it when you brought it in to Disguise DeLimit. You knew the pants were torn, right? You must have gotten them caught on something at the party."

Amy was silent on the other end of the phone. "Amy? Are you still there?"

"I have to go. We have customers." She hung up.

There was no doubt in my mind that I'd said shaken Amy

up. Was it simply that I'd tracked her down? Or was it the mention of the tear in the pants? Maybe she didn't know the garment had been torn—which would be a problem only if she'd been doing something incriminating when the tear had happened.

I'd succeeded in accomplishing one thing: I'd made her nervous. If she had nothing to hide, she would have reacted entirely differently. I didn't believe for a second that she'd thrown the costume out. Now, the first chance I got, I was going to go to Candy Girls to see if it was somewhere in their inventory, and if so, if I could match the torn fabric to that costume.

I spent the next hour undressing the mannequins in the front window and redressing them in the newly acquired sailor outfits. I envisioned a *South Pacific* theme. By store opening, not only did I have three mannequins dressed in crisp (and pleasantly smelling) uniforms—two men and a woman—but also a female mannequin in the middle dressed as Nellie Forbush. I measured the backdrop of the window and made a few quick sketches of a tropical scene with palm trees, blue water, and sailboats. Now all I needed were materials and a skilled set painter.

It was a slow day in the shop. The highlight was a woman who came in with a small brown wiener dog under her arm. She wanted a custom Robin Hood costume for him. He stood still on the counter while I took his measurements and then wrapped him from neck to tail in brown butcher paper and marked out where his leg holes would have to go. I recorded everything in a notebook and quoted her a price. She paid her deposit and we agreed she could come back to pick up the costume on Thursday. She tucked the wiener dog under her arm and left.

For the next few hours, I used a blank page in the notebook to work out the six degrees of separation from Blitz Manners. The problem wasn't the lack of suspects, it was the high number of them. Anybody who'd attended the party would have had the opportunity to get into the kitchen and kill him—at least anybody who knew when the kitchen would be empty.

I flipped through the pages clipped to the clipboard until I found the list of custom costumes I'd made for the party. Grady's credit card slip was stapled to the upper left-hand side of the page, and his phone number was written alongside of it. If only I could think up an excuse to ask him about who wore which costume.

Maybe I didn't have an excuse to call Grady, but I had a perfect excuse to call Detective Nichols. Now that I knew that she and Tak were a couple, I couldn't shake the look on her face when she discovered us at Hoshiyama's the previous night. I didn't need there to be any bad blood between us, not while she was investigating Blitz's murder.

Ebony's vandalized car was an isolated incident that Ebony had asked me not to report, and that meant not reporting the empty black hair spray cans and torn piece of fabric. That didn't mean I couldn't bring up Amy's suspicious behavior.

I called the number on the card the detective had given me at the party. "Detective Nichols, this is Margo Tamblyn. You asked me to call you if I had information related to Blitz's murder."

"Does this have to do with Ebony Welles?" she asked.

"No. It has to do with Amy Bradshaw. She works at Candy Girls Party Store."

"What about Ms. Bradshaw?"

"She was at the party on Saturday."

"I already know that. I have a copy of the guest list. Is that all?"

I cleared my throat and spoke up. "She came into my store on Sunday morning and wanted to sell me her costume, but when I told her I needed her name, she changed her mind."

"Sounds like you already knew her name."

"I didn't find out who she was until after she left. But don't you think that's suspicious? That she's in a relationship with Blitz, but the day after he's murdered she comes here to try to sell her costume? I mean, why wouldn't she take it to her own store?"

"Ms. Tamblyn, it isn't a crime to shop the market."

"No, it isn't," I said. Every impulse told me to hang up the phone before I annoyed the detective and made things worse, but I didn't. The image of Ebony saying good-bye and driving off that morning appeared and I squeezed my eyes shut to pretend it hadn't happened. But it had. And it was up to me to resolve things so she'd come back.

"Detective, it's possible that Amy Bradshaw has a very good reason for trying to sell me her costume. I just don't know what it was. When I told her I needed her name, she changed her mind about selling and took off. I could understand if she didn't like the price I offered, but that wasn't the case."

"You said she wore this costume to the party on Saturday?"

"Yes. She was one of Charlie's Angels." I didn't really think her choice of costume was relevant, but there it was.

The detective thanked me and hung up. She made no mention of last night at Hoshiyama Kobe Steak House and neither did I.

* * *

KIRBY showed up a little after four o'clock. The first thing I did was run upstairs for a much-needed bathroom break. When I returned, I found him looking at my sketch.

"Are these for the new window that you did?" he asked.

"It was just an idea."

"They're great. I bet the drama club would be willing to paint the background for you if you gave them a discount on costumes for their next play."

"I didn't know you were in the drama club," I said.

"I'm not," he said. He kicked the toe of his Converse sneaker against the floor. "Rehearsals are the same time as afternoon swim team practice. I heard some of the drama club talking about fund-raisers on the bus ride home."

"Are you friends with them? Would you be willing to ask if they'll do it?"

He looked up. "I could ask the girl in charge if you want."

"Great," I said. "I'll give them a fifty-dollar store credit in exchange for the backdrop."

"Man, Varla's going to flip. Can I call her now?"

"Varla?"

Kirby reddened. "She's the stage manager. She's cool."

"Sure, go ahead and call her."

Kirby went into the back room to make the phone call. I suspected Varla was more than just another girl who rode the bus with him.

I straightened the colorful display of crinolines when the door to Disguise DeLimit slammed open. The door hit the rack of feather boas, knocking it backward into the makeshift wall that separated the store from the stockroom. Feathers from the orange boa came loose and flitted through the air. One caught on the sleeve of the sun-kissed woman who entered. She shook her arm vigorously to free it, and then, when it refused to let go, she picked it off with her thumb and forefinger and flicked it in my direction. Being a feather, it caught the wind and glided away.

"Are you Margo Tamblyn?" she demanded.

"Yes. Welcome to Disguise DeLimit."

"Don't give me that crap. I want you to stop harassing my employees and stop talking about my company. Do you understand? My husband is an attorney and if you keep up the smear campaign against us, I'll press you with defamation of character charges."

"I don't know who you are, but maybe you should mind your own business," I said.

"I am minding my business. Candy Girls is the most important party supply and costume store in Proper City and your rumors are chasing away customers." She turned to leave and tripped over a box of foam clown noses that sat on the floor. Brightly colored balls spilled out around her orange platform shoes.

She kicked the balls away and turned to leave. She stopped at the door and looked over her shoulder. "And in case nobody's told you yet, you look stupid in that hat," she said, and then she left.

I followed her to the door. She climbed into a sporty blue convertible and drove away.

Kirby came out from the back room. "Jeez, Margo, what'd you do? I've never seen the Casserole lose her cool like that." He tucked his phone into the back pocket of his jeans and stared out the front door.

"The *Casserole*?"

"Gina Cassavogli. We all call her the Casserole. Behind her back."

"Who's we? The kids at school?"

He gave me a funny look. "No. Jerry and Ebony and me." He paused. "And some of the kids at school," he added.

"Let me guess. Gina owns Candy Girls," I said.

Kirby nodded. "You must have done something big to get her to show up here and acknowledge Disguise DeLimit exists. Normally she acts like they're the only game in town."

"Candy Girls is only five years old," I said. "Disguise DeLimit has been here since 1975. It would make more sense for us to pretend *they* didn't exist than vice versa."

"You know women," Kirby said. "Sometimes they don't always see what's right in front of them." He bent down and corralled the clown noses back into the box. I didn't ask how his conversation with Varla had gone. I had a feeling I could guess.

After we closed the shop, I went upstairs and sat at the dining room table, staring at the envelope of cash. I still couldn't figure out how it had ended up with Ebony after I'd given it back to Blitz on Wednesday night. But was it the money Blitz had tried to use to pay for the costumes? Or was it money that he was planning on donating to Bobbie's foundation? It couldn't be coincidence that the amounts were the same and they were both stashed in envelopes. It had to mean something, only I didn't know what.

I traced my finger around the edge of the envelope. "Where have you been?" I asked it. "Did Blitz give you to Ebony after I gave you back to him? Or am I missing something?" I pulled the cash out of the envelope and fanned it in out in front of me, feeling only slightly silly for talking to it. Now would be a great time to discover that money really did talk.

No closer to answers twenty minutes later, I put the money back into the envelope and set it next to the fabric and the empty hair spray cans. Grady had paid for the costumes, so our fee from the party had been covered. All this time I'd thought that Blitz had stiffed Ebony, but maybe he hadn't. And if that was the case, then her motive for murder would be gone.

But she'd told me at the party that she still had to work out the details of his payment. So how was it the envelope of cash had turned up in her possession after he was dead?

Chapter 14

I WAS EAGER to leave the store once we closed on Monday night. I hopped onto my scooter and drove to the fire hall where the party had been. It was, by all accounts, the scene of the crime, and even though I'd been there when the body had been discovered, I wanted to look around now to see if there was something I'd missed.

Several white vans were parked by the curb in front of the building. Two men stood on the sidewalk, smoking. They each had clear plastic shields pushed up on the top of their heads. Remembering how Tak had spotted my scooter, I passed them and wedged the scooter into an available space on a residential street two blocks away.

A small man with a fringe of hair around an otherwise bald head stood in front of the building. His arms were crossed as he glared at the smokers. I watched from the side of the road as three additional men dressed in blue plastic containment suits came out of the building. They were carrying large red plastic bags marked with a black biohazard symbol.

I approached the bald man. "Excuse me," I called out in a friendly voice. "What's going on in there?"

"What's supposed to be going on is crime scene cleanup. It's bad enough that this—this *thing*—had to happen in my fire hall. The police wouldn't let me touch the place until they were done. Can you imagine what that's going to do to my business? My future rentals?"

"Your future rentals? Oh, you must be the owner," I said. "With all due respect, sir, I don't think you're thinking of the bigger picture here."

He turned his attention from the smokers to me. The anger in his face softened to understanding. "You're right. That young man's death is far worse than my loss of income," he said.

"Are those men part of the crime scene cleanup crew?"

"Yes. They've been at it for most of the day. Usually it's the party planner who gets the job of cleaning up the day after. Ebony got lucky this time." He looked at me again. "I'm sorry. I'm not usually this insensitive," he said. He raised his hand to his forehead and his eyes fluttered dramatically. "I think I've blocked the whole thing out of my mind."

"I can see why you'd want to," I said. It would be hard for me to reenter the kitchen, having seen Blitz's body facedown in a puddle of blood. "Do you know how much longer they'll be at it?"

"I told them to keep working until the job was finished, but it's after seven and I expected them to be done by now."

"Do you have to stay here?"

"No, but I want to do a final walk-through before they leave. No sense in having to get them back out here and lose another day of work."

"Wait here and I'll find out for you." I left the little man before he had a chance to change my mind.

The smokers watched me approach. One tossed his cigarette onto the ground and stomped it out. The other held his behind his back.

"Hi," I said. "The owner over there wanted to know how much longer you guys think you'll be."

"Job's almost done," said the taller of the two men. "Everything's been bagged and bleached. The crew inside is coming out with the waste now. Once they're clear, we'll take him for the tour and if he signs off, we're outta here."

The shorter man put his cigarette out on a nearby trash can and then tucked the butt into the pocket of his shirt. "We leave the place cleaner than we found it. Company motto."

I looked at their T-shirts and jeans. "Why aren't you wearing blue suits like the other guys?"

"Suits are for inside. Once you leave the building, you dump the suit so you don't track chemicals outside."

"So what happens if you have to go back in?"

"You put on another suit." He tapped the pack of cigarettes in his T-shirt pocket. "Expensive habit. Some days I go through five or six suits."

A crew of men came out of the fire hall. Each man stripped his blue plastic suit off while standing on the front step, and then shoved it into an additional red bag held open by the first guy who had exited. The men remained gloved, and after the suits were off, they carried sealed red bags to the last white van and loaded them in through the back. If there was any evidence left over that the detective hadn't found, it would be in one of those bags. I imagined two-day-old goose that hadn't been refrigerated, bloodstained towels, and bleach-covered rags, and I shuddered. The ick factor was off the charts.

When the last bag was loaded, one guy slammed the van

door shut. "Yo, Bartlett! We're done," he called out. Smoker #1, Bartlett, nodded at him and then turned to me.

"Does your boss want a suit for the walk-through?" he asked me.

It took only a moment to realize his erroneous assumption that I worked at the fire hall. "Yes," I said quickly. He reached into the front seat of the van and pulled out a flat square sealed in clear plastic. "And one for me too, please," I added.

He grabbed a second package. "One size fits all," he said, thrusting the packages at me. "Let's go."

I waved the owner over to us and held out a suit. "They're ready to do your walk-through," I said.

"Why do you have a suit?"

I smiled my most charming smile. "I thought you might like a second set of eyes, you know, to make sure they didn't miss anything. I mean, no sense in having to get them back out here and lose another day, right?"

"Good thinking."

The professionals didn't bother putting suits on for the walk-through. I didn't really expect to find any clues in the fire hall after the professional crime scene crew had done its job, so I wasn't disappointed when the walk-through netted nothing more than the less-than-flattering blue plastic jumpsuit. The owner accepted that the job had been completed with a high level of satisfaction. He thanked the men and left. I stepped out of my own suit after he was gone and balled it up.

"Do I need to do anything special with this?" I asked the smoker who shall be called Bartlett.

"I already told you, the place was clean. We wear them to avoid contact with the chemicals and with any of the biological waste. Chuck it in the trash or keep it as a souvenir." He elbowed his friend and they both laughed.

"Are they expensive?" I asked.

"Why? You planning on making a fashion statement?"

"No. I run a costume shop, and we don't have anything like these." I thought about the alien costumes my dad was bringing back from Area 51, and envisioned a dedicated science fiction display in the store.

"I thought you worked for the bald guy."

"No, I was just helping him out."

"Well, if it's the costumes you want, you can get 'em online. Most medical supply stores have them too." Bartlett slapped Smoker #2 with the back of his hand. "The game's starting in twenty minutes. Let's go."

Smoker #2 nodded. "Hey, lady, sorry about the costumes."

"What costumes?"

"We found a couple of costumes shoved into the back of the oven in the kitchen."

"Where are they now?"

He nodded toward the back of the truck. "Incinerated. They went with the first round of stuff we pulled out of the place. Once the crime scene was released, we were told to gut the place and burn everything."

He headed around the back of the van and I chased after him. "Wait!" I said.

"For what? Listen, lady, it's late and we gotta get out of here."

"Before you go, can you tell me anything about these costumes?"

"Sure. There was a hat, like one of them plaid ones that Sherlock Holmes wears."

My heart sank. Blitz was wearing the classic Sherlock costume when I'd found him, but the hat had been missing. It must have come off and rolled away in whatever it was that had amounted to his last seconds of life. "That hat was part of the victim's costume," I said. "I guess it fell off before he died."

"Guess so." He climbed into the driver's side and started the van. "Did his costume include a trench coat?"

"No. Why?"

"Found one of them too. The coat was in worse shape than the hat."

The van pulled forward. I put my hand on the door handle and jogged alongside. He slowed to a stop. "Lady, you gotta let go of the car."

"Just one more thing," I said. "Can you describe the trench coat?"

"Yeah. It was rumpled and it was dirty. That mean anything to you?"

It did. It meant Columbo had been involved in Blitz's murder. Now all I had to do was find out who had worn the Columbo costume.

Chapter 15

I WAS HALFWAY to Grady's house in Christopher Robin Crossing before it occurred to me to think up an excuse for showing up unexpectedly and asking about who wore what to the party. Payment wasn't a valid excuse. Plus, I'd already made it clear that the costumes weren't returnable if purchased, so I couldn't offer to buy the costumes back without undermining the store's return policy.

Police sirens sounded behind me. I glanced in my rearview mirror and saw the flashing lights. *Fine time to get a ticket!* I pulled over to the shoulder, my heart racing. The police car shot past me and turned into the development. I followed. The flashing lights disappeared around the corner. I took the same turn. There was no question where the police were headed. Two black-and-whites were parked willy-nilly in front of Blitz Manners's house on Pooh Corner.

Blitz's mom stood out front. Again she was tastefully dressed, today in a somber black skirt suit. Her driver stood next to her, his arm on her elbow. She hugged her body and kept her eyes focused on the ground. Even though the sun had descended, she wore heavy black sunglasses. Considering her son had been murdered only a few days earlier, I suspected she was hiding the evidence of her grief.

Among the officers who got out of their cars was Detective Nichols. Today she wore a snug black T-shirt under her black blazer. Her blond hair hung loose in soft curls. She'd parted it on the side and tucked it behind her ears.

I watched from the side of the road. The detective approached Mrs. Cannon, who looked up and pointed at the house. She shook her head in answer to something Detective Nichols asked. The detective went inside the house. Mrs. Cannon and her driver stayed behind in the driveway.

A car with dealer plates screeched into the development and pulled up behind the police cruisers. Black Jack hopped out and raced over to his wife and she crumpled into his arms.

"If I didn't know any better, I'd say you were spying on the rich and famous." I recognized Grady's voice before turning to confirm my suspicion.

"Maybe I was just out for a nighttime ride," I said.

"Pretty bold of you, considering you got lost in our development only yesterday."

"*Lost* seems like such a strong word, don't you think? *Temporarily disoriented* is better."

"Okay, so what does your temporary disorientation have to do with the scene in front of the Cannon house? That is why you're here, isn't it?"

"Actually, I came out here to see you." At the surprise on his face, I smiled. "I wanted to talk to you about the costumes from Saturday."

He waved his hand in front of me. "Forget about it. You

made it clear that they weren't refundable. I'm not going to fight you on that."

"That's not what I meant," I said. "I was hoping you could tell me who wore which one."

"Why do you want to know?" he asked.

I searched my mind for something—anything—to say and I came up empty. I wasn't comfortable enough to tell him the truth.

"Listen, I get it. What happened to Blitz at the party was horrible and I can't shake it either. The police have a list of everybody who was there. If they needed to know who was dressed as each character, they would have asked. You have to try to let it go."

I nodded as if he'd figured me out. "I can't help thinking that one of those people is a killer. You know? A dress-up party is supposed to be fun, but one person saw an opportunity to hide their true identity so they could get away with murder. It doesn't make it any better that everybody was dressed up as a good guy. I mean, who was it? One of Charlie's Angels? Charlie Chan? Or maybe it was Kojak or Columbo?"

Grady stepped away from me and his face changed. I waited for him to let it slip that he knew who those people were, but he didn't. "Nothing good will come from asking those questions." He put his hand on my arm and turned me around to face the Cannon house. "Besides, wouldn't you rather find out what's going on over there? Come on," he said. He passed me and turned back, holding out his hand for me to join him.

"Grady, this isn't my neighborhood and it isn't my business."

"It's my neighborhood, which makes it my business. And you're with me, so what's the problem?"

There were so many ways I wasn't with Grady that I would

need extra fingers and toes to count them. I still couldn't place the expression that had crossed his face when I mentioned the costumes, but his attention had been hijacked—assuming I'd ever had it to begin with—and I had to agree with him. Something was going on across the street and I wanted to know what it was.

I set my helmet on the floorboards of my scooter. Grady was almost to the sidewalk on the other side of the street. I jogged to catch up with him. A small crowd of neighbors had spilled from their respective houses and created a gathering by the perimeter of the Cannon house. Grady joined them. Black Jack kept his arm around his wife, and I crouched down by the end of his car. A man in a checkered shirt and straw fedora turned his back on Black Jack and walked across the driveway to the crowd.

"What happened?" Grady asked.

"Robbery. Black Jack says the place was trashed. The police are going through it now, mostly to make sure nobody's still in there," said Checkered Shirt.

"What did they take?"

"Mrs. Cannon said her jewelry was missing. Other than that, I don't know."

An image of Amy Bradshaw wearing a giant diamond engagement ring flashed into my head and I felt my eyes go wide. "Grady," I said, stepping out from behind Black Jack's car. Several heads turned toward me. "Can I talk to you?"

"Who's she?" someone asked.

"I think the better question is what is she doing here?" asked the detective.

I turned around. Detective Nichols stood facing me with her hands on her hips. "Unless my records are incorrect, you live on the other side of Proper City, don't you?"

"I came out here to talk to—" I scanned the crowd for

Grady, but he wasn't there. "I wanted to talk to a friend," I finished.

"Does this friend have a name?" she asked.

"Grady O'Toole."

"Ms. Tamblyn, how long have you and Grady been friends?"

"I only just met him a few days ago."

She studied me for a second and I wished I'd taken the time to put my captain's hat back on. Silly as it sounded, elements of costume made me feel more invincible than I was as my regular self.

"Ms. Tamblyn, I can appreciate the fact that you're trying to make new friends, but I caution you against using a murder investigation as grounds for common interests. What happened to Blitz Manners was a crime, both literally and figuratively. I would hate to find out that you're hindering a homicide investigation so you can expand your social circle."

"Does the robbery at the Manners house have anything to do with the murder?" I asked.

She studied my face for a second before answering. "Cannon, not Manners. And it would be premature to comment on that."

"But you're not ruling it out."

"Ms. Tamblyn, I want to make myself perfectly clear. If you know something about the murder at the fire hall or about the robbery here, I want you to tell me. If you don't have anything new to contribute, then I suggest you leave."

My phone rang, interrupting her. She scowled. The screen said *Don Digby*. I held up an index finger and answered the call.

"This is Margo," I said.

"Margo, this is Don. Are you at the shop?"

"No, I'm out. Why? Is everything okay?" The immediate

silence that met my question told me the answer was no. I felt light-headed and dizzy, and the view of the strangers on the yard in front of me blurred and distorted.

"I think you should sit down," Don said.

"Did something happen to my dad?"

"I need you to try to stay calm. We're in a hospital about two hundred miles outside of Proper."

"A hospital? What's wrong?"

"Margo, I'm so sorry. Your dad had a second heart attack."

Chapter 16

I MUST HAVE screamed, though I don't remember. The phone fell from my hand. My heart rate doubled in a second and my knees gave way underneath me. I landed on a patch of grass to the side of the driveway. Detective Nichols repeated my name, but I couldn't answer. Every fear, every nightmare, every ounce of helplessness I'd ever felt over what had happened when I was born magnified. I couldn't lose my dad too.

Numbness radiated from my heart and traveled to my fingertips. I became aware that the detective was talking. I forced myself to look at her. She pointed to the house and then to me. I grabbed Black Jack's bumper and pulled myself up until I was standing. Slowly, methodically, I looked for my phone. Detective Nichols returned to my side and held it out.

"How about I give you a ride home?" she said. The edge of her voice had been replaced with compassion. I nodded, the only thing I was capable of.

I followed her to the police car. "Sit in the front," she said.

Before I climbed in, I looked across the street at my scooter. "I'll make sure it's safe," she said.

I built a barrier against my emotions during the drive to Disguise DeLimit, staring at the white line on the side of the road as if it were one of Magic Maynard's hypnotic tricks meant to put me into a trance. Occasionally Detective Nichols looked at me, but I kept my forehead pressed to the passenger-side window. If I spoke, I'd lose all control.

A tidal wave of tears built up as we approached the store. Detective Nichols swung the car in an illegal U-turn and parked in front of the shop. I took a deep breath, preparing myself to thank her, when she pulled a piece of paper from her uniform pocket.

"Margo, I spoke to Don after you collapsed. Your dad's in a hospital in Moxie. Here's the number. Don said you can call him anytime, but he wanted to make sure you got home safely."

I took the paper. "Thank you for the ride," I said in a clipped voice. My bottom lip quivered and my voice cracked.

"If you need anything, you can call me. Even if you just want to talk."

"I have to go." I got out of the car and into the shop. After the door was locked behind me and the blind was pulled down to cover the window, I sat on the floor with my back to the door. I pulled out my phone and called Ebony.

The call went to voice mail. "My dad had another heart attack," I said. "He's in a hospital in Moxie." I didn't know what else to say, so I hung up. And then I started to cry.

SOMETIME after that—minutes or hours, I didn't know which—I dragged myself upstairs to the apartment. Soot sat on the other side of the door. He followed me to my bedroom and jumped on the bed. I stripped off my sailor outfit and fell asleep in my underwear.

I slept in fits and starts and climbed out of bed at the first sign of sunlight. The clock read 5:47. A glance in the mirror confirmed that what little mascara hadn't come off when I'd cried had been smudged in my sleep. It wasn't a pretty sight.

After a steaming-hot shower, I called Don. "I'm sorry it's so early," I said.

"Margo, are you okay? The detective said she drove you home."

"I'm fine. How is he?"

"He's in critical condition. This is a small hospital, but they're taking very good care of him. His blood count is low. He's had one transfusion, but they don't want to move him until they see some improvement."

"I want to come see him."

"I don't think it's a good idea for you to drive that little scooter this far," he said.

"I won't take the scooter. I'll find someone who can give me a ride."

"I'll take you," said a voice from the hallway.

I spun my chair around. Ebony stood in front of me. Her Afro was full, with a copper scarf tied around her forehead. The ends of the scarf hung down her back. She was dressed in a brown paisley tunic, faded bell-bottom jeans, and platform sandals. I jumped up and threw my arms around her.

"Don, Ebony's going to bring me. Tell her what we need to know while I get ready." I thrust the phone at her and hugged her a second time.

I dressed in a late '60s sheath dress and pink ballerina flats. The dress, like most of the other pieces of noncostume clothing that I owned, had originally belonged to my mother. My dad didn't talk about her much—too painful, I guessed—but he had kept her clothes in case I wanted them when I grew up. They were the only things I had to tell me about who she was. Now, with my dad's health in jeopardy, I wore it to feel like she was with me. I dried my hair into a bouncy flip and joined Ebony in the kitchen.

"That's one of your mom's dresses, isn't it?"

"Yes."

"I bet she looked just like you when she was your age."

I avoided Ebony's eyes. Her intention, I suspected, was to make me feel connected to the mother I hadn't known, but instead it served as a reminder that my mom had never gotten to be older than the age I was.

"Listen, Margo, never fear, because Ebony's here. Nothing bad's gonna happen on my watch. You got that?" From the floor by Ebony's ankles, Soot meowed. She looked at his grumpy little gray cat face and then looked at me. "You might as well pack him up too," she said. "This here's turning into a family affair."

THE four of us, Ebony, Ivory, Soot, and I, were on the road by six thirty. Soot sat in my lap. It took ten minutes for him to stop howling. Ivory was, for now, in the backseat. The window was rolled down enough for him to peek his nose out and feel the air rushing past his face. If ever the two animals had to coexist, this was the time.

I considered asking Ebony where she'd been, why she'd left, and what her connection was with Blitz's family, but ever since receiving the news about my dad, I felt detached from the homicide investigation. For the next two hours while we were on the road, it was just us. No murder investigation, no detectives, no hidden agendas. I didn't want to say or do anything to upset the balance.

We arrived in Moxie a little over an hour later. I suspected Ebony had played fast and loose with the speed limits, which, under the circumstances, was fine by me. She stayed behind in the car with the animals first while I went inside, and I promised to relieve her shortly.

The Moxie Hospital was a small, white building on the outskirts of a desert town. I entered through the main doors. Don sat in the lobby with his face buried in a book. Aside from a family with two young children, he was alone. He looked up at me, his expression quickly changing from concentration to recognition and relief.

"Margo," he called out. He tossed his paperback onto the chair and met me by the coffee machine.

"How is he?" I asked.

"He's awake. His heart rate has been stable for the past few hours. I told him you were on your way. I thought it was better not to have any big surprises."

A woman in salmon scrubs walked past us and fed a bunch of coins into the vending machine next to us. She punched the button for a cinnamon Danish wrapped in plastic. The spinning coil that should have released the Danish didn't, and her pastry dangled inside.

She turned to me. "You do not know how badly I need that Danish," she said.

Without thinking, I whacked the machine. The Danish fell and the woman looked at me, at Don, and then back at me.

"This is Jerry's daughter," Don said. "She and her friend drove up from Proper. Can they go in?"

"Sign in at the front desk and I'll give you a pass. Where's your friend?"

"Outside with the cat and the dog."

Don shook his head in disbelief. "You brought the animals?"

"They're part of the family."

"One at a time," the woman said. "And I mean one. No animals allowed in the rooms." She took her Danish from the machine and stared at it for a second. "If Jerry's up for it, maybe we'll let him take a walk outside and visit with them in the parking lot."

I followed the woman to the desk and signed in. Don escorted me to my dad's room, where he lay in the hospital bed, tubes connected to his nose and arm. Machines surrounded him like guard dogs. His face lit up and then grew serious.

"Margo," he said. He held his hand out. I sat in the chair next to the bed and held it. His fingers were swollen and the skin was rough. I fought against asking questions that had no answers: Why did this happen? And how can we make it so it never happens again?

After a minute or so, he jiggled my hand. "This might be it for me," he said.

"Don't talk like that," I said. I squeezed his fingers and tried to pretend the tubes that were connected to his nose and arm weren't there, but I couldn't. Tears spilled down my cheeks even though I'd promised myself that I'd be strong for him. I brushed the tears away and a new set took their place.

"I've had a lot of time to think while lying here in this bed. The doctors say I have to take it easy for a while. They won't give me a specific time frame. As much as I hate to say it, running the store is going to be too much. I'm going to have to give it up."

"No," I said. "Kirby can work longer hours while you're getting better—he wants the money for college and his dune buggy—and I can help out until I have to go back to Vegas—"

He set my hand on the bed and patted it. "Margo, I'm going to listen to what the doctors said. They know what they're talking about. And if they're right, if cutting back on the stress of running a business helps me get this under control, then I'm going to do it. There's a lot I haven't seen yet. I didn't realize until this trip how much I want to see America. If the shop closes, life will go on. You have your life with Magic Maynard, and Candy Girls can pick up where we left off."

I wanted to protest again, but I couldn't bring myself to tell him—the man who had sacrificed his whole life to raise me mostly by himself and then encourage me to move away from our small town so I could see a bigger world myself— that he didn't deserve the same experience.

He patted my hand and pulled his away. "The store has been my whole life for so long. These last couple of days on the road with Don were the most fun I've had since—"

He didn't finish his sentence. He didn't have to. Sure, I wore costumes to school when other kids had clothes from the mall, but that wasn't what counted.

"Dad, Ebony's waiting to see you. She's in the parking lot with Ivory and Soot. I should give her a chance to come in and visit."

A man in blue scrubs entered the room. "How's my favorite patient?" he asked.

"Practically brand-new," Dad answered.

The man got ready to take my dad's temperature and turned to me. "You should have seen this place last night. Jerry's friend brought in a bunch of alien heads for the staff to wear. Sure did cheer up the kids when we walked into their wing. Imagine that, a hospital staff in papier-mâché alien heads. Those kids—some of them are terminal. They needed that laugh." He chuckled to himself and thrust a thermometer in my dad's mouth. He—the nurse, not my dad—waited until it beeped and recorded the result on a chart that hung from the foot of the bed.

I went out to the parking lot and sent Ebony in. "About time," she said. "Thought I was going to have to pack these two up in my handbag and smuggle them in."

We took turns in the hospital room until well beyond visiting hours. Between my skill with the partially operating vending machine and the compliments Ebony drew on her outfit and accessories, the staff quickly warmed to us. They even relented and let Dad come outside to visit with the animals. Soot started purring the second he hit my dad's lap. (He was in a wheelchair—my dad, not the cat.) Ivory stood on his back legs and put his paws on the side of the chair, whimpering for attention of his own.

By the end of the day, my dad's spirits were high, but the doctors said he wasn't out of the woods yet. Often a second heart attack would follow on the heels of the first. I told them that this was already the second. They told me that was part of the reason for their concern. Jerry Tamblyn wasn't heading back to Proper City just yet.

I found Don in the cafeteria. "Ebony and I have to leave," I said. "I kept the store closed today, but I should open it tomorrow."

Don agreed. "Margo, Jerry's been talking about selling the store when you go back to Las Vegas," he said. "I get the feeling it's an extra source of stress, and he doesn't need any stress on him right now."

"He shouldn't worry about that." Don's eyes narrowed and he tipped his head to the side. I looked away so he couldn't read my thoughts. "How about Ebony and I take the trailer back to Proper City now so you won't have to worry about the extra weight on the car when you hit the road?"

"That would be a big help. Are you sure Ebony's car can handle it?"

We walked to the exit and looked at the trailer and then at Ebony's Cadillac. The Caddy was twice as long as the trailer. "She probably won't even notice," I said.

"Notice what?" she said, surprising me. I jumped.

"We're taking the trailer. Can you help Don hitch it to your car while I say good-bye?"

"There's nothing crazy in that trailer, is there?"

Don and I looked at each other. "Nothing too far out of the ordinary," he said.

I went back inside. My dad's head was turned to the side and his breathing was even. I approached the bed and put my hand on top of his. "I'm going to make everything okay," I said.

He looked up at me, and for a flash, it felt as if I were the parent and he was the child. I swatted at the fresh set of tears that ran down my cheeks, kissed him on his forehead, and left.

IT took Ebony five miles to get the feel for the additional weight hitched to her car. Every once in a while the trailer swayed. Each time she muttered under her breath about the idiocy of carting interplanetary species along behind us.

Ebony was more superstitious than most people. Not only did she avoid ladders and black cats, she had her tarot cards read weekly, took feng shui to a new level, and knocked on wood a *lot*. She even maintained that her medallion had special powers of protection. I wasn't up on the superstition handbook, but I had a feeling towing a trailer filled with relics that had heretofore been stored in the highly secret Area 51 made her nervous.

The Caddy and trailer combination evened itself out

around mile twelve, not that I was counting. That's when Ebony relaxed enough to talk. "It's nothing bad," she said.

She could have been talking about anything from my dad's health to the slightly aggressive noise her engine made every time she accelerated past sixty miles an hour, but I knew instinctively that she was talking about her history with Blitz. I suspected she knew I knew it.

"I didn't think it was," I said, confirming what I thought she thought I thought.

"People will talk. They always do. But it's nothing I should be ashamed of," she added. "The truth is, there is a history there. One that not many people know about."

"A history with Blitz?"

"A history with his family. What most people don't know is that I had a relationship with Blitz Manners's dad long before Blitz was ever born."

Chapter 17

I SAT VERY still. Ivory squirmed in my lap and I ran my open hand over his fur to calm him down. He turned around and hung his head out the window. Soot slept by my feet.

"My mother worked for Mr. Manners's father when I was a little girl," she said. She reached up to her throat and ran her fingers over her clavicle until they found the chain that held her medallion. She followed the chain to the pendant and rubbed her thumb and forefinger over the smooth brass surface while she spoke. "This would be Blitz's grandfather. It was the '60s and it was hard for a single mother to find work. Mama took odd jobs—laundry, cleaning, cooking, whatever she could get hired to do. She brought me with her to these jobs and a lot of people had a problem with that. Truth was, there was no place else for me to go."

"How old were you?"

"Five. Blitz's dad—Brody Manners—was a teenager at

the time. He sure was popular. Girls were always around the house to flirt with him. I remember one time a couple of cheerleaders hung around while he washed his car. They said they'd wash it for him and he said no, that he wanted to teach me how to do it. They didn't believe him. Truth? I didn't believe him either until he handed me the hose and asked me to rinse off the bubbles. Imagine that—a rich white boy and a poor black girl washing a car together in 1965." She smiled to herself more than to me, and I could tell the memory was one she cherished. "The whole family was like that. They treated me and my mom like we were no different than they were."

"Where are they now?" I asked.

"They moved to Palm Springs after Brody graduated from college. That must have been '72, I think. I was twelve. You know what Brody did? He gave me a set of keys to his Mustang. He told me to find him when I turned sixteen and he'd teach me to drive. I think he really planned to keep his word too."

"But you didn't seek him out," I said.

Ebony's mother had gotten sick when she was in high school. It was one of the reasons Ebony stayed behind in Proper City after her graduation. Her classmates moved away, and she started Shindig. Somewhere in the six years between Blitz's father promising to teach Ebony how to drive and Ebony graduating from high school, her life had been turned upside down and nothing, not even the promise of being taught how to drive on a 1965 Mustang, was going to make it right.

"My mama taught me to drive. It's one of the last things we did together before she got sick. She died two weeks after I graduated. I was officially on my own and nobody was going to take care of me but me. I did odd jobs myself and saved up what I could. I started Shindig when I had enough money."

"And it's a good thing too, because Shindig is the best party planning company in Nevada," I said. "You have a knack for it."

Ebony's ringtone—the opening bars to "Shaft"—sounded from her handbag. She fumbled around inside her oversized hobo bag for it, glanced at the screen, and dropped it back into the bag. Almost as soon as the ringtone ended, it started again. This time she ignored it.

Conversation lapsed into silence. Even Ivory and Soot seemed to understand that we were in serious mode. I stared out the passenger-side window, wishing we were passing something interesting instead of miles upon miles of flat, brown desert, but that was the trouble with Nevada. Most Vegas-adjacent towns were either blinged out with garish casinos and neon signs or left as undeveloped stretches of dirt roads occupied by geckos and prairie dogs.

"I should have gone to the bathroom before we left the hospital," Ebony said. "We're going to have to make a pit stop."

She took the next exit and glided into a fast-food restaurant at the first intersection. Before she got out of the car, I put my hand on her arm.

"Ebony, you don't owe me any explanations. We don't have to talk about any of this."

"You're right, we don't have to talk about my bathroom break, but you might have gotten suspicious when I took the exit. You want anything from the restaurant? Chicken nuggets? Apple pie?"

"French fries," I said. "And Ivory and Soot want to split a burger."

Ebony grabbed her handbag and left me in the car. She

had her phone in her hand before she reached the doors to the restaurant.

Bathroom break, my aunt Fanny.

I got out and stretched my legs. Ivory relieved himself on a rusted metal trash can. I checked the time on my phone and saw that I'd missed two calls from Bobbie. She left a message the second time that told me to call her as soon as I could.

Ivory extended the length of his leash to sniff around the exterior of the building. Inside the fast-food restaurant, Ebony was next in line. I kept an eye on her while I called Bobbie back.

"Margo! Jeez, where have you been? The store's closed and you're not answering your phone. I got scared that something happened to you."

"Not to me, to my dad. He had another heart attack."

"Is he okay?"

"For now." Conversation with Ebony had effectively pushed concerns about my dad from my mind, but now the fear came rushing back. I dropped into the passenger seat. Ivory, sensing the tug on his leash, returned to the car. He jumped in and put his dirty paws on my knees. "He's in a hospital outside of Proper City. Ebony and I drove out this morning. They think he's going to be okay, but I'm still scared."

"If the doctors say he'll be okay, then he'll be okay," Bobbie said with unjustified certainty. "You have to have faith."

"Faith in what?" I said. My temperature rose and anger at the unfairness in the world took over. "Faith in the world that took my mom from me the day I was born? Or faith in the world that took Blitz Manners on his twenty-sixth birthday? Or how about my dad, who's in the hospital for a second heart attack? Where am I supposed to put my faith, Bobbie? Everywhere I look, I see people suffering who shouldn't be."

"Listen to me," she said. Her voice was steady and strong. "Focus on the sound of my voice and listen to me, because I have something important to say to you and I want to make sure you hear it." Bobbie had always been the one person who could adopt a calm tone to counter my emotional outbursts, and today was no different. "Are you listening?"

"I'm listening."

"Okay. Here's what I want you to think about: the universe gives you the lessons you're supposed to learn."

"Meaning what?"

"Meaning there's a reason this is happening. You're in a class called Life and this is a midterm. Figure out what you're supposed to learn, and then everything will make sense."

"But none of this is about me," I said.

"It's your life, Margo, and that makes it partially about you."

The doors to the restaurant opened and Ebony walked out. She balanced a cardboard drink carrier loaded with two beverages and three bags on her hip. Her medallion swung from side to side. Large sunglasses were propped on her head on top of the copper scarf. It had gotten too dark for sunglasses, and as I suspected, she'd been wearing them to hide the now-visible redness around her eyes.

"Bobbie, I have to go."

"Wait. There's something you should know before you get back."

"What?"

"Tak Hoshiyama was looking in the windows of your store when I went out there to check on you. He was worried about you too. I think maybe you and he should talk."

"I don't see that there's anything to talk about." Ebony pulled open her door and set the food and beverages inside. Ivory smelled the food. He charged across the front seat, putting his paws on Ebony as she bent down. His paw got caught in her chain.

"I have to go," I said again.

"Call me when you get home."

I stole a glance at Ebony. She'd freed Ivory's paw and was now feeding him a piece of hamburger patty. I looked in the other two bags and found my French fries. As healthy as I tried to be (don't let the Fruity Pebbles fool you—they're gluten free and high in vitamin D), I had a weakness for potato products. Potassium, I told myself.

Ebony finished her own burger and Ivory and Soot nibbled on theirs. We wasted twenty minutes in the backing-up-with-a-trailer process before leaving the parking lot and getting back onto the road. Ebony found her rhythm behind the wheel faster this time. The mile markers told me we were fifteen miles outside of Proper.

"You haven't told me everything, have you?" I asked.

"No."

"Are you going to?"

She put on her blinker and checked her side mirror several times before changing lanes. Three cars passed us on the wrong side. "Can't see with those darn aliens on our tail," she muttered.

"Ebony," I prompted.

"I think we've had just about enough with the trip down memory lane for tonight," she said. "Besides, what good is it going to do?"

I sat back against the leather seat. Soot and Ivory had curled up on the seat between us. The excitement of a road trip had tired them out enough that they coexisted in sleep. I stroked one, then the other. Something had happened when we were at the rest stop. Ebony had been moved to confide in me after our visit with my dad, but now she was closed up again.

It was the phone call. It had to be. But who had called her? And why? And what did it have to do with her connection to Blitz Manners or his family?

Ebony pulled her Caddy up to Disguise DeLimit and let the engine idle. I was about to ask her if she wanted to come in when she spoke quietly.

"It was the early '90s. I almost lost Shindig," she said. "I was in debt up to my eyeballs. Living on advances from my credit cards so I could keep the store afloat. People were turning to big chain stores to get whatever they wanted for their parties and all of a sudden, having a novelty party store in a small town wasn't the best investment in the world. I had two choices: close my doors and sell off everything I owned or ask an old friend for help."

"You went to Brody Manners," I said.

She nodded. "He and his wife were in that big house on Christopher Robin Crossing. Blitz was just a kid, maybe four years old. He was a little devil, that one. One minute he was running around the place screaming at the top of his lungs, the next minute he was hiding behind the sofa, waiting to jump out and scare you."

And suddenly Blitz's comment the day he walked into Disguise DeLimit—the opinion of a spoiled four-year-old boy that had been cemented in his mind ever since—made sense.

"Blitz saw his dad give you money."

"Blitz and his mother both saw. They overheard Brody say that it was for old times' sake, that nobody had to know what happened in our past. The two of them suspected the worst. They didn't know the circumstances and they wouldn't listen to me. I haven't been welcome in that house ever since."

"But if Blitz held a grudge against you, why would he hire you to plan his party? And why would he hold that knowledge over your head?"

"Seems the little devil finally reached a point of maturity. Blitz hired me because he finally got tired of not knowing the truth."

Chapter 18

"HOW DO YOU know that?" I asked.

"He told me. After I said I'd plan the party, he came to Shindig on his own. He apologized for making a scene at your store. You know, I actually think it never occurred to him that I'd tell him the truth if he came to me like a normal person and asked about what happened."

"So you told him? About the loan and how his mother always suspected the worst?"

"I didn't have a chance to get into specifics. He said we'd talk at the party. But he finally understood that his dad always considered me to be somebody special. That boy almost cried when he talked about Brody. He said he'd give back all the money he inherited if it would bring back his father."

But it wouldn't. That money could make a difference for Bobbie's fund-raisers, and it could keep Ebony from debt, and it could throw the biggest detective-themed costume party that Proper City had ever seen, but the one thing it couldn't do was bring someone back from the dead. Nothing could. I'd made similar proclamations myself, so I knew.

"You said Blitz planned to talk more at his party?"

"He said he'd come find me when he had a chance to get away. I think deep down, even with all of those people around him, he was alone. He probably came to the kitchen to find me. And then somebody killed him and he'll never know the truth."

"He must have suspected that it wasn't as bad as his mother said if he wanted to talk to you. What Brody did for you was totally legitimate. There's nothing to be embarrassed about," I said.

"I wasn't embarrassed. Brody was never anything but nice to me. He wrote me a check that allowed me to clear my debts and stay in business. I don't know if he ever knew what a difference that money made to me. The only thing I regret is that he died before I was able to pay him back. I wanted to tell Blitz that I tried to pay back the money."

"When?"

"I made one trip to that house after Brody passed away. Blitz's mom, Linda, refused to accept it. She wouldn't acknowledge that any such loan had taken place and she asked me to leave and never come back. She treated me like I was a dirty secret from Brody's past. I always wondered if Blitz knew the truth, or if he thought I was back to ask for more money from her. The day he walked into Disguise DeLimit was the first time he ever mentioned it, and that's the day I realized what his mom must have told him about me."

When I remembered that day, I was struck again by how strange it had seemed at the time that Blitz wanted Ebony to plan his party and Disguise DeLimit to provide the costumes. And again I found it hard to justify the person who had

walked into our store expecting to toss around money and get
what he wanted with the person Bobbie Kay had told me she
knew—the tortured rich boy who made donations to her nonprofit with no expectations in return.

Certainly Blitz could have turned to a number of different
people to make his birthday party happen. As far as costumes
went, what my dad always said was true. We had a vast inventory and our reputation as a costume shop had spread beyond
the perimeter of Proper City, but I hadn't been able to understand why Blitz would hire someone he didn't appear to like.
Now I understood. He wanted to get to know her—get to
know the story behind her relationship with his real father—
and he'd used his party as an excuse to open that door. His
attitude had been for show, a proud kid who hid his vulner-
ability behind an act of false bravado.

"You awake over there?" Ebony snapped her fingers in
front of my face.

"I was just thinking about things."

"You can think all night if you want, but it's late and I'm
tired," Ebony said. "How about we unpack the contents of
the trailer so I can take off?"

Ebony wasn't the only one who was tired. The emotional
drain of the day, combined with the particular stiffness that
comes from spending extended amounts of time on a road
trip, were setting in. I unlocked the store and picked up the
assortment of colorful flyers that had been shoved underneath
the door. Soot ran inside. I changed out of my mom's dress
and into the tracksuit I'd worn when I went to Hoshiyama's
with Tak. The scent of fried rice clung to the stretchy fabric,
making me both hungry from and annoyed at the memory
at the same time.

Ebony and I didn't talk much while we unloaded the

costumes. I sensed we both wanted to get the job done. I would have left it for the next day, but after everything my dad and Don had gone through to acquire the costumes, it didn't seem like a good idea to leave them sitting in the trailer out front.

We took turns loading dollies of boxes and rolling them into the already-full stockroom. Until now, I'd largely ignored the massive disorganization in the back room, but tonight I wished that I hadn't. Our only choice was to put the boxes wherever we found space, and most of that space was in the center of the room. At least now I'd have a project for the morning. We brought in boxes labeled ALIEN HEAD, ALIEN TORSO, and ALIEN AUTOPSY and stacked them floor to ceiling. A quick calculation determined that there were approximately seventy-five boxes in all. Maybe instead of the tracksuit, I should have dressed in the sailor costume and downed a can of spinach first.

When we were done, I said good night to Ebony and went upstairs, changed into pj's, and climbed into bed. I'd hoped that exhaustion would make the transition from awake to asleep seamless, but it didn't. Without any other distraction, my mind opened up the floodgates of the concerns I'd been able to hold at bay. My dad's heart attack, Ebony's history with Blitz's dad, Tak Hoshiyama's relationship with Detective Nichols, the robbery at the Manners house . . . It was a never-ending loop that kept me wide awake.

It was like the whole town of Proper was cut out of cardboard and someone had gotten it wet. Everything—and everybody—was either crumbling or falling apart. I was having a hard time keeping the faith.

After two hours of staring at the bedroom ceiling, I got up in search of a distraction. I poured a glass of half orange juice and half sparkling water and flipped through the mail, tossing piece after piece into the trash.

And then, there it was. An oversized, full-color postcard with a photo of Blitz Manners in the center. I flipped the postcard over. It was an announcement of a memorial service hosted by Candy Girls. Below their name was the tagline: *Look to us for costumes, catering, and condolences.* If it wasn't so atrociously inappropriate, it would have been laughable. General activities were listed on the card: informal reminiscences and mingling. Food and beverage service courtesy of Roman Gardens.

Roman Gardens—the location where Blitz had been planning to throw his party. To hear Blitz tell it, when the pipe burst and Octavius told Blitz the party would have to be rescheduled, Blitz canceled everything and redirected his attention—and his money—to Shindig and Disguise DeLimit. You would think Octavius would be angry at the loss of income.

So why was Octavius Roman involved in Blitz's memorial service?

The first reason that sprung to mind involved the kind of grand illusion Magic Maynard liked to attempt. Diversion, he'd said. Get people to believe you're doing one thing and then you can pull the wool over their eyes. Was Octavius playing the generosity card in order to make the whole town think he was one of the good guys while behind the scenes he hid his involvement in a homicide?

I leaned back in the chair and thought about Blitz. The more I learned about him, the more of a conundrum I found him to be. So much of his public persona—the brash person who had come to the costume shop and set a ridiculous timetable, the spoiled man-child who threw around $20,000 and insulted Ebony's integrity, the disgruntled drunk who tossed the custom-made Sherlock Holmes costume on the floor because it wasn't to his liking—those actions fit one person. But then there was the person Ebony described tonight, a young man who felt alone in his own crowd. That person fit with what Bobbie had said: he donated his money freely to her charity without expecting any sort of return. In fact, he'd asked her to keep it quiet. He resented being popular for his money and he'd never gotten over the death of his dad.

And while Ebony had gotten out of debt and built Shindig up to an established party planning business and Bobbie had gone to a treatment center voluntarily to confront her problems with drug abuse, Blitz hadn't fought against his demons. He'd hidden behind his money while withdrawing from everyone around him.

In ways more than one, Blitz and I were similar. He had acted out for his attention. I dressed in costumes for mine. He never got over the death of his father and I lived with the knowledge that I'd never get to know my mother. Thanks to very different circumstances, we were both isolated. Was this how Blitz had felt underneath the surface? Alone, afraid to trust anybody? Living with the fear of losing the few people who he had? I felt an unexpected sense of loss at the knowledge that someone who might have understood the way I felt was now gone.

I woke to Soot chewing on my hair. At first I swatted him away but, persistent ball of gray fur that he was, he kept coming back. I sat up and looked him in the face. "Leave my hair alone," I said. He stuck out a paw and swatted at my cheek. The clock told me it was after nine. I scooped Soot out of my way and got out of bed.

The first thing I did was call the hospital. "This is Margo

Tamblyn, Jerry Tamblyn's daughter. I was there yesterday. How is he?"

"I'll connect you with his room and he can tell you himself."

Seconds—and three and a half rings of the phone—later, he answered.

"Dad? It's Margo. How are you feeling?"

"I feel good. Hungry, but good."

"If you're hungry, then eat something."

"It's not that easy. This place seems to own stock in green Jell-O. I'd give my signed Blues Brothers necktie for a hamburger."

"You must be delirious. No way you'd part with that for a hamburger."

"Maybe not a hamburger. But make it a filet mignon and all bets are off."

We chatted for a few more minutes, innocuous father-daughter stuff that had the desired result of leaving me feeling like everything was normal. After half an hour, he said a nurse needed him to hang up so she could use him as a human pincushion.

There was barely time to get showered and dressed before opening the store. So much for having time to organize the aliens.

This morning's smoothie was a banana, a half cup of almond milk, a half cup of orange juice, and a heaping tablespoon of plain yogurt. I added a handful of crushed ice and hit liquefy. While the blender whirred, I wondered if Blitz's memorial would have any impact on business.

I dressed in a white T-shirt, black pants, and a pair of red plaid suspenders left behind from a ladies of the '80s costume. I knotted on a pair of red canvas Converse high-top sneakers, pulled my hair into a side ponytail, and went downstairs to unlock the doors. Gina Cassavogli stormed down the sidewalk toward me.

"What are you doing?" she demanded.

"I'm getting ready to open. What does it look like I'm doing?"

"You can't open today. You'll spoil everything!"

"The store was closed yesterday for—for personal reasons. I have to open today."

"Show some respect, Margo." She thrust one of the over-sized Blitz postcards at me.

"Someone already put one under my door," I said.

"Well maybe this time you should read it." She flipped it to the side with Blitz's photo and pointed a shiny red talon at a barely legible font that ran down the side. "It says right here that all of the businesses in Proper City are going to remain closed to pay respects to Blitz. Candy Girls coordinated this whole memorial on very short notice and it's only appropriate for you to acknowledge what we did and support us like everybody else."

Heat flamed over my face. "Give me that," I said, and snatched the postcard from her fingers. I looked closely at the tiny words along the side of the postcard. I'd missed that last night. I looked up and down the street. None of the other stores appeared to be opening. "Everybody agreed to this?" I asked, waving the card.

"Well, of course they did. At least most of them did. It's the right thing to do. Besides, it would look even worse if you opened, considering your role in his murder."

"My role? I had no role in the murder. Blitz hired us to provide costumes for his guests and we did. If you ask me, it's a little strange that he didn't hire Candy Girls, considering his fiancée works for you."

"His fiancée? Blitz wasn't engaged," Gina said.

"Maybe somebody should tell that to Amy Bradshaw. She seems to be quite happy flashing a giant diamond ring that she says Blitz gave her."

"I already warned you to leave my staff alone. Now, you're welcome to come to the memorial today. Everybody in Proper is invited. But don't come if you plan to show up and spread rumors." She pinched the postcard with her shiny red-tipped fingernails and slid it out of my hand. "You said you already had one, so I'll take this back."

She put the postcard on top of the stack she had in her hand and walked away, leaving me on the sidewalk. Her short pink skirt swished back and forth while she teetered on turquoise platform sling-backs. For all I knew, she was policing the rest of the storefronts for signs that other business owners had talked to me and were planning to open as well.

It was a few minutes before ten. I slipped back inside and called Bobbie.

"Is this whole Blitz memorial for real?"

"A lot of people aren't happy about the loss of business, but once they heard that Candy Girls had the blessing of Blitz's family, they agreed to stay closed. If I were you, I wouldn't try to stop it from happening. It'll draw attention to you in a negative way."

"Okay, fine. I have one more question," I said.

"What's that?"

"Do you mind if we show up together?"

CARS lined the perimeter of the park. Bobbie circled around the block twice before giving up and handing her keys to a valet attendant. I stepped out of the car and smoothed the creases out of the black cotton dress that I'd changed into. Ladies of the '80s suspenders and red Converse sneakers hadn't felt appropriate for a memorial service, but I was surprised to discover that I was one of only a few people who had chosen to wear black.

"There's a valet attendant at a memorial service at a public park?" I whispered.

Bobbie shrugged. "Everybody has to make a living."

The Proper City Park, or PCP as it had inevitably been nicknamed, was a large, flat stretch of public property that was a combination of dirt and patches of yellow grass. It would have taken our entire water supply to grow the kind of lush grass that was popular in less-arid states, so a group of community gardeners had banded together in the '90s and leveled the ground, created a two-foot-tall rock border, and built small shaded areas out of tall tree trunks and corrugated aluminum.

Picnic tables filled the area under the aluminum roofs. Small fire pits, blacked with soot, sat at ten-foot intervals, smoking with freshly lit charcoal. Clusters of people stood talking to one another while looking around as if trying to figure out what they should be doing. I kept my round, black plastic sunglasses on and scanned the crowd for familiar faces. Linda and Black Jack Cannon talked to Gina Cassavogli next to a four-foot-tall picture of Blitz that rested on a wooden easel.

It wasn't until I spotted Detective Nichols standing off to the side taking note of those who arrived that I realized what I'd overlooked about the occasion. If everybody who was tangentially connected to Blitz was here, then it stood to reason that the person responsible for his death might be here too.

Detective Nichols caught me looking at her. I looked away too quickly, which I'm sure made it obvious that I'd been watching her. She started toward me and I turned to Bobbie.

"I don't want to talk to Detective Nichols," I said. "Do you mind running interference?"

"No problem," she said. She met Nichols halfway while I went in the opposite direction. "Hi, Detective," I heard Bobbie say. "I've been meaning to talk to you about a fundraiser for the police force. Do you have a minute?"

When I was clearly out of her line of vision, I stood back and scanned the crowd again. Grady O'Toole waved. I waved back. He said something to the men he was with and then joined me.

"I was hoping to see you today," he said. "I have something for you."

He put his hand on my waist and guided me away from the crowd. "Grady," I said. "I don't think it's the best idea to sneak off in the middle of a memorial."

He reached into his suit jacket and pulled out a sheet of paper. "You asked me about the costumes at the party," he said. "I made you a list like the one I gave the detective." He smiled, less thousand-watt smile like before and more aw-shucks. "This seemed kind of important to you the other day. I know you got some bad news and I thought—well, I thought you might rather have this than a bunch of flowers."

"Thank you," I said. I unfolded the papers. His pen must have died halfway through the list because the color of the ink switched between *Veronica Mars* and *Jupiter Jones*. The crime scene cleanup crew had said that they found a wadded-up trench coat in the back of the oven, and that trench coat went to one very specific costume. I scanned over the names— including Sherlocks #1–#4—but didn't see Columbo listed.

"This list isn't complete."

"Sure it is. I put everybody on there."

"What about Columbo?"

Grady looked surprised. "Why are you asking about him?"

"I specifically remember making the Columbo costume. He was one of my favorites. It struck me as odd that he's not on here."

"I thought you already knew." He shoved his hands in his pockets and looked at me sheepishly. "The guy in the Columbo costume was me."

Chapter 19

"YOU WERE COLUMBO?" I asked. I stepped backward to put distance between us and looked around for Detective Nichols, for Bobbie, or for anybody familiar.

"Sure. Why is that so important? At first I let Blitz think I was going to take the Sherlock costume that he wanted to wear, but that's too cruel even for me."

"When did you give it to him?"

"We spent Friday going over his invite list and assigning costumes to different people. A couple of the women wanted to do their own thing—you know, the ones who work for Candy Girls—but other than that, just about everybody liked what we picked out."

I looked at the list again, this time scanning for Tak's name. "What about Tak Hoshiyama?"

"I don't know what he was doing there. Blitz invited him when he heard he was back in town, but neither of us thought he'd show. He said he'd figure out his own costume. Who was he?"

"Charlie Chan."

"Man, he did a good job with that. I wondered who was under that mustache."

The longer I stood at Blitz's memorial talking to Grady, the more I felt like a mask had been pulled over my eyes, hiding the truth about the people around me. Only it wasn't so much that the truth was hidden, it was that an alternate truth had been fabricated and fed to me like a fistful of candy corn. If Grady was involved in Blitz's murder—a fact that I wasn't yet ready to discount—his current golly-shucks attitude now seemed diabolical. I snuck a look at him from under my curled eyelashes and caught him staring back at me. This time he grinned the same smile that had put me on alert a week ago when he was in the shop.

I turned around again and spotted Bobbie talking to Black Jack. He wore the same cowboy hat and bolo tie he'd worn when I met him at the gas station.

"Thank you for the list," I said to Grady. "I want to pay my respects to Black Jack and Mrs. Manners."

"Mrs. Cannon," Grady corrected. "She took Black Jack's name when they married. Blitz was pretty angry about that. He stayed at my house for a month so he wouldn't have to talk to her."

"But surely he understood that there was nothing wrong with her falling in love with Black Jack after Mr. Manners passed away, right?"

"Blitz didn't see things that way. He never forgave his mom when she remarried."

"So Blitz and Black Jack didn't get along?"

"No, they got along great. That made his mom even more

angry. Black Jack never acted like he wanted to be Blitz's dad. He let Blitz do whatever he wanted. Even gave him a black Ferrari from the dealership when he graduated high school. That just made things between Blitz and his mom worse."

I nodded as though I was listening, but I couldn't stop thinking about the wrinkled Columbo coat. Could I trust anything that Grady said? I didn't know. Kirby had said that the friendship between Grady and Blitz was less than perfect. If they did have a deep-rooted competitive rift between them, what would keep Grady from making up stories about Blitz's family that would throw suspicion away from himself?

I thanked Grady again and headed toward the shaded picnic tables. The more I thought about that Columbo coat, the more another question nagged at me. Why hadn't the police found it when they went over the crime scene? A murder had been committed. Every person at that party had been interviewed. According to the crime scene cleanup crew, the fire hall had been left in postparty state for forty-eight hours because the police wanted to make sure they'd gotten every piece of evidence that had been left behind. So how was it that a rumpled and dirty trench coat, balled up and shoved in the oven in the corner of the kitchen, could have gone unnoticed?

Either the Proper City Police Department had done a very sloppy job on the investigation or somebody wasn't telling me the truth.

I walked across the yellow-green patchy ground and plucked a bottle of water from a large silver bowl filled with rapidly melting ice cubes. Gina Casserole—I mean, Cassavogli—narrowed her eyes at me but said nothing. She hadn't changed out of her pink skirt and turquoise shoes, and she stood out like an extra from *Miami Vice*. For a fleeting moment I regretted not adding Crockett and Tubbs to the costumes at the party.

Water from the wet bottle ran down the palms of my hands and dripped onto my dress. I peeked around to see if anybody was watching me and then ran the bottle over the side of my dress to dry it. When I looked back up, I saw Tak Hoshiyama staring at me from the charcoal pits.

Figured.

I would have turned around and walked away except that Detective Nichols was standing beside him. It was the perfect opportunity. Tak and I hadn't spoken since the fried rice incident, and this would establish to both of them that I was just another person in Proper City who was participating in a Proper City event.

It was also the perfect opportunity to ask the detective about the Columbo coat, and since Tak had been at the party, maybe he could contribute something to the conversation.

"Detective Nichols, Tak, nice to see you both," I said. My voice came out higher than usual.

Tak stepped toward me, putting himself between us. "I heard about your father. Is everything okay?"

It was the one question I hadn't been prepared for. The ground shifted underneath me and I swayed. Tak put a hand out around my waist and stabilized me. I looked over his shoulder at Detective Nichols, who had focused her attention on the grill.

"He's in stable condition," I said. "The hospital in Moxie is keeping him. They don't think it's a good idea for him to be in a car for the amount of time it'll take for him to get home. Not yet. How did you know?"

"Word gets around. I saw that the shop was closed yesterday and I was worried."

"I don't think you should be worrying about me," I said. I cut my eyes to Detective Nichols again, who had joined a crowd of people by the poster of Blitz.

"I can't help it."

The tone of his voice caught me by surprise and I looked back into his eyes. For the first time since I'd met him, I noticed how dark brown they were, how the color almost dissolved into the iris. I felt the same way I did the first time Magic Maynard held his spinning wheel up in front of me and told me to focus on the center. Disoriented and dizzy and a little bit drunk. I hadn't realized how close we were standing to each other, but all of a sudden Tak was the only person I was aware of.

"Your dad's going to be okay," he said gently. And with that, my eyes filled with tears like they had at the hospital and overflowed down my cheeks. He brushed them away. I stepped back and his hand dropped.

"Will you be at the store later tonight?" he asked. "We should talk about what happened at the restaurant."

"I don't think there's anything to talk about."

"I do."

"Why? I didn't know, but now I do, so it's fine."

"It's not fine. Whatever you think you know, you don't."

Just what I needed in my life. Another person who spoke in riddles.

"Tak, I came over here to talk to Detective Nichols. She was here a second ago. Do you know where she went?"

"She's sitting at the picnic table with Linda Cannon."

"Okay, thanks." I turned away and he reached out and caught my hand. "Tonight. Eight o'clock?"

"Fine."

I left while I still had most of the control over my emotions. I wasn't the only person shedding tears—it *was* a memorial—but having known Blitz Manners for less than a week made my tears seem forced. I didn't want to talk about my dad's heart attack in this crowd. It felt private, like if I kept it a secret from the rest of the world, I could pretend it never happened.

Detective Nichols was finishing up with her burger when I reached her. It struck me as an odd choice to serve hamburgers and hot dogs at a memorial service, but who was I to criticize? Several hundred people had shown up to pay their respects. I suspected everyone in the town of Proper felt unease over the murder of one of the residents. On some level, this was what everyone needed.

I sat across from Detective Nichols before she stood up. "Don't leave. I want to talk to you."

She crumpled up a black paper napkin and rolled it into a ball between the palms of her hands. Finally, she leaned back and set the ball down in the middle of the empty, black paper plate. Everything that Candy Girls had provided—the cups, napkins, plasticware, and plates—was black. The only color in the area was the floral arrangement that sat next to the photo of Blitz, a three-foot-wide burst of oranges, reds, and yellows that had been donated by Packin' Pistils.

I leaned forward. "There was a crime scene cleanup crew at the fire hall yesterday. Did you know that?"

"I'm not surprised. Once we process a crime scene, it's up to the businesses to decide how they want to handle things." She shook her head and made a face like her hamburger wasn't sitting well. "It usually doesn't take that long to clear a scene, but with that many people at the hall when the murder happened, we wanted to make sure that we didn't miss anything."

"Do you feel confident that you didn't?"

"Ms. Tamblyn, maybe you want to stop beating around the bush and ask whatever it is you came over here to ask me."

I rested my elbows on the table and propped my face in my hands. To anyone watching, I was just a regular person having a conversation with a patron of the event.

"You say that you processed the crime scene, and you're confident that you didn't miss anything. But the crime scene cleaners found the trench coat from the Columbo costume and the deerstalker hat that Blitz wore shoved into the back of the oven in the kitchen. They said you released the crime scene. If that's true, then how did those items get there?"

Chapter 20

DETECTIVE NICHOLS'S EXPRESSION changed from annoyance to defensive. "No way. Not possible."

"According to the men I spoke to two days ago, it's not only possible, it's the truth. And if there's evidence that someone else was in that kitchen with Blitz when he died, then I think you're going to have to lay off Ebony as your main suspect."

She sat up straight and looked around at the crowd. "This is an open investigation and I'm not going to discuss suspects with you. But since you brought up Ms. Welles, where is she? I don't believe I've seen her here yet."

"We were out of town yesterday and maybe she didn't find out about the memorial in time to come."

"You knew about it," she said.

"Gina Cassavogli came to the store this morning."

"And you didn't mention it to Ebony? Seems kind of odd." Her tone was calm and inquisitive, not snitty or accusatory, as I would have expected. But despite her even tone, the insinuation was there. She found it curious that Ebony had chosen not to attend the memorial to honor Blitz, her most recent client. And while I knew Ebony was innocent, I found it curious too.

The detective pushed her plate away from her. "You didn't come over here so we could talk about Ms. Welles's decision to stay away from the memorial, so let's get back to these costumes. Where are they now?"

"They were being incinerated. From what I understand, that's how these things work. The fire hall was left unattended for two days after the murder. The cleanup crew dealt with the whole place, not just what was left in the kitchen. Food was left out, garbage was overflowing. I watched them carry at least a dozen bags of hazardous waste out of the hall before they declared it clean."

"Was it?"

"The owner proclaimed that it was."

"What about you? Did you agree?"

I could have lied or pretended that I didn't know, but what would have been the point? Going on that walk-through hadn't been against the law, and besides, it was clear that Nichols knew I'd been there. As long as she was treating me with respect I'd return the favor.

"Yes. They did an excellent job. You'd never know a crime took place inside the building."

She stared at me as if trying to read my thoughts. Just in case she *could* read my thoughts, I put forth the internal musings that Ebony was innocent interspersed with the fact that I wasn't interested in her boyfriend. After several uncomfortable seconds, she sat back in her chair and crossed her arms.

"Are you staying much longer?" she asked.

"No. I want to offer my condolences to Black Jack and Linda and then I'll leave."

"I meant in Proper City," she clarified.

"I don't know."

"If you do, plan to get used to me poking around your business. I like to know the residents of the town so I can protect them." She gave me a quick smile, lobbed her trash in the aluminum can that sat to my right, and then stood up and walked away.

I'd never had a police officer tell me that he or she planned to poke around my business, and I wasn't sure what to make of it. Now hardly seemed the time to discover that I was somehow special.

Black Jack and Linda Cannon stood off to the side of the crowd. For the first time since I'd arrived, they were alone. I approached them with a nonthreatening manner.

Recognition flashed across Black Jack's face and he stepped toward me. "Hello there, little lady," he said. "Margo, right? Have you met my wife, Linda?"

"No, I haven't," I said. I held out my hand.

"Hello," she said.

Linda Cannon's face was vacant. Her eyes were dilated and her cheeks and mouth drooped slightly. Not having met her up close and personal prior to today, I wasn't sure how much of it was because we were at a memorial for her recently deceased son and how much of it was the result of a heavy dosage of antidepressants to keep her emotions under control. Whatever was responsible for her expression, it was creepily effective in hiding whatever she might have been feeling.

She took the tips of my fingers with her own and held them for a few seconds before letting go. Her skin was cold to the touch and I flinched.

"I'm very sorry for your loss," I said. "Both of you."

Black Jack put his arm around Linda. "Thank you," Linda said. "It was lovely for so many of Blitz's friends to turn out today. How did you know my son?"

"I only met him recently. My father owns the shop where he ordered the costumes for his party."

The blank expression changed and Linda became animated. Surprise. Anger. Outrage. The emotions moved quickly across her previously vacant face. She turned to Black Jack. "Did you invite her?" she asked.

"Honey, your son was an important member of Proper. I told Candy Girls to invite everybody in town. You knew that."

"Yes, but if you'd shown some common sense I wouldn't have had to warn off that Ebony woman."

"What do you mean you warned off Ebony?" he asked.

"The woman was standing over my son's body with a knife in her hand. Whoever found his body told the police. They hardly have to look any further than her to find the killer."

I spoke up. "Mrs. Cannon, I found Blitz's body, and Tak Hoshiyama called the police. And since you very clearly haven't been told the facts, you should know that the knife Ebony held was pristine. She was about to cut the goose for the partygoers."

Black Jack and Linda stared at me, as did a few of Blitz's friends whom I recognized from the party. Tak appeared from out of the crowd and put his arm around me.

"Margo, I've been looking for you. We should be going or we're going to be late," he said.

I looked at him like he was wearing the two-headed lizard mask that sat in the corner of the costume shop. In the split second that passed, I realized how absolutely inappropriate my outburst had been, even if its motivation had been just.

Tak watched me, and as I processed the information his face relaxed. It was like he could read my thoughts and he knew that I knew that he was trying to help me out.

"I lost track of time," I said to him. I turned back to Black Jack and Linda. "I'm very sorry. For what I said and for what happened to your son."

"Never you mind," Black Jack said. His arm was around his wife, but he reached his other hand out and rested it on my forearm. "This past week has shaken all of us up. You go on. And thank you for coming."

Tak and I turned away from the Cannons. Neither of us spoke until we reached the perimeter of the park.

"Do you want to tell me what that was about back there?" he asked.

"That depends. Are you going to use what I tell you in your investigation against Ebony?"

He looked confused. "What investigation?"

"I already know you and Detective Nichols are, well, I don't know what you're doing, but I know you're dating her, and I know you keep showing up and asking me questions that probably have to do with the investigation. So I figured you're reporting in to her on everything you've found out. I appreciate your help back there, but I don't like being used."

"Margo, please get in the car and let me give you a ride home."

"I came here with Bobbie Kay," I said.

"And Bobbie had to leave so she asked me to keep an eye on you."

"Bobbie wouldn't leave without telling me."

"It's possible that she was trying to find you when she saw you talking to Nancy."

His use of Detective Nichols's first name confirmed

everything I thought I knew. You just don't go around calling police officers by their first names unless you're dating them, right?

"And just because I used her first name doesn't mean I'm dating her," he said. I was starting to get seriously spooked by the way he could see right through me. "I'd rather not have this conversation on the edge of a public park where most of the residents of Proper City are in a position to watch."

He was right. Amy Bradshaw, whom I hadn't seen so far, stood off to the side with Grady. Gina Cassavogli was behind them, holding the silver bowl of water bottles. An unexpected breeze blew the picture of Blitz from the easel. Gina thrust the bowl at Amy and ran across the patches of yellow-green grass to pick it up before anybody else noticed.

"I need to call Bobbie first," I said.

He bowed his head slightly and held one hand out, palm up, in a gesture that said, *Go ahead if you think that's necessary.* I did, so I did.

"Bobbie, where are you?"

"Hi, Margo. Didn't Tak find you?" she asked. I looked at him and caught a smile. I used my thumb to lower the volume of the phone until I almost couldn't hear her. "He's standing right next to me, but I thought I should check with you first before leaving."

"What did you think? That an employee from the district attorney's office did away with me at a public gathering?" She giggled. "You're just as funny as you were in high school."

I didn't tell her that humor hadn't been the driving force behind my accidental comedy routine. "I'm just making sure nobody's signals got crossed. Yes, I'll catch a ride home with him."

"Don't be mad. You were talking to Detective Nichols and I didn't want to interrupt you."

I assured Bobbie that I was fine with the way things had panned out, even if the new arrangement left me feeling out of sorts. I'd been planning to go back to the store and call the hospital before I got to work on the stockroom reorganization project. Now, with Tak by my side, I wasn't sure what I'd get done.

THE trailer was gone from the front of Disguise DeLimit and a note from Ebony, explaining that she'd taken care of it, was tucked in the front door of the shop. I folded the note and Tak followed me inside.

"I'm going to be busy in the stockroom for the next couple of hours," I said.

"Do you need any help?"

I shook my head no before thinking, and then changed my mind. "Yes," I said.

"That wasn't the clearest of signals."

The thing was, the signals I was getting from Tak weren't exactly clear either. It had been a long time since I'd been attracted to someone, so I found myself second-guessing the way I felt about him and the way he treated me. Las Vegas wasn't known for its pool of eligible bachelors—the bachelors who partied in Vegas weren't exactly eligible—so maybe I was rusty. Maybe my intuition was on the fritz. Maybe my judgment was out of whack because of everything crazy that had happened since I'd arrived back in Proper.

"I want to change. Will you wait here until I get back?"

"Sure."

I ran up the stairs and changed into my clothes from earlier. My hair went back up into a ponytail. Soot sat in the middle of my comforter, cleaning his face with his paw. I sat down on the corner of the bed and placed my index finger directly between his ears. He stopped cleaning himself and looked at me, his paw suspended in front of his grumpy gray face.

"Soot, do you think it's a good idea for me to trust Tak? He's downstairs now. He seems understanding, but maybe it's a mistake."

Soot tipped his head back and my finger slid down to the tip of his nose. He swiped at it with his paw. "I don't trust a lot of people. I trust my dad and I trust Ebony and I trust Bobbie. That's pretty much it. I don't even really trust Crystal to do the magic act the right way and keep my job safe. And now here I am, about to confide in a total stranger. What's wrong with me?"

I scooped Soot off the comforter and planted a kiss on his head. He responded with an annoyed meow and a yawn. I made up for interrupting him up by scratching his ears while I carried him downstairs.

"Sorry to keep you waiting," I said to Tak. I set Soot on the concrete floor.

Tak's eyes went from my face to my head and back to my face. "No problem," he said. "You wouldn't have left me alone down here if you didn't trust me."

"Were you listening to me?"

"No. Why? Were you talking about me?"

"No. Never mind." I turned my back on him and reached for one of the big boxes. It was large but light. I shifted it from on top of a stack to the floor. Tak grabbed the other side, overestimating the weight of the box. Because he'd expected it to be heavy, his effort to help support it resulted in the box flying from my hands into the air. He looked stunned. I stepped forward and caught it.

"What's in there?" he asked.

"An alien," I said. He raised his eyebrows. "Okay, I think

it's an alien but I don't know. All of this came from the
scouting trip my dad and Don went on. I have to figure out
how to get it to fit in this room."

"Don't you want to empty the room out first?"

"No, I'm not getting rid of anything. I need to make it fit
with everything else that's already here."

He scanned the room. White metal shelves lined the
perimeter, with boxes stacked on top and garment bags hanging below. There appeared to be no rhyme or reason to the
organization, just a general sense of put-it-in-the-back-ness
that kept the off-season merchandise out of view and allowed
the costumes in the shop to stand out. Aside from my dad,
Kirby, and now me, nobody really knew what we had in our
inventory at any given time. Judging from the condition of
the stockroom, I was willing to bet that maybe none of us had
a clear picture of the scope of it.

"I have an idea," Tak said. "Do you have a tape measure
and a notebook?"

"Sure." I found both by the register and brought them back.
Tak asked me to hold one end of the tape measure. He measured the length of the walls, the height of the ceiling, and the
depth of the shelves, and wrote all of the numbers into the
notebook. I watched, assisted, and waited while he worked.
He appeared to have a plan in mind, and far be it from me to
interfere with a plan.

After taking the last measurement, he retracted the tape
measure and set it on top of the first box we'd unstacked. "I
don't want to tell you how to run your business, but if you
reorganize this back room, you could pick up a pretty sub-
stantial amount of storage space."

"Our store has functioned with this room as our stockroom for over forty years now. What makes you so sure your
way is better?"

He rested his elbow on the top of the box and smiled. "Like I said, I don't want to tell you how to run your business. But if you want, I can help you."

"Might as well hear you out. It's not like I have any better offers."

He drew a couple of lines on the notebook and then added some notes. I moved around the box and stared over his shoulder. Within seconds, he'd rendered the stockroom.

He set the notebook down and measured the width, height, and depth of a few of the boxes from the trailer and then added some additional notes at the bottom of the page. It quickly became apparent that his way was better than ours, in terms of storage optimization.

"How'd you learn how to do that?" I asked.

"What, sketch?"

"No, walk into a room and figure out how much will fit when it's organized."

He set the notebook and pen down. "It's something I've done since I was a kid. Spatial relations, math variables, calculations, they all come naturally to me."

"So you parlayed your natural aptitude for math variables into a job at the district attorney's office."

He looked serious. "How'd you know about that?"

"Word gets around." I smiled. "I don't remember who told me."

"After I got my engineering degree, I landed a job in the planning division of the DA's office."

"Organizing their stockrooms?"

He grinned. "Something like that."

"No, really, what do you do?"

"Mostly process applications for variances and rezoning. I enforce county codes and applicable laws. Sometimes I get to review plans for ordinance regulations, and I work closely with other engineers, architects, contractors, developers, and property owners on procedures."

"So that's how you ended up solving Don Digby's property line dispute," I said, half to myself.

"I forgot about that."

"Do you have any other talents I don't know about? Besides assessing small spaces at a single glance?"

"And making fried rice," he added.

"Yes, there is that. So, math and fried rice. You must be popular at parties." As soon as I said it, a flash of Tak dressed as Charlie Chan popped into my head. I didn't get the feeling that Tak was part of Blitz's crowd, and even Grady had said that Blitz invited Tak to his party but never expected him to show. I still didn't know what he'd been doing there. And if it wasn't in some official district attorney/spatial relations capacity—not that I'd know what that was—then I didn't know why he'd attended. Which put me back to where I was this afternoon, not sure exactly why he was going out of his way to spend time with me.

"I've known the Mannerses and the O'Tooles my whole life. My dad likes to play the slots and Grady's dad owns a casino in the old part of Vegas, so, in time, I was thrown in with that group."

"But you're older than they are," I said. "Aren't you?"

He grinned. "Older, wiser, better-looking . . ."

"I see Grady isn't the only one around here with a healthy dose of self-confidence."

"I'm kidding. I'm more like a friend of the family, I guess. My dad's restaurant is popular, so people accepted me."

Even though we had a lot of work ahead of us if we were going to implement Tak's plan, I pulled out a box that was packed full of Styrofoam wig heads and sat down on top of it. "I grew up here in Proper. How come we never met?"

"My parents moved here while I was finishing up my master's degree. That was about ten years ago."

"Where'd you live before that?"

"I was born in Hawaii." He crossed his arms over his chest. "Do you want my GPA or transcripts? Because I can arrange that if it makes you feel more comfortable."

I stood back up. "I didn't mean to interrogate you," I said. "I was just curious."

"You're trying to figure out why I was at Blitz's party, aren't you?"

"I don't know what you're talking about." I turned my back to him and pretended to be busy with one of the boxes.

He tapped me on the shoulder until finally I turned around and faced him. "What?"

"You should be happy I *was* at that party. Otherwise your friend Ebony would be in a lot of trouble."

Chapter 21

"**HOW DO YOU** keep knowing what I'm thinking?" I asked.

"Because you're easy to read. It's refreshing to meet someone who is so comfortable being exactly who she is."

In the past week I'd worn elements from go-go dancer, cowgirl, clown, and sailor costumes, and today I sported ladies of the '80s suspenders. I didn't know who I wanted to be until I woke up in the morning, and I dressed to suit that mood.

"I think you have me mistaken with someone else," I said.

"Margo, you're so busy watching everybody else that you never noticed me watching you. I knew there was something different about you, but I didn't put my finger on it until I saw you at Blitz's party."

"I was checking out the costumes to make sure everything turned out okay."

"It's not just that. You're aware of everything around you. Do me a favor. Close your eyes and describe this room."

"Why?"

"Indulge me," he said.

He seemed to have earned something by way of redesigning our stockroom, so I closed my eyes and kept a hand on the box next to me. "There are white metal shelves mounted to the walls around the perimeter of the room. Boxes filled with wigs and costume accessories are stacked on top of them. Most of the boxes are labeled in black marker. Nobody likes to reach up, so the boxes up top are things that we don't sell very often. Under the shelves are more boxes. We used to keep fairy-tale characters on the back-left side, and I think they're still there because I saw Little Bo Peep's cane on the floor. And two nights ago, Soot caught a mouse back here, but I don't know where it could have come from."

I opened my eyes and looked at him. "How was that?"

"Now close your eyes and tell me what you remember from Blitz's party."

Whether it was the relative privacy of the stockroom or the fact that Tak had been nothing but nice to me since arriving, I didn't know, but I did as he asked. The memory was tangible, as if I were standing inside the fire hall smelling the circulating appetizers of roast beef with horseradish dressing.

"There were clusters of people around the interior. Rockford, Nancy Drew, and Kojak. Tom Swift was showing Miss Marple how to work his rocket pack and the Bob-Whites were dancing." I remembered spotting Tak at the back of the fire hall and appreciating his costume. "You were there, but you weren't talking to anybody. Charlie's Angels were by the door and Columbo was talking to Veronica Mars." My eyes popped open. "But that's not possible."

"Why?" Tak leaned forward.

"Because Grady told me he was Columbo, and the person I saw talking to Veronica Mars wasn't Grady."

"Maybe there were two Columbos?"

"No. Grady gave me a list of who wore what and Columbo wasn't on the list. When I asked him about it, he said that was his costume. I'm pretty sure if another Columbo showed up Grady would have asked him to go change."

"Why did you ask Grady about the Columbo costume?"

I felt stiff and awkward as a new thought about Grady filled my mind. "I—I needed to know who was Columbo, that's all," I said.

"What just happened?"

"Nothing."

Tak and I stared at each other in silence. If I was as easy to read as he claimed, then he would have seen that I'd thought something that I didn't want to share.

The information about the trench coat found balled up in the kitchen of the fire hall was the one significant clue that said someone other than Ebony had been back there. The trench coat went with the Columbo costume, but now . . . now it didn't make sense. Grady had made a big deal of saying he was Columbo, and he'd wanted to know why I wanted to know. Had he planted a double at the party, someone to impersonate him while he snuck away and killed his friend-slash-rival?

I broke eye contact first and turned away from Tak to think it through. If what I suspected was true, then Grady could have been anywhere while the fake Columbo was out front. He could have murdered Blitz and left out the back, traded trench coats with the double, and reentered the party in time to be questioned by the police. His double could have disappeared long before anybody noticed.

Nausea twisted my stomach and triggered a wave of dizziness. I put a hand on the box next to me to steady myself.

"Are you okay?" Tak asked.

"I'm fine. Let's get to work." When I turned back to face him, he showed confusion and hurt. I put my hand on his arm and looked up at his face. "I can't talk about this right now. I'm sorry. It's not because I don't trust you"—okay, it was a little, but I didn't say that—"it's that I'm scared for Ebony and . . . and . . ." I grappled for the next thing to say, but couldn't figure out how to express what I was thinking without telling him everything. "Please," I added, immediately aware that it didn't fit the situation.

He picked up the notepad and stared at his sketch for a few seconds. "Here's what I had in mind," he said. He stood next to me and pointed out his plan for reorganizing the shelves to accommodate more merchandise. When he finished, he turned back to face me. "If you want to go ahead with this, I can start moving the merchandise so you'll have a place to store these boxes."

I agreed. One by one I sliced through the packing tape and peeked inside. Not only had we gained several alien costumes, but also an array of dark suits with government identification clipped to the lapel and a couple of cardboard models of scientific equipment that would make great backdrops for the windows. Three of the boxes were filled with panels that fit together to depict a laboratory. Another box held fog machines and jugs of the juice that went in them. I filled one of the machines and plugged it in. While the machine warmed up, I snuck out to the shop and squirreled Soot into the stockroom with me. I set him down when a cloudy layer of fog crept across the floor, and I ducked behind one of the larger boxes.

"What the heck?" Tak said. Fog swirled around his

ankles. Soot walked over to him and Tak jumped like he'd seen a ghost. When he recovered, he looked from side to side and finally saw me peeking around from behind a stack of boxes. I stood up and stepped away from my cover. I switched the fog machine off and smiled.

"You don't grow up in a costume shop and not learn to enjoy the props," I said.

"It must have been fun growing up in this world. I bet your parents threw the best parties in town."

"It's just my dad and me. My mother died when I was born. Ebony started looking after me when I was five, and she's been the closest thing I've had to a mom ever since." I'd surprised myself. Usually I didn't like to talk about my family to strangers, but with Tak, something was different.

He didn't say anything at first. He didn't offer to hug me like guys I'd dated who saw that admission as a cry for consolation. I liked him a little bit more for that. He reached up and held on to the bracket to one of the metal shelves.

"My dad and I aren't talking right now. He doesn't understand what happened with my job at the DA's office. There's some questionable activity going on there and I didn't want to be a part of it, so I resigned. My boss wouldn't accept my resignation, so it's on the books as an unpaid leave."

"What does your mom think?"

"My mom wants me to be happy. And she wants my dad to be happy. And she wants us all to get along, which might never happen. To him, quitting is a sign of a poor work ethic. You just don't do it. He thinks I should put my nose to the grindstone and barrel on through, regardless of what's going down."

"Do you think whatever's happening there is illegal?"

"No, but I think there's some stretching of the law, and that makes me uncomfortable. It was best for everybody if I left and they found someone better suited for the job."

Tak's story was oddly comforting. It made me feel less alone in my struggle to help the two people I loved the most. It also let me see that he was an ordinary guy with ordinary problems. Suddenly, it didn't seem so important to keep everything to myself.

"Would you like to go out to get some dinner?" I asked suddenly. "No strings attached and we don't have to talk about anything important."

He reached up and tucked his longish black hair behind his ear and then smiled. "I'd like that."

TEN minutes later, Tak and I shared a booth at Catch-22, a restaurant that boasted twenty-two different ways to serve fish. For a seafood restaurant in the middle of the desert, it was surprisingly popular. Tonight the featured "Catch of the Day" was shrimp, so I ordered the Salvadorian shrimp salad, and Tak ordered his shrimp Cajun style. We filled the time between ordering and the food arriving with chitchat that came surprisingly easily. Despite the fact that it was the two of us out to dinner, there were no first-date nerves. Still, I couldn't help notice the looks we attracted from the other diners in the restaurant. I figured only about half of them were due to my ladies of the '80s suspenders and side ponytail.

"How's your dad?" Tak asked.

"He's steady. The doctors said they might release him by the end of the week. The only reason they haven't yet is because it's his second heart attack in two weeks and they want to be sure he's stable. I want him to come home, but I hope things calm down before he gets here."

"Does he know about everything that's been happening?"

"He knows Blitz was murdered at the party and he knows

something's up with Ebony. But she's not involved. Detective Nichols is being stupid if she thinks she is." As soon as I said the words, I regretted them. "I didn't say that because she's your girlfriend. I really mean she's wrong if she thinks Ebony is involved."

"Detective Nichols isn't my girlfriend," Tak said. "She was, but it's—we're—we broke up."

"Oh," I said, clearly losing the ability to converse.

"I—you thought I'd say yes to a date with you if I had a girlfriend?"

"This is a date?"

"I thought it was. Isn't it?"

All of a sudden, everything I'd thought about feeling not-a-date natural went out the window. I ran my tongue over my teeth to make sure there was no lettuce caught between them and reached for my glass of water. I accidentally knocked it over. Water and ice spilled out on the table toward Tak, drenching the side of his shirt and the leg of his pants. Several patrons looked our way.

"I'm sorry," I said, and handed him my napkin. He blotted the fabric and then motioned for the waiter.

"Can we get a second glass of water over here?" he asked.

"That's not necessary," I said.

"I'll be right back," said the waiter.

"Margo, it was a glass of water. I don't think the conservationists would be all that upset over it, so you shouldn't be either."

I barely heard him. "That napkin isn't going to do any good. I'll be right back." I slid out of our booth and headed toward the hostess station. As I reached the counter, I looked to my left and saw Amy Bradshaw sitting alone in a booth in the back corner.

That was either highly coincidental or she was there because of us. I grabbed a stack of napkins from the bar and took them back to Tak. "These should help."

"That's the beauty of living in the desert," he said. "The air's so dry out here the water already evaporated."

"Great," I said, barely paying attention. "Can you excuse me for a second? I saw someone I know and I want to say hello."

He looked at me as if I were crazy.

I handed over the napkins and took a circuitous route to Amy's table so she wouldn't see me coming. She was drinking a glass of wine when I reached her, and as soon as she recognized me, she choked on it.

"Amy, isn't it? Nice to see you again," I said. I pointed to myself. "Margo Tamblyn, from the costume shop."

"I know who you are."

"Great. I wasn't sure if you'd remember me. You were a little flustered the day you came into Disguise DeLimit."

She set down her glass and looked from side to side. "What are you doing here?"

"Probably the same thing as you. Having dinner. If you haven't already ordered, the Salvadorian shrimp salad is pretty good."

"I'm having the scampi."

"Okay, well, maybe next time." As awkward as it felt, standing in the aisle next to Amy's table, I couldn't help thinking about how very possible it was that she was involved in the vandalism on Ebony's car or, even worse, in Blitz's murder. And if she was, then she wasn't going to get away with it. She turned her head toward the window—dismissing me, I imagined—and folded her hands in front of her. There was no ring on her finger.

Bingo.

I slid into the booth opposite her. "I'm not going to join

you, if that's what you're worried about. I'm just curious. What happened to the engagement ring you were wearing when you came to Disguise DeLimit on Sunday morning?"

She curled her right hand around her left and dropped them both into her lap. "What ring?"

"The giant diamond ring. It was pear shaped, wasn't it? You said it was from Blitz's family."

"That was all true. The ring belonged to Blitz's mother. He used to say he was going to give it to me."

"But he didn't give it to you, did he?"

"Blitz was a selfish man-boy who thought he was the center of the universe. We were together for two years. And then one day he cheated on me. Just like that. I might not have ever known if I hadn't found them together at his party."

"You caught Blitz with another woman at his birthday party?" I asked, surprised.

"Close enough. I caught him making out with Gina Cassavogli in the back of the big, brown gas guzzler that was parked out front."

Chapter 22

"THE CADILLAC?" I asked.

"I thought it was a prop for the party. There were so many detective shows in the '70s that it made sense."

"That's Ebony's car."

Amy looked stunned for a second, and then she recovered with a look of disgust. "I don't care how much Blitz paid her for the party, she should have shown a little more class about loaning out her keys."

That was the thing. Ebony wouldn't loan her keys to a couple of kids who wanted to make out at a birthday party. Especially not the owner of Candy Girls. Not even if the birthday boy was the one who wanted it. That Caddy was her pride and joy. She'd owned it since high school. In the past forty years she's probably paid more to maintain it than Black Jack Cannon charged for a brand-new car off his lot.

But if Amy thought Ebony had loaned out the use of her backseat and she—Amy, not Ebony—caught her rich boyfriend of two years with her married boss back there, she would be angry. Angry enough to confront said boyfriend in the kitchen of the party? Angry enough to wield a knife? Angry enough to stab him and leave him for dead? I didn't know. What I did know was that it all boiled down to one thing: Amy had a motive.

I excused myself from her table and rejoined Tak at ours. A small bowl with two scoops of half-melted ice cream sat in the middle of the table. Tak held a spoon in one hand. There was a dent in the side of the scoop closest to him. A clean spoon sat on my place mat.

"I thought you'd like to split some ice cream," he said. "Better hurry, though. It's almost melted through."

I picked up my spoon and then set it back down. "Amy Bradshaw is sitting at the booth in the back corner. Sunday morning she came to the store and tried to sell me her costume from Saturday night. She was wearing a giant diamond ring and she made it seem like Blitz had given it to her. Today she not only says that I misunderstood her, but admitted that she caught Blitz and Gina Cassavogli in the backseat of Ebony's car at the party."

Tak stared at me with open admiration. "You found all that out in, like, five minutes?"

I felt pretty good about it myself. I picked up the spoon and scooped a sizable amount of ice cream into my mouth. I savored the sweet creaminess of it and swallowed. "What flavor is this?"

"Cherry vanilla."

"Mmmmmm." I took another scoop and closed my eyes. When I opened them up, Tak was grinning.

"What would you have had for dinner if we weren't here?" he asked.

"A bowl of Fruity Pebbles, probably," I said. "Daily supply of vitamins and minerals."

"I don't think the son of a restaurant owner can be seen in public with a woman who eats Fruity Pebbles for dinner."

"Don't knock it till you've tried it."

We finished off the ice cream and the waiter brought the bill. I snatched it from the table before Tak could get to it and made a show of leaving cash in the black folder.

"I thought this wasn't a date?" he asked.

"It's not. If it was a date, we'd go dutch."

The tension from the spilled water incident had dissipated and Tak and I were back to the comfortable getting-to-know-you feeling from earlier at the store. Sadly, the tension came back when he pulled his SUV up in front of my store, because someone else was already parked there.

Detective Nichols.

She was dressed in a pair of black stretchy yoga pants, a sports bra, and an open zip-front sweatshirt. As if she hadn't already won the employment round (detective trumps magician's assistant in almost everybody's world), she pulled ahead in the body-fat round too. As in, a lot less than I had. Whereas I was far from comfortable in my own skin, the detective proved she was not only comfortable in hers, she wanted everybody to see it. She unpacked my scooter from the back of an old, beat-up pickup truck.

"Tak," Nichols said.

"Nancy," Tak said.

Detective Nichols turned to me. "How's Jerry?" she asked.

"He's still at the hospital in Moxie. I'm hoping he comes back by the end of the week."

"Are you going back up there to visit him tomorrow?"

"No, I need to be here to open the store. I didn't count on the lost business from today."

She nodded as if she understood. "I finally had a chance to get your scooter."

"Thank you. You didn't have to bring it here."

"Don't mention it," she said with a wave of her hand.

I looked back and forth between Tak and Detective Nichols—Nancy—and felt more tension than I had when I'd knocked over the glass of water at Catch-22. Whatever the terms of their breakup were, I sensed they were unresolved. Now hardly seemed the time to get on the officer's bad side.

"Thanks for helping me out in the store tonight," I said to Tak. I pulled out my keys. "Detective Nichols, do you have a couple of minutes? I think we need to talk."

Tak looked surprised but recovered quickly. The same could not be said for Detective Nichols, which caused me, at least internally, to smile. Tak climbed back into his SUV and drove off, leaving us two gals hanging out on the sidewalk. I unlocked the store and she followed me inside. I turned on the lights and set my keys on the counter.

"If I remember correctly, the reason you were at Christopher Robin Crossing on Monday was because somebody robbed Black Jack and Linda Cannon's house, right?" I asked.

"Hold up," she said. She put her hands up, palm-side out. "You want to talk to me about the investigation?"

"What did you think I wanted to talk to you about?"

She looked at the door and then back to me. "Yes, that's right. Linda Cannon called the police when she came home. The place had been tossed."

"Do you know what was missing?"

"Her jewelry. Why?" She turned her head to the side and assessed me out of the corner of her eyes.

"Amy Bradshaw came here on Sunday morning. She was wearing a giant diamond ring and, when I commented on it, she led me to believe she and Blitz were engaged. I ran into her tonight and she wasn't wearing it anymore. When I asked her about it, she said it was Blitz's mother's ring. She never told me why she had it in the first place. I don't know what happened to it now but it seemed odd, that Amy would even have a piece of jewelry that belonged to Blitz's family."

"Describe this ring," she said.

"It was a big, pear-shaped diamond. I've never seen a ring that big before."

"This all happened on Sunday morning when she came in here and tried to sell you her costume?" she asked.

"Yes," I said, chewing my lower lip the way I did when something bothered me. "And she let something else slip. Not Sunday, but tonight. She said she caught Blitz and Gina Cassavogli—the owner of Candy Girls, who is married, by the way—in the back of Ebony's Cadillac at the party. Amy and Blitz had been dating for over two years. I can't figure out why she'd act like they were still a couple—not just a couple, but pretend that they were engaged—when she came here on Sunday, unless she was trying to cover something up, you know?"

Detective Nichols stared at me. Her fingertips were in the pockets of her yoga pants, with her thumbs hooked on the outside. "The timing on the ring doesn't make sense," she said finally. "The robbery was on Monday."

"What if someone who had every right to be in that house has been stealing from them all along? If Amy was dating Blitz, nobody would have questioned her being there. She could have stolen the ring. She could have stolen a lot of things. But now that Blitz is out of the picture, there's no reason for her to be there anymore. What if she staged it to look like someone came in and robbed the place on Monday so she'd be off the hook for the missing jewelry?"

"Seems far-fetched."

"Do you have any other theories?"

"With all due respect, it's not in my job description to discuss 'theories' with the locals."

"With all due respect, I think this information gives you a reason to follow up with Amy Bradshaw and talk to her about her relationship with Blitz."

"I'm curious. What took *you* out to the Cannon house the day of the robbery? Seems like you were there just in the nick of time."

"I went to see Grady," I said.

"Any particular reason?"

"I wanted to know who wore which costume at the party. I already told you about the trench coat that the crime scene cleanup team found in the kitchen. Did you check into that yet? Or is there a reason you're ignoring the information I've been giving you?"

Detective Nichols cocked her head to the side for a second and then righted it. "Okay, I'll check this out. Thank you for the tip."

"You're welcome. Thank you for bringing my scooter."

"You're welcome."

After she left, I went upstairs and stared again at the collection of items I'd amassed on the kitchen table. The empty hair spray can that I'd found in Ebony's Cadillac. The scrap of plaid fabric. And the $20,000. Was I withholding evidence? Technically, I thought no. The hair spray and the fabric were in Ebony's car, which had been parked out front of the store. That crime of vandalism hadn't been reported. And the money . . . well, I still needed to ask Ebony about that.

THE next morning I dressed in a black T-shirt with a ruffled shirt, bow tie, and tux lapels printed on the front and wide-legged black trousers. I fed Soot and called the hospital.

"Margo! Good news. They ran out of green Jell-O so they're letting me leave."

"Today?" I asked.

"Tomorrow. I'm pretty sure Don had something to do with it. When he's not with me, he's out there playing poker with the hospital staff. They're probably tired of him taking their paychecks."

My dad and Don had bonded over three things: card games, the blues, and conspiracy theories. I wanted to call up the nurses' station and tell them they were lucky Don was in a poker phase. Otherwise they'd be listening to his argument about how we never actually landed on the moon.

"When will you be here?"

"As soon as they let me go, we're leaving. I don't like being cooped up in this bed all day. I want to get home and take a look at those costumes I bought. Did you unpack them yet?"

"No. I'm in the middle of reorganizing the stockroom. Once that's done, we can tackle the aliens together."

"As long as they're not armed," he said and then laughed at his own joke.

When the call was over, I made a cherry and banana smoothie to go and left by quarter to eight. I hopped on the Zip-Two and got off in front of Dig's Towing.

Today Dig was dressed in a turquoise bowling shirt with red flames on the back. The sleeves, as usual, had been torn out, and the anchor tattoo on his formidable biceps was on display. His jeans were dark wash, wide leg, and cuffed over CAT boots. Dig didn't seem to care that the temperature in Proper was ninety degrees in the shade. Dig was so cool the heat didn't touch him.

He was bent over the engine of his tow truck. When I said hello, he jumped and banged the back of his head on the raised hood.

"Where'd you come from?" he asked, rubbing the back of his bald head.

"The Zip-Two."

"Something happen to the scooter?"

"No, I thought it would be easier to scare you if you didn't see me coming."

"You got your dad's sense of humor, that's for sure. How's Jerry doing? Ebony told me he's back in the hospital."

"He's going to be fine. I talked to him this morning and he said the doctors expect to release him in the next day or two."

As comforting as it was to know how many people in town cared about my dad, it was hard to keep answering the question that I was only barely allowing myself to think about. I hoped if I repeated "he's going to be fine" enough, it would become true.

"Jerry's not ready to cash in his chips yet," he said. "Not until he gets to Florida."

"Florida? What's in Florida?" I asked. I'd never once heard my dad mention an interest in going to Florida.

"He's got a pen pal out there who has a collection of pink flamingo costumes. Can you believe that? Apparently there was some kind of stage production and a local artist made ten of them. Adult sized. Now who else in this whole country would be interested in ten life-sized flamingo costumes? I don't know. Those pink flamingos have Jerry Tamblyn written all over them."

"If it takes pink flamingos to keep my dad going, then pink flamingos are my new favorite bird," I said.

"Word," he said. He stood back from the truck and crossed his arms over his chest. Now I could see half of both of his tattoos: the anchor and the Tweety Bird on the other side. "You didn't come out here this early to give me an update on your dad's health, did you?"

"No, I didn't. I wanted to talk to you about Ebony's car."

He lowered the hood of the truck and wiped his hands on his jeans. "You're talking about the vandalism, right?"

"Right."

"Let's go inside."

I followed him to the open garage. He went straight for a small table that held a fresh pot of coffee and an assortment of powdered creamers. "You want some?" he asked. I shook my head. He poured himself a mugful, dumped in a ski-slope-sized amount of powdered creamer, and stirred it all with a brown plastic stirrer. He ran the stirrer through his lips and tossed it before turning back to me.

"What do you know about that vandalism?" he asked.

"Not much. I came out of the shop and there it was. The window was broken, the car was spray-painted, and the tires were flat. I thought I knew who did it, but now I'm not so sure."

"Turns out you're not so sure about a couple of your facts. The paint, as you figured out, was hair spray. Came off with soap and water just like you said."

"That's only one fact that I was wrong about," I said, knowing that he was building up to something.

"The window wasn't broken."

"Yes it was. I saw it."

"Somebody wanted you to think the window was broken." He drank from his cup, made a face, and added more creamer. "There are two things I know that you don't. The back lock on the passenger side of Ebony's car doesn't work. Looks like it's locked, but if you try to open the car and jiggle the handle, the door pops right open."

"So anybody who wanted to get into her car could." I

thought about what Amy had said about Blitz and Gina in the backseat at the party. That explained how they'd gotten in there. "But what about the broken glass?" I asked.

"That's where somebody got creative. Ebony's window was rolled down and glass was inside and outside of the car. Whoever did the vandalism wanted you to think that the window was broken."

"So you just rolled the window up?"

"Pretty much. The crank sticks a little, but if you know the trick like I do, you can get it to work." He flashed a proud smile at knowing how to work Ebony's car. It was cute.

"Why would somebody do that? Make it look like her window was broken when it wasn't?"

He shrugged. "I can't figure that part out. The whole thing is off if you ask me. The paint washed off, the window wasn't broken, and because the back door wasn't locked, she can't claim somebody broke in."

"What about the flat tires? Somebody sliced them."

"Nope. Somebody let the air out, but the tires were intact."

"You mean you just filled them back up with air and they were fine?"

"Yep. Craziest thing I ever saw. It's like somebody was playing a practical joke on her. Everything was temporary. No permanent damage."

"Except that I don't know a lot of practical jokers who would write the word *Murderer* on her car hours after a dead body was found."

"True, that."

"Is there anything else that you noticed?" I asked. "Anything at all?"

"There's one more thing, but this is between you and me."

"What?"

"I found an envelope of money under the seat. A lot of

money. Hundreds in an envelope. When I asked Ebony if she knew anything about it, she looked like she'd seen a ghost. But then she took it and said she'd been looking for it. She took the bills out of the envelope and tossed the envelope in the trash."

"What aren't you telling me?"

He reached under the counter and pulled out a cream-colored envelope with the letters *BM* embossed on it. "This is the envelope and those are Blitz Manners's initials."

I relaxed. "Blitz hired her to coordinate his birthday party," I said. "That was probably how he paid her."

Dig turned the envelope over and showed me a smear of something red on the back. "So then you want to tell me why it has somebody's blood on it?"

Chapter 23

THE SMEAR ACROSS the back of the envelope could have been a lot of things: ketchup, barbecue sauce, hair dye, or, yes, blood. And considering where it was found and who it had come from, the obvious answer wasn't that Blitz had been eating a plate of ribs without a napkin before he'd been killed.

"Dig, did you tell anybody about this?"

"No, and you can't either."

"It's not that simple. This is evidence," I said.

He snatched it back from me. "No it's not. It wasn't found in the fire hall, it was found in Ebony's car. Nobody searched her car. It wasn't part of the crime scene."

"Because I drove it away," I said. "Maybe they would have searched it. We don't know."

"It's too late for that now. I detailed the thing after I finished cleaning up the exterior."

"Did she ask you to do that?"

"Nope. It was on the house."

Depending on how thorough Dig had been—and I was guessing he'd been very thorough, considering how he felt about Ebony—he'd negated the principle that forensic science was based on: every contact leaves a trace. Because if there was trace evidence in her car, it had been vacuumed up and dusted off with a coating of Armor All.

"This means she's in trouble, doesn't it?" he asked, waving the envelope back and forth like a fan.

"Not necessarily." I checked the time on my phone. I'd planned to go to Ebony's house before opening the store. I needed to catch the next Zip-Two or I wouldn't have enough time to make it back to Disguise DeLimit by ten.

"Remember—not a word about this," he said. He tucked the envelope into his back pocket and I looked away.

The Zip-Two was filled with people on their way to work. All of the seats were taken. I stood by the doors about a third of the way back and kept myself balanced by holding on to a silver pole that protruded from the floor while I thought about this new information. According to Amy, Blitz and Gina had occupied the backseat of Ebony's car at the party. So it wasn't a stretch to think that Blitz could have had the envelope of money in his costume and that the envelope had fallen out. And continuing that train of thought, he could have gone inside and been confronted by someone—maybe someone who expected that very envelope of money—who killed Blitz for it.

But who at that party would have expected Blitz to hand over twenty grand?

There was Amy, who was noticeably angry at Blitz for cheating on her after a two-year relationship. A woman scorned was not to be taken lightly, and if she was angry enough, she could have snapped. But what did that have to do with the money?

Then there was Octavius Roman, who had been burned by

Blitz's last-minute cancellation. There was no easy explanation for why he'd been at the party in the first place, and $20,000 would have been a significant amount to him to absorb for the loss of business, even if his insurance covered the broken pipe. Had he snuck into the party and confronted Blitz in the kitchen over the money? It's doubtful someone would have questioned him. Just like Black Jack had said, anybody could have gotten into the party if they were dressed in the right costume. Who would have known if there'd been a stranger among us?

Gina Cassavogli's involvement had come out of left field. At first defensive over how I'd talked to Amy, I now knew that Amy had caught her with Blitz in the backseat of Ebony's car. And hadn't Gina threatened me with a lawsuit because her husband was an attorney? I wondered how that played into her master plan of having Candy Girls take over our business? I could hardly imagine that she'd want her activities with Blitz to become public knowledge.

I hadn't given much thought to Black Jack and Linda Cannon. Was it a coincidence that they'd been robbed days after Blitz's murder? Or had someone, not finding the money on Blitz at the party, broken into their house looking for it? Or had it all been staged, a way to bury them under community sympathy instead of looking too closely at their possible involvement?

The bus jerked to a stop. The sudden movement snapped me out of my thoughts. What was I thinking? I was so eager to find another suspect that I was practically accusing a family of murdering their son. But blood was thicker than water. I knew that better than most. Even though I'd moved away, at the first sign that something was wrong with my dad, I'd dropped everything and come back. And I'd stay as long as it took to make sure he was okay.

I climbed off the Zip-Two a stop early and walked the rest of the distance to Ebony's apartment. Her Cadillac was parked out front. I went around the back and knocked on the door that led to the kitchen. She answered a few seconds later, like she'd been close by.

"Hey, girl," she said. She wore a pair of faded denim bell-bottoms with patch pockets, platform sandals with cork soles, and a maize-colored shirt that was knotted at her waist. A long, tribal-looking scarf was knotted around her head. Ivory, who looked like little more than a dumped-out bag of cotton balls on the kitchen floor, sniffed her purple toenails. "What brings you here so early?"

"We need to talk," I said.

"Come on in."

I followed her through the back door to a small love seat out front. She paused when she reached the sofa. Ivory looked up at her and yipped, and she ran the palm of her hand over his puffy white fur.

"I know about the twenty thousand dollars," I said. Her head snapped up. First shock, then relief, and then an attempt to pretend she hadn't reacted at all flashed across her face in pulses. "You must have dropped it when you were loading or unloading your car. I found it after you drove away on Monday. I have it—not with me, but it's in the costume shop."

"You've had it all this time?"

"Ebony, I don't understand why *you* had it. You said Blitz didn't pay you. But I talked to Dig and he told me he found the envelope with Blitz's initials on it in your car. An envelope that had something dark and red smeared on it. And he told me how you took the money but threw the envelope out. What's going on?"

Ebony walked around the side of the sofa and sat down

next to Ivory. He settled down on the cushion next to her and put his paws on her thigh.

"Blitz told me he had my money. He said there was one thing he wanted for it. He wanted to know the truth about me and his dad. He didn't give it to me. I found it in my car. After."

"After what?"

"After he was murdered." She looked down at Ivory, who looked up at her. For a few seconds, it felt like they were having a wordless conversation. I liked to think that Ivory was the voice of reason, telling her to tell me what was going on. Perhaps he was, because when she looked away from him, she stood up and reached her hand down between the cushions of the sofa and pulled out a knife.

"What is that?" I asked. I needed to hear her say it to confirm my worst suspicions.

"It's the knife that I had in the kitchen. The one I was about to use to carve the goose. When I saw Blitz's body, I dropped it and it landed in the blood."

Her eyes were wide, the whites of them standing out against her coffee-colored skin. Her mouth was shaped like an *O*, which made her already-pronounced cheekbones stand out even more. Terror emanated off her in waves. Like a contagion, it made my throat restrict almost immediately.

"Why is it here?" I asked, fighting to keep my voice calm.

"I found it in the bushes behind my house. I don't know how it got there, but I know it means one thing. Somebody planted it to make me look guilty."

"But if you were holding that knife, then it wasn't the one used to kill Blitz."

She sank back down on the sofa, her hand wrapped around the handle of the knife. "Oh my God, oh my God, oh my God. What's gonna happen to me?"

"Ebony, you have to calm down." I leaned forward and put my hands on her wrists. The tip of the knife pointed down and poked me in the thigh. I moved my knees to the side. "Set the knife down here and tell me what happened."

She released it and it clattered to the coffee table in front of us. "When I went into the kitchen, I went straight to the oven to check on the goose. The oven is behind the kitchen island," she said. "In the corner. I pulled the goose out and set it on the counter, and then I got the carving knife out of the drawer. When I turned back, I saw Blitz's body on the floor. You came in and I dropped the knife. I was in shock."

"Then this knife should have stayed at the fire hall. Somebody else knew your fingerprints were all over it. They wanted to frame you. Where did you say you found it?"

She stared at it as if hypnotized. "In the bushes behind my back door. Sitting among the leaves, like someone tossed it when they walked past." She reached into the neckline of her tank and ran her fingers over her clavicle.

"Why aren't you wearing your medallion?" I asked suddenly.

"I can't find it."

The doors to Shindig opened and three uniformed police officers came in. One of them was Detective Nichols. I didn't know the others.

"Ms. Welles, Ms. Tamblyn," Detective Nichols said, nodding at each of us. "Ms. Welles, I'd like for you to come with me so we can have a long talk."

The knife sat on the table in front of us. It was the only thing on the table, and if the detective looked down, she'd see it. There was no way to hide it without making my actions obvious.

Detective Nichols looked down.

When she looked back up, her expression changed. "Ms.

Welles, do you want to tell me what that is on your coffee table?" she asked in a tight voice.

Ebony looked at me. The strongest woman I'd ever met looked terrified. I put my hands on her shoulders and squared her so she was facing me. "Now, listen to me. Never fear, because Margo's here. Nothing bad is going to happen on my watch. You got that?"

"You got enough on your mind with your dad that you don't need to be worrying about me too. I've gotten myself out of worse jams than this." She tried to smile, but tears filled her eyes.

"I will fix this," I said. The tears were contagious and my own eyes welled up.

Ebony turned to face the detective. "That knife came from the kitchen the day Blitz Manners was killed," she said.

"Am I going to find your prints on it?"

"Yes. And I agree. I think it's time we had a long talk."

The detective pulled a white handkerchief out of her pocket and picked up the knife. She didn't look at me. She gestured to Ebony, who stood and followed her out the front door, leaving Ivory and me alone inside of Shindig.

Yesterday, Detective Nichols had brought my scooter to Disguise DeLimit and had acted like a normal, nice human being. Twelve hours later, here she was, carting Ebony away like a common criminal. What had happened in that short amount of time? Just last night she'd agreed to look into what I told her about Amy Bradshaw. Clearly, she hadn't.

I was shaking. There was one person who would know how Detective Nichols thought, and that person was Tak. As much as I didn't want to make the call, I did.

"It's Margo. I'm at Shindig. Detective Nichols was here. She took Ebony away—" My voice caught and I coughed.

I did not want him to hear how upset I was. "Do you know anything about this?"

"I'm sorry, I don't. I had a meeting this morning and I left early. What did Nancy say?"

"Someone planted a knife at Ebony's house and the detective saw it. She and Ebony left to talk. What does that mean? Is a talk just a talk, or is it worse? You know how this stuff works from working for the district attorney, right?"

"Depends on what led Nancy to Ebony's house. Right now she's probably going to interview her, but if they left Shindig together, then Nancy has enough to hold Ebony overnight. After that, she's going to need a warrant to make an arrest."

"How long will that take?"

"She can only hold her for twenty-four hours."

Which meant if Detective Nichols was planning on arresting Ebony, she would need a judge to sign off on a warrant by tomorrow morning. Which meant I was going to have to find some answers tonight.

Chapter 24

"I DON'T KNOW what time I'll be back in Proper, but stop by the restaurant when you close the store. I'll try to meet you there," Tak said. I couldn't promise anything, so I thanked him and hung up.

My efforts to navigate Proper City via the bus had left me at the mercy of its every-twenty-minute schedule, and from a glance at the clock, I saw that I was between twenty-minute intervals. Besides that, I was now the temporary caretaker of one fluffy white bichon frise. I found Ivory's leash in a kitchen drawer and clipped it on, grabbed a bag of dog food, and then locked up Shindig behind me.

By the time I returned to Disguise DeLimit, the store was twelve minutes late in opening. A woman in a flowy floral dress and cowboy boots stood outside, staring into the windows at the sailor and *South Pacific* costumes. I said hello and unlocked the store while Ivory lifted his leg on the front of the building. The woman stepped over the small puddle and followed me inside.

I flipped on the lights. The stockroom door was open the width of one cat. Seconds later a guilty Soot appeared with Styrofoam pellets stuck to his whiskers. He took one look at Ivory, hissed, and ran upstairs.

"I'm sorry I was late getting the store opened," I said to the woman.

"Time is such an abstract concept," she said. "Five minutes here, five minutes there. Not a big deal."

I set Ivory behind the counter and prepped the register for a day of sales. The woman flipped through a rack of Hawaiian attire behind the window. She moved on to the picked-over wall of flapper dresses, and then to the display of clown clothes next to it.

"Please let me know if I can steer you in a direction," I called out. "I'm Margo, and this is my family's store. Sometimes people like to wander and get ideas, and other times they know exactly what they want."

"I'm a wanderer," she said. She let the sleeve of a brightly colored muumuu fall from her fingertips and looked at me. "I'm Willow. I just moved to Proper a few days ago, and I'm thinking about throwing a small get-together for a few clients. After I saw the photos from the other costume parties people have had on the Proper City website, I thought dressing up might be fun. Help break the ice."

I smiled. One of these days I'd meet the person who maintained the Get to Know Proper page on our website and I'd thank him or her. The photos that residents submitted of their parties showed off some of the best costume concepts we'd ever thought up. No way was I letting Candy Girls be the only game in town.

I welcomed the distraction of talking about costumes.

After building a barrier out of clown shoes to keep Ivory contained, I gave Willow my full attention. "If you're looking for costumes, you've come to the right place. We sell or rent. With rentals, there's a refundable deposit. If you rent and decide to buy, you can. If you buy and decide you wished you'd rented, well, I can't really do much about that after the fact." I stopped talking long enough to realize that I'd just hit her with a lot of sales jargon in a short amount of time. "Have fun looking around. We just acquired the sailor costumes that you see in the window, and there's lots of other stuff in the back stockroom."

Willow had a genuine look of curiosity about her. She pointed at the stockroom. "Anything back there that I don't see out here?"

Bobbie had mentioned the acquisition of ice cream shop uniforms, but I hadn't come across them yet. Who knew what else my dad kept back there in the disorganized mess?

"Aliens and G-men," I said. "We just acquired a collection from a sci-fi collector in Area 51. There's the usual, the little green men and some government-type outfits, but also some unique items that were handmade."

"Little green men! That sounds perfect. Is there any way I can see them?"

I looked at the stockroom door. Tak and I had made a little progress, but I wasn't comfortable letting a new customer get a behind-the-scenes look at the way we did business. Besides, there was the matter of the dead mouse that Soot had found, and the last thing I needed was for a customer to stumble upon one of those!

"I was going to work on a display of them today. If you don't mind waiting, I'll bring a sampling out front."

"Take your time," she said.

It occurred to me that a flowy floral dress and cowboy

boots was a good outfit for someone who wanted to appear nonthreatening. Soot must have thought the same thing. He wandered into the shop and brushed his fur up against Willow's ankles. She squatted and held her hand out for him to sniff. When he reached the same conclusion I had, he stepped forward and bumped his head into her open palm.

I left them alone and ducked into the stockroom, stacking several boxes onto the dolly. I added two white Tyvek suits that hung on hangers, and the single blue plastic suit that I'd gotten from the crime scene cleanup crew, and then wheeled the cart back out front.

"The boxes have heads inside, but this is a sampling of what someone could wear for the body of their costume," I said. I handed her the hanging costumes and unfolded the flaps of the cardboard box. From inside I pulled out three papier-mâché heads: two with antennae that bobbled around the top, and one vaguely peach-colored headpiece designed to look like a classic *SNL* Conehead. Her eyes lit up and she picked up the Conehead. "I haven't seen one of these in forever. Do you have any more?"

I looked in the bottom of the box. "To be honest, I don't know. When I said this collection was a recent acquisition, I wasn't kidding. I drove them here two days ago." I opened the next two boxes and peeked inside. Three more Coneheads.

"So far, there's four. Chances are good that there's more in the back. How many costumes do you need?"

"Eight, I think." She handed me back the Tyvek suits on hangers. "This seems a little heavy for the kind of weather we're having, but this blue thing looks like it might be perfect. Do you have eight of them too?"

"That's a sample," I said quickly. "I'd have to order them for you."

"That's fine. I have a couple of weeks."

"Great. Let me check for more Coneheads." I moved the remaining two boxes off the dolly and wheeled it toward me. The wheels locked up. I moved it back and forward to no avail.

"It's caught on something," Willow said. "Hold on." She bent down and picked up a chain with a shiny round medallion hanging from it. "Does this go with one of the costumes?" she asked, holding it up.

Ebony's lost medallion! I glanced at the ceiling and gave a silent thank-you to Saint Anthony. "That's Ebony's favorite necklace," I said, forgetting that Willow didn't know who Ebony was. "She said it was missing. I guess it fell off when we unloaded the boxes."

"She'll probably be happy to get it back. I don't think that's just any old necklace. That looks like a talisman." At my confused look, she continued, "A good luck charm or, more likely, something that comforts her."

"That's exactly what it is to her. How'd you know? Most people think it's just a necklace."

"I can tell from how the brass is shiny at the base of it that she probably rubs it regularly. Most people who have a favorite piece of jewelry become so accustomed to it that throughout the day they take a subconscious inventory to make sure it's where it should be."

"I've never heard that before," I said.

She blushed. "It's my theory."

"Do you always make up theories about people and what they wear?" I asked, wondering what she thought of my tuxedo T-shirt.

"It's kind of my job. I'm a counselor," she said.

"Like a shri—psychologist?" I asked.

"I'm not licensed like that. But sometimes people need people to talk to, and I try to provide a safe, confidential place where they can."

"Do you have a lot of clients?"

"I don't have any," she said. "I moved here from Texas, where I lived for the past twenty years. Time for a fresh start," she said. I sensed that there was more that she wasn't telling me, but it felt too personal to pry. "I rented a small bungalow at the edge of Proper City where I'll meet with clients." She pulled two textured, dirt-brown business cards out of her wallet and handed them to me. "Word of mouth helps, so if you know anybody who wants to talk, give them my card."

I ran my thumb and forefinger over the texture and read the lettering. WILLOW SUMMERS, read the card, and underneath, in italics, it said *TALK IS CHEAP*. A phone number followed.

"Thank you. I might," I said, and tucked the cards into the pocket of my trousers.

"If you don't, then plant them."

"Excuse me?"

"The cards. They're made from recycled paper and they're infused with seeds. Bury them in the dirt and you'll get the beginnings of a houseplant." She smiled. "Some people might prefer to talk to a houseplant than to talk to me. I figure it's good to have options."

Willow Summers had such a pleasant disposition that I was tempted to tell her all about Ebony on the spot. But I didn't. Instead, I wheeled the cart into the stockroom and loaded it up with three more boxes. We had to open only two to find the remainder of her Coneheads.

She reserved the heads for rental and ordered several of the blue plastic suits for pickup. I made a notation and promised to call her when they were in. Already the alien costumes were proving to be a nice addition to our collection.

As soon as she left, I called Ebony's cell to tell her that I'd found her medallion. She didn't answer. I tried the landline at Shindig, but I already knew that she wouldn't be there. Which meant Detective Nichols might be closer to getting that arrest warrant than I thought.

BY the time Kirby showed up at three, I was eager to leave the store. In addition to Willow's rental, I sold a dozen boas to a group of ladies who stopped in after a luncheon. I'd long ago learned never to underestimate the shopping power of a group of women who were powered by champagne and shrimp cocktail.

"Hey, Margo, any word on Jerry?" Kirby asked.

"He's coming home tomorrow," I said.

"That's great! That means things can get back to normal around here."

"Normal, right." If normal meant Ebony in jail for a murder she didn't commit and my dad selling the store so he could travel the country.

"Are you going to leave when he comes back?"

"I don't think that's a good idea. He has to learn to take it easy."

"Oh, okay, sure." Kirby's shoulders dropped. He walked past me and put his dune buggy magazine and keys into a cubby behind the counter.

I was taken aback by his reaction. As far as I'd figured it, he and I had gotten along just fine since my father's heart attack. Maybe he didn't like me telling him what to do. If that was the case, he'd have to get over it sooner rather than later. I didn't have time to get into that conversation because I'd been waiting for him to show up for hours. Now that he was here, I could finally get out of the store and try to help Ebony.

"I meant to tell you, I talked to Varla. She's stoked about the discount and the background. She asked if I could take measurements of the window so she could start working on something," Kirby said.

"Why don't you tell her to come and see it for herself? She can still take measurements, but it might help to see it in person."

"You want me to ask her to come here?" He turned beet red.

"Don't you think that makes the most sense?"

"I guess so."

"Great. Call her now if you want. I need to head out for a bit and I don't want to wait until it's too late."

He perked up. "You're going out? Sure, I'll take care of everything."

I scanned the store for a project to delegate, but Kirby was already opening the boxes that he'd carried inside. "If I'm not back by seven, are you okay closing up?"

"Yep." If I didn't know any better, I'd say that Kirby liked working in the store a lot more when I wasn't around. Was I such a bad boss? I shook it off, grabbed my keys, and left.

I took my scooter this time and drove directly to the house of Linda and Black Jack Cannon. The same black town car sat in the driveway as before. I parked the scooter and walked up the sidewalk, preparing to knock on the front door. I adjusted the hem of my tuxedo T-shirt and stood straight. The door was answered four seconds after I rang the bell, something I knew only because I counted out the Mississippis to help calm my nerves.

Linda Cannon answered the door herself. Today she was elegant in a light blue skirt suit set off with deep blue earrings, necklace, and ring set in gold. Her blond hair was up in a French twist and her lipstick looked freshly applied.

"May I help you?" she asked with no apparent recognition.

"Mrs. Cannon, I'm Margo Tamblyn. We met at your son's memorial service."

"The costume woman," she said.

"Yes, that's right."

She glanced at my T-shirt. "Won't you come in?" she asked, indicating a path behind her.

"Thank you." I entered the grand foyer and glanced up. The chandelier that hung over my head must have been at least twelve feet in the air. For a paranoid second I feared her hospitality was motivated by an elaborate plan to have the chandelier fall on my head, eliminating me from her life. I shook off the thought. It had been too long since my last therapy session.

"May I offer you something? Tea? Water? Wine?"

"No thank you," I said. "I came here to talk to you."

She picked up a glass filled with ice and took a sip, leaving a faint smudge of coral lipstick on the rim. "I'm afraid I may have been rude to you at the memorial," she said. "My husband thought it would be a good idea to throw a public memorial for our son, to help me grieve. At the time I agreed with him, but perhaps there are things that should be kept in the family."

"Mrs. Cannon, I understand that you were upset. I may have been a little upset myself. My father is hospitalized with his second heart attack in two weeks."

"That must be hard on your family," she said.

"My father is my family. My father and Ebony Welles."

"She's not your mother!" she proclaimed.

"She's the closest thing I have to one. My real mother died when I was born," I explained. "Ebony became friends with my dad when I was five. She was the most consistent female role model I had." Linda Cannon looked away. "I don't know what I would have done without her," I continued. "She taught me to be strong, honest, and hardworking. She's the person I turned to when I couldn't talk to my dad. And now—"

Linda set the glass down. "You seem like a fine woman, but I'll credit your father with your upbringing, not Ms. Welles. She has been nothing but trouble for this family since I first knew her. And after my late husband's generosity, what she did to my son . . . I just can't forgive her. I cannot."

"Ebony is innocent," I said quietly. "She didn't hurt Blitz."

"Margo, your loyalty is misplaced. Ebony Welles blackmailed my late husband, killed my son, and robbed my house. Now, I've been hospitable and invited you into my home, but if you are going to insist on defending that woman, then I must ask you to leave."

I stood up. "How can you convict a person without proof?" I asked.

She stood up with me. "The police have all the proof they need. Ask yourself: who was standing over my son's body with a knife in her hand?"

"That wasn't the knife that killed Blitz. The police know that."

Black Jack stepped into the room and put a consoling arm around his wife. "Margo, we can both understand that it's hard for you to accept what happened, but there's just too much evidence pointing to Ebony for us to ignore it. Maybe we could if she hadn't been linked to the robbery, but now"—he shrugged—"there's just no denying it."

"The robbery?" I asked. "What about Amy Bradshaw?"

"She's the one who put two and two together for the police," Linda said. "She found my engagement ring at a local pawnshop. She even spent her own money to buy it, the poor thing. It was awfully brave of her to come forward like she did, but she knew it was the right thing to do."

"When did this happen?" I asked. The information didn't fit together the way it should.

"Amy came to us yesterday," Black Jack said. "Once we spoke to the police, they tracked down the pawnbroker. He made the ID. Ebony Welles was the woman who pawned my wife's jewelry."

Chapter 25

EBONY COULD NOT have been the person to bring in Linda Cannon's jewelry. The robbery had taken place on Monday night and Ebony had been—Ebony had been missing all day. Before I tried to defend her, I needed to know where she'd gone.

I quickly assessed that it would do more harm than good to admit that I didn't know Ebony's alibi for the day of the robbery. What I did know was that Amy Bradshaw had been wearing that engagement ring on Sunday morning, a full day before the Cannon house was broken into. Maybe she hadn't expected me to notice, but I did. I'd even commented on it. And what had happened days later when I mentioned the engagement? Denial. Which meant one thing: she knew the presence of that ring on her finger on Sunday morning was going to create problems for her.

There was nothing more to be gained from an afternoon at Linda and Black Jack's house, so I made as polite an exit as I could under the circumstances. Across the street, Grady's silver sports car sat in the driveway. He would have easily seen my scooter when he parked his car. A friendly hello might have been in order, but all I wanted was to get out of Christopher Robin Crossing and find out what was going on.

It was after five. I hadn't eaten since my smoothie that morning and I was hungry. And I had to go to the bathroom. Not the best combination when driving a scooter over a road with potholes and ruts. Main Line Road was backed up with cars, and I'd never been the type of scooter driver who was comfortable easing my way up the aisle between two lanes of traffic. On the right, I saw the glowing sign for Hoshiyama Steak House. As soon as I got close enough, I pulled off and parked in the back.

Truth be told, it wasn't just the possibility of a bathroom that led me there, or the fact that Tak had asked me to stop by. My mind was a loop of problems with no solutions, and the best way think outside of the box was to get outside of the box. In short, I needed unfamiliar surroundings to shake me out of what I already knew.

I'd been a fan of teppanyaki restaurants since my sixth grade graduation. Dad, Ebony, and I had driven into Las Vegas for the day. He'd promised that I could pick any restaurant I wanted for dinner. After a day spent wandering around the strip, I think he expected me to choose McDonald's or Burger King, but I didn't. I spotted an old wooden building with a low gabled roof. MORI'S RESTAURANT read the sign over the door. A pretty lady in a pink satin kimono opened the front door and looked out. Her black hair was pulled back in a bun that was secured with sticks. She smiled at us. I thought she was the most beautiful woman I'd ever seen. My dad must have noticed, because he asked if I wanted to eat there.

"That's a restaurant?" I had asked.

"Yes. They make the food in front of you like a show," he said.

Ebony clinched the deal. "I love their fried rice. Let's go!"

They were right. I loved every aspect of it, from the outfits on the serving staff to the volcano that the chef made out of a sliced onion. After I moved to Las Vegas, I'd treated myself to lunch at Mori's every year on my birthday, even when the cost of the meal could buy my groceries for two weeks.

Tak's truck wasn't in the lot. I approached the door to the restaurant and prepared myself for the experience of dining alone. The table, I knew, would accommodate eight people. Me being a party of one, I'd be slotted into an empty seat at a table of strangers. I didn't mind—I never had. Sometimes sitting with strangers felt more comfortable than trying to force conversation with people I already knew. I ducked into the restroom out front and then approached the hostess station.

A woman greeted me. She had long, straight, brown hair streaked with gray, and was dressed in a green linen dress that ended just above her ankles. Tasteful flat brown sandals were on her feet. She wore very little makeup and her natural attractiveness shone through. Despite the creases by her eyes and laugh lines by her mouth, there was a youthfulness about her that kept me from pinpointing her age.

"How many?" she asked.

"One."

"Name?" She bent over the seating chart with a pen.

"Margo. Margo Tamblyn," I said.

She looked up quickly and smiled. "Follow me," she said.

She led me to a back table with three couples. Two empty chairs sat along the side of the table. I thanked her and sat in the chair to the right, leaving an empty chair between me and the couple to my left. Some people preferred their privacy, even in such a festive location. I scanned the menu, looking for my usual—sesame chicken—and cringed when someone sat in the chair next to me. I focused on the menu even though I already knew what I was ordering.

Dining alone in Japanese steak houses had become a way for me to practice being myself among strangers. Odd as it seemed, I was comforted by the anonymity of the people around me. But tonight, I couldn't stop thinking about the accusations against Ebony. I picked at my salad, rolling the single grape tomato around the bowl with my chopsticks, while the chef sliced and diced our food. He finished the whole presentation before I was done with my soup.

A woman in a kimono stepped up to my left. She held a black and red laminate tray. One by one she picked up my plate, my salad, my bowl of fried rice, and my glass of water.

"I'm not done," I said.

She nodded. "We have a better room for you," she said. "Come with me."

Three conversations stopped. Six pair of eyes watched me stand up and follow the woman to the side of the room. She went behind a large screen and I followed. I hadn't known there were private rooms in the back until she slid a wood-and-muslin panel to the left and exposed a low table flanked by even lower seats. She set the tray on the table and bowed slightly. I reciprocated. Moments after she left, Tak appeared in the doorway.

"Mind some company?" he asked. "Don't be mad," he said quickly. "My mom told me you were eating alone. If you want to be alone, I'll get out of here."

"Your mom?"

"The lady who took your name at the door."

"How'd she know who I was?"

"I may have mentioned your name around the house," he

said. He picked up the menu and studied the entrees with phony concentration.

I set my menu down and folded my hands in front of me. "I'm a big teppanyaki fan, so if you need me to recommend something, just let me know," I said. He set down his menu and shook his head.

"I mean it. You didn't ask for me when you came in, so if you prefer to eat alone, I'll leave."

I turned to face him and felt the weight of worry surround me like a giant, waterlogged teddy bear costume. I put my hand on his upper arm. "Stay," I said.

He put his hand on top of mine. "Okay."

We sat on opposite sides of the table. A man poked his head into the room. "I'll have what she's having," Tak said. The man looked at my plate and disappeared.

"Do you want to talk about Ebony?"

I set my chopsticks down. "She didn't do it. Any of it. I don't know why someone is out to get her and make it look like she did, but I'm going to—" I stopped abruptly. I still didn't know how much I could trust Tak. If he was here to pump me for information for the detective, I wasn't going to deliver.

"Remember how I told you that I was on leave from my job in the DA's office?" he asked. "That was only partially true. It's true that I'm on leave. The part that I left out was that it wasn't entirely my choice."

Tak took a drink of his water. "I became friends with one of the prosecutors. We both put in long hours and sometimes ran into each other after work. He had some structural issues with his house and asked me to come over and take a look. When I got there, he introduced me to his girlfriend. She was a county judge."

"They're hardly the first two people who met in a work environment and started a relationship," I said.

"In most companies, interoffice relationships are frowned upon. In the DA's office, that issue is magnified. Hal asked me not to say anything. Susan was up for pension in a few months and she was planning on leaving the bench after that.

"A couple of weeks later I heard a rumor that a judge was showing favoritism to one of the county prosecutors. That judge was Susan. When I asked Hal about it, he said opposing counsel was spreading the rumor so the case they were working on would be tossed."

"Sounds like a dirty tactic," I said.

"Maybe it was. Or maybe there was some truth to it. I don't know. The case was thrown out and a suspected murderer went free." He looked down at his plate and spun his chopstick around with his fingers. "Detective Nichols was the arresting officer. It was pretty bad when she heard the news and worse when she found out I knew about Hal and Susan's relationship."

He didn't say if he and Detective Nichols were still a couple then, but I put two and two together and assumed this was the catalyst for their split.

"Did Detective Nichols have something to do with you being put on leave?"

He looked up at me. His brows pulled together over dark brown eyes that looked troubled. I reached across the table and put my hand on top of his—the one not playing with the chopstick.

"I'm not the guy who runs to the principal and rats on the cheater. I'm the guy who works hard to get ahead. I mind my own business and I expect everybody else to do their job too. I don't know if the rumors were true. I don't know if opposing counsel manipulated things. I don't even know if Susan really was up for pension or if she and Hal discussed the case or if the suspected murderer was guilty. My job in the district attorney's office was to plan the expansion of Clark County, and I ended up learning something that I had no business knowing. Lives were changed because of that. My supervisor found out that I was friends with Hal and Susan. I was suspended pending review. And here we are."

"You didn't tell your parents the truth, did you?"

"No. I can't shame them. My dad thinks I wanted to quit. That's bad enough."

"What does your mom think?"

"My mom knows something about the job is troubling me. She doesn't know what it is and she respects my privacy. Since I came here, she's said that it's more important for me to be happy and live a life I can be proud of than it is to suffer under someone else's rules."

"Why did you tell me the truth?"

"This is going to sound pretty selfish, but I needed to tell someone. It's like it was building up inside of me and I was going to burst. Ever feel that way?"

Again with the mind reading.

Tak set down his chopsticks and turned to me. "Margo, there's something about you that's different from the people I worked with. They work hard to get ahead, sometimes sacrificing their personal lives for opportunities. Those people will start rumors to undermine a defender's case or get a judge pulled from the bench. They care about winning more than they care about the truth. But you—you're driven to find the truth no matter what it takes. You've got this spirit about you, this sense of loyalty to Ebony that I don't see every day. You believe in Ebony's innocence so strongly that I want to believe it too."

"That's because I know Ebony is innocent. She didn't kill Blitz Manners."

"But what if she did?" he asked.

"She didn't."

"It's that clear-cut to you, isn't it?"

I nodded. "Think of it in math terms. Imagine someone told you that the Pythagorean theorem was wrong. That C squared didn't equal A squared plus B squared. And they try to show you evidence to support their argument, but you know there's no way their evidence can be right, because you *know* the Pythagorean theorem is a fact. Do you see what I'm saying?"

"I think so."

"Tak, it's pretty simple for me. I know Ebony didn't do it. So somebody else did. I don't know who or why, but I know they did. And now people are making up evidence against her and it's making things worse."

"Tell me about this evidence."

"Amy Bradshaw came to Disguise DeLimit on Sunday morning and she was wearing a giant diamond ring. She made it sound like she and Blitz were engaged. Today I learned that she told Black Jack and Linda Cannon that she recognized the ring when she saw it in a pawnshop and bought it so she could return it to Blitz's mom. There's something wrong with that, but I can't figure out what."

"Why does it feel wrong? Talk me through it."

I leaned back and looked at him. "You really want to help me figure this out?"

"It might do us both some good to try."

Maybe it was the admission of what had really happened with his job in the district attorney's office or maybe it was the fact that he'd sensed how out of place me and my thoughts were in the middle of his father's restaurant, but I forgot about my trust issues and used him as a sounding board.

"For starters, Amy was wearing the ring on Sunday. The house was robbed on Monday afternoon. So if the ring was taken during the robbery, how'd she get it a day early?"

"Devil's advocate: what if somebody's been robbing the house over a period of time?"

"I thought that too. But why not tell someone about it right away? Why wear the ring at all if you planned to come forward with information about the robbery?" I sat back and moved the mushrooms around on my plate. "There's something wrong with Amy's story. And now the pawnbroker told the police that Ebony was the person to sell him the jewelry, so every other suspect has dropped off the list."

I ate a piece of sesame chicken. The flavors of garlic and butter melted in my mouth. For a second, my thoughts were reset and the only thing on my mind was the fantastic food in front of me. I ate another piece of chicken and then speared a piece of zucchini. Hunger returned in a way I hadn't expected, and conversation ceased while we ate. And then, as if the nutrients from the food had been the missing factor in the problem-solving part of my brain, a plan formed.

"If Amy Bradshaw bought the ring from the pawnbroker, then he should have something to say about her. I have to find out what he knows." I dabbed the corner of my mouth with my napkin. "I have to talk to the pawnshop owner. Are you with me?"

Chapter 26

"MARGO, LET ME ask you something. Do you really think Amy Bradshaw killed Blitz?" Tak asked.

"I believe that Amy Bradshaw knows more about the murder than she's telling. And I don't know why she's keeping secrets, but she's the one who led the police to the pawnshop, and the pawnbroker told the police something that led them to Ebony. I know Ebony isn't guilty, so I have to know what the pawnbroker told the police before I can figure out where everybody went wrong."

"You're solving for Y," he said.

"Sure, I want to know why, but I'll settle for who first."

"No, not *why*, Y. Like an algebraic equation. This comes up a lot in engineering. There are basic equations that you use when you know some variables but not all. You plug in what you know and solve for the rest of the information." I must have looked confused, because he continued. "It's like the Pythagorean theorem you mentioned. C squared equals A squared plus B squared, right?"

"Right."

"That's what everybody's working with. C squared is Ebony. Everybody thinks she's guilty. So they're finding the values for A squared and B squared that fit the picture where Ebony is the killer."

"But I know Ebony isn't guilty, so I'm looking for A, B, *and* C," I said, finally understanding.

"Right. Only you don't have to find A and B. All you have to do is prove that A squared plus B squared *doesn't* equal Ebony. You don't have to find the killer, you just have to show that Ebony *isn't* the killer."

That's where Tak and I disagreed. Because as long as the killer was out there, he or she would have the power to make life miserable for Ebony. People would continue to believe in her guilt until the real murderer was found.

I moved my napkin from my lap and set it on the table. It was after eight. Kirby would have closed the store over an hour ago. My dad was due from the hospital tomorrow morning, and I wanted to make sure everything was perfect before he and Don arrived. Which meant if I was going to talk to the pawnbroker, it was going to have to happen now.

"Will someone bring our check back here?" I asked.

"Don't worry about it."

"I didn't come here because I was looking for a free meal."

"Margo, forget about it. You're not going to pay for your dinner if you're dining with me in my family's restaurant."

I glanced at my watch again. I didn't have time to argue. I pulled $40 from my wallet.

"Don't insult me," he said.

"How is this an insult? It's a seventy-four percent tip."

A smile tugged at his mouth. "Okay, fine. I can tell you want to leave. Give me the money and I'll take care of it."

I pulled the money back. "No way. I don't trust you. I'll give it to your mother."

I scrambled up from the low seat and slid the closed screen open. The pretty woman from the hostess station was escorting a family to a table. In her place was the man who had called the police on Tak and me the night we came here for fried rice. Now that I'd spent a little more time with Tak, I could tell this man was his father. He was shorter than Tak and had a head of neatly trimmed gray hair instead of longish black hair, but the shape of his face, the sculptured cheekbones and jawline, the heavy brow, the deep brown eyes, they were all the same.

He looked up at me and recognition flashed in his eyes. I stood a little straighter and went directly to him.

"Mr. Hoshiyama?" He nodded once, slowly. "I'm Margo Tamblyn. I just finished dining in one of the private rooms with your son. I have to leave and I didn't have a chance to get my check. This will cover my dinner." I held out the two twenties. "I had sesame chicken and fried rice. I drank water."

"Did you enjoy your meal?"

"It was all very good." The same smile that I had seen on Tak's face tugged at the corners of his father's, but he didn't take the money. "I really do have to be going." I set the two bills on the hostess stand and left before he could stop me.

I drove away from Hoshiyama's and pulled the scooter into the parking lot next to Bobbie Kay's office. The lights were on. I hopped off and unbuckled my helmet while I was walking inside.

Bobbie sat on the floor in front, surrounded by patches of brown fur. A bag of fiberfill the size of a beer keg sat next to her. Behind her, a sewing machine sat unattended on the desk.

"Teddy bear fund-raiser coming up soon. I have to build up inventory." She held up her right hand, hidden inside a half-stuffed bear. His head had taken shape, but his arms and torso dangled limply. His legs hadn't been sewn together yet, so the fabric flopped around like that of a puppet. "You want to help?"

"I can't—not tonight. I have to go to the pawnshop."

She set the bear down. "Margo, there are better ways to get money than to pawn your possessions. You could donate them to charity and take the tax write-off. And you'd be helping those in need."

"I'm not going to sell," I said.

"You're going to buy? What could you possibly need to buy from Rudy's Pawn Shop?"

"I need to talk to the owner. His name is Rudy?"

"Rudy Moore owns the pawnshop out Main Line Road. It's the last stop out of Proper, or the first stop if you're coming back in. Does this have something to do with Ebony?"

"Yes." I walked past her and sat down in the chair behind her desk. "Apparently the pawnbroker said Ebony came in and sold him a bunch of jewelry that was stolen from Linda Cannon's house. I need to find out why."

"Sounds risky." She turned the teddy bear on her hand toward her face. "Doesn't it?" she asked him. He nodded his fully stuffed head twice. She turned him back to me.

I picked up one of the frames on Bobbie's desk. It was a picture of her in high school, the day she'd gotten a letter from the president. Two days later she'd checked herself into the recovery center. I admired how committed she was to her life of fund-raising and helping people. Her grades and her acclamations would have landed her a job with a Fortune 500 company after college, but she'd veered off that track when she went into rehab. As I watched her push another wad of fiberfill into the teddy bear's torso, I couldn't help but be proud.

I left Bobbie's office with a promise to call her in the morning and drove back to the costume shop to change into something that might make Rudy more apt to talk to me. I pulled a navy blue shirt and pants from the wall of uniforms and changed in the stockroom. The patch on the shoulder was generic; the word *security* was stitched in red thread against a white background. While technically it was a costume, we often rented this kind of thing out to people who were too cheap to hire real security guards but had recruited a volunteer to dress up and help maintain the presence of law and order at their event.

The pants were big in the waist, so I belted them with a belt from the gangster section, and then laced on a pair of black boots. I pulled my hair back into a low ponytail and left.

RUDY'S Pawn Shop was a small brick building that sat off to the left of an abandoned Laundromat. There was ample parking for what must have once been a thriving strip mall. I drove through the lot and parked close to the entrance.

Neon lettering in the front window of the redbrick building said RUDY'S PAWN SHOP—THE END OF THE LINE. I wondered how many of his customers thought that was funny. Underneath were the store hours: noon until midnight. The pawnshop customer wasn't an early riser. I locked my helmet to the seat of my scooter and went inside.

I wasn't prepared for the bright interior and blinked several times as my eyes adjusted. Once they did, I looked around. Rudy didn't seem to have much of a specialty. Walls were covered in colorful guitars, large paintings, framed sports jerseys, and wedding dresses. The latter surprised me. For some reason, the concept of a pawnshop had a masculine feel to it. I hadn't spent much time thinking about the women who needed to make money fast, and the reasons someone might be willing to hock their wedding dress in exchange for money gave me pause.

"Can I help ya?" asked an old, shriveled man from behind the counter. He had no hair on his head, but he more than made up for it with his bushy eyebrows. He wore a white undershirt and faded jeans held in place by a thick black belt with a tarnished silver buckle. He tucked his thumbs into the front pockets of his jeans and faced me with his shoulders rounded and his chest concave.

"I'm looking for Rudy," I said.

"Whatcha want him for?"

"I have a couple of questions for him. About the jewelry pawned from the Cannon house." I stood tall and mirrored his body language by placing my hands in the front pockets of my pants.

"You weren't here with those other officers," he said. "You look different than they did."

I had to be careful not to lie. Impersonating a police officer was a serious thing and I couldn't help Ebony if I needed help for myself. I pointed to the patch on my uniform. "Security," I said. "Not a police officer." I rolled my eyes. "I spoke to Linda and Black Jack Cannon earlier today and a couple more questions came up." All true. I held my breath and waited to see how the man would react.

"Those cops were a pain my butt," he said. "They knew I didn't want to talk to them. I didn't have much of a choice. Cops make people nervous and my business runs on trust."

Trust and pennies on the dollar. There's a business plan.

"I'm Rudy. What can I do ya for?" he said. His hands came out of his pockets and he leaned down on top of a case filled with guns. I hadn't noticed them earlier, and now the presence of so many weapons so easily obtained made me uncomfortable.

I started with a few basic questions. "If I understand correctly, the jewelry that was stolen from the Cannon residence came in here yesterday?"

"Yeah, that's right."

"Did you know where it was from?"

"The day I start asking questions is the day people stop bringing me inventory."

"When did you find out that it was stolen?"

"Last night. The cops showed up and asked me a bunch of questions."

"You told them about the woman who brought the jewelry in. Did she give you a name?"

"No, but she didn't have to. I described her to the police and they knew exactly who I meant. Ebony Welles, the party planner."

"So you know Ebony—I mean, Ms. Welles?"

"Well enough. I told the police it was her and described the medallion she was wearing and that was enough for them to put two and two together."

I reached out for the counter to steady myself. Ebony couldn't have been wearing her medallion—it was sitting at home on my counter. If that was the clue that brought the police to her door, then I'd just found a way to prove that when you put two and two together, you didn't always get four.

Chapter 27

"YOU NEVER SAW that medallion, did you?" I asked. Rudy stepped away from the counter. He didn't answer right away. "Can you describe it?" I added.

"I have to make a phone call." He went to the back. As soon as he disappeared, I took off out the front door. I'd gotten what I came for. Now I had to piece it all together and prove it.

EBONY had worn that necklace to the hospital on Tuesday. Several members of the staff had complimented her on it, and even Ivory had gotten his paw caught in the chain when we were at the rest stop. Probably, security cameras all over the hospital could verify it. When we'd returned from the hospital, she'd helped me carry the boxes from the trailer into the stockroom, and that's where I found the medallion this morning when I loaded the dolly with boxes from the trailer and the wheels jammed up. It must have been there since Tuesday. Even better, I hadn't been alone when I found the medallion. Willow, the new age therapist, had been there too.

So either Rudy Moore had encountered a different black woman who dressed like Foxy Brown and wore a gold medallion in his shop on Wednesday, or he was telling untruths to the police. But Amy Bradshaw had been the one to lead the police to him in the first place. Time to figure out why.

I drove from the pawnshop to Candy Girls, arriving around eight thirty. Only two cars sat in the lot: a black Lexus and a red Prius. The store's sign, a giant neon lollipop, spun around in a circle next to a smaller illuminated rectangle that said CANDY GIRLS—SUGAR AND SPICE AND PARTY PLANNING. Under that, in italics, it said *WHAT MORE COULD YOU WANT?*

I parked my scooter in a well-lit corner of the lot and locked up my helmet. The lights inside the store went out and two women exited. One was Amy. She and the other girl parted ways. Amy locked up the store and headed toward the red Prius. I waited until the other car drove away before calling out to her—Amy, not the girl who had left.

She was startled at first, but relaxed when she recognized me. "We're closed," she said. "Come back tomorrow."

"I'm not here for the store. I'm here to talk to you."

"I don't have anything to say to you," she said. Her voice trembled with nervousness, not the defiance I had expected. She glanced at my outfit. "Why are you dressed like that?"

"Like what?" I looked down at the security guard uniform. "I always dress in costumes from Disguise DeLimit. Everybody knows that."

She appeared to accept that, though her expression said something about what she thought of my style.

"I won't keep you long, but I have to talk to you. I know

the pawnbroker doesn't have proof that Ebony pawned Linda Cannon's jewelry. You took that diamond ring in to his store, not Ebony. Why did you lie?"

"I didn't lie," she said. Her voice shook again, worse this time.

"Then you won't mind telling me what you told the police." We stood that way, facing each other in the middle of the Candy Girls parking lot, for a few more seconds. I needed to say something to shake Amy up, to either scare her into making a mistake or touch a nerve inside of her so she'd help me.

"I know you were the one to vandalize Ebony's car. I found a scrap of plaid fabric caught in the car door. The pants of the costume you tried to sell me were torn. I also found an empty can of black hair spray from Candy Girls in the backseat, and I know it's what you used to write *Murderer* on her car. Those things connect you to that. So far, only a few people know about the vandalism, and nobody knows about the piece of fabric, but I won't hesitate to go to the police with it and show them that you've been trying to make Ebony look guilty since the day after the party."

Under the glow of the blue neon sign, Amy's pale face looked sick. Her eyes were wide, and dark circles under them made her look like she was wearing clown makeup to age her twenty-something face.

"Either you're guilty or you're covering for somebody," I said.

Her face tightened up, and then her eyes filled with tears. She tipped her head back and the tears fell down the sides of her temples. When she looked back at me, more tears spilled down her cheeks. She wiped them away with her fists, leaving smudges of eye makeup to further darken the circles that were already there.

"Nothing that I did to Ebony's car was permanent. I told

you, I caught Blitz with Gina in the back of that car. After I went and put together our Charlie's Angels costumes, that's how she repays me! I was so angry. When I found Blitz, we got into an argument." She wiped her nose with the back of her sleeve. "I left before he was killed. Later that night, when I saw the car parked in front of your store, I—I just snapped. I had the hair spray in my car and I just started spraying it."

"Why did you write *Murderer* on Ebony's car?"

"I didn't! I sprayed the doors and the roof. And then I smashed empty glass bottles against the side. I was trying to break the window, but it didn't break. The glass fell all over the sidewalk. I was afraid to walk over it, so I opened the back door and crawled through to the other side to get out."

"How did the fabric get caught in the window?"

She cursed. "Why can't you leave it all alone? The vandalism doesn't have anything to do with the murder!"

"I think the police should be the judge of that," I said. I stepped backward as though I were leaving.

"Wait," she said. I turned back. She balled her fists up in the hem of her lime green T-shirt and twisted the fabric until it was stretched out. "I wanted it to look like the window was broken so I rolled the window down from the inside. The hair spray can fell out of my hand and I hung out the window to grab it. I didn't know my pants tore, but they must have gotten caught on something—a piece of metal trim inside the car or something else sharp—I don't know what. And then I tossed the cans in the back and I left out the other side. It's the truth. I'll tell the police. I promise. I will! I want this all to be over."

"What about the flat tires?"

"I held the core of the stem in with a screwdriver. My brother taught me how to do that when I was a kid. I'm telling you the truth."

It wasn't the time to point out to Amy that a broken window would have left glass inside the car and not outside on the sidewalk or to advise that the next time she uses hair spray to vandalize a car she should take the Candy Girls price tag off the can. Her story explained a lot of things, but not enough. If she hadn't painted the word on Ebony's car, then who had? And if Blitz had cheated on her at his party, why had she shown up at Disguise DeLimit the next day pretending they were engaged?

"Amy, where did you get the ring you were wearing when you came to my store on Sunday?"

Her fists dropped to her side and she looked at the ground. "I saw the ring at the pawnshop last week." She glanced up at me as if to gauge if I was judging her or not. I kept as impassive a face as I could so she would continue. "That night, I asked Blitz about it. He said it couldn't be his mom's because that was her most precious possession from his real dad. I don't know what happened on Friday, but Friday night he came over to my house and gave me something wrapped in several layers of tissue. He said he had just done the most important thing of his life and not to let anything happen to the package."

"When did you look inside?"

"Sunday morning. After I heard the news. I knew he wasn't coming back for it." She hung her head. "Two years together—that's a long time. Enough that he trusted me with that bundle. I had to see what it was, because I didn't know if it was something that would get me killed too. When I saw it was his mom's ring, I figured he bought it out of hock. I know it was wrong of me to put it on and act like we were engaged, but he wouldn't have asked me to keep it for him unless maybe he thought that one day he really would give it to me."

"Why did you leave when I asked for your name?"

"You were asking too many questions. I thought you

somehow knew the ring wasn't mine to wear and I didn't want to get in trouble with Blitz's family."

"So when the Cannons were robbed on Monday, you talked to the police."

"I had to. They thought the robbery on Monday was the first one. I was the only person who could tell them that the ring had been hocked sometime last week. I told them when I saw the ring at the pawnshop, and I told them that I told Blitz. I gave the ring back to Mrs. Cannon on Wednesday."

"That's why you acted so funny when I asked about it at the memorial."

"I didn't tell them that I wore it for a few days. Nobody knows that but you and me."

I bit at my lower lip. "Amy, there's just one thing I don't understand. Why did you come to my store on Sunday?" If everything Amy was telling me was true—and it did have a note of authenticity to it—then showing up with her torn costume while wearing Blitz's mother's ring was a pretty dumb move.

"Gina wanted me to donate our costumes to Candy Girls. After she helped Blitz cheat on me, I wanted to make her mad. I knew it would drive her crazy if I sold it to you."

I thanked Amy for talking to me and drove home. Back at Disguise DeLimit, I changed out of the security officer uniform and into my alien-printed pajamas. I sat at the kitchen table, staring at my clues. Piece of plaid fabric. Empty can of black hair spray. Twenty thousand dollars. And now Ebony's medallion. Four things that told the story of who murdered Blitz Manners—or rather, who didn't. Amy's story explained away the hair spray and the fabric. They implicated her in the vandalism, but not the murder. I separated them from the money and the medallion so I wouldn't consider them evidence. Amy had also said that Blitz got the ring out of hock on Friday. But the supposed robbery hadn't taken place until Monday. Maybe I'd been right about someone had been stealing from Linda Manners all along.

I added a piece of paper to the table and wrote *Columbo trench coat* along the bottom. It was a clue that would have pointed the finger at Grady if I had it, but I didn't. It had been incinerated along with everything else that came out of the fire hall after the party. That cleanup crew had made sure the crime scene could never be revisited.

I picked up the chain of the medallion and let it dangle from my fingertips. What had Willow called it? A talisman. Something that Ebony wore to give her strength. I didn't have a talisman. I changed my accessories and my overall look the way most people changed nail polish. If it was true that a person's identity could be gleaned from their personal style, then I was a lost cause. I put on and shed identities of fictional characters because they were easier to adopt than to look inside myself and identify what made me who I was. And here, it was Ebony's talisman that poked a hole in the story that the pawnbroker had told the police.

I called Detective Nichols. "This is Margo Tamblyn. I have some new evidence in the Blitz Manners murder case."

"Why does that not surprise me?" she said. "What do you have?"

"Ebony Welles's necklace. She wore it all day on Tuesday when we were at the Moxie Hospital, and the chain must have broken when she helped me unload the trailer we brought back here. I found it in the costume shop this morning. The pawnshop owner said that a black woman with a medallion pawned the jewelry, but that's not possible. Ebony didn't have her medallion on Wednesday or today. He's lying."

"I think it's safe to say that Ms. Welles might own more than one gold necklace," she said.

"But this isn't just any old necklace. It's a talisman. She wears it everywhere."

"Ms. Tamblyn, I can appreciate that you don't want your friend to go to jail, but I've already taken the evidence to a judge and I'm expecting a warrant for Ms. Welles's arrest to come through tomorrow morning. That means she stays in the county jail. And don't worry too much about that necklace. We don't allow inmates to wear jewelry."

I was so angry I wanted to scream. "You're going to let a killer go free because you're too caught up in believing Ebony is guilty. What do I have to do to show you she's not?"

"Ms. Tamblyn, I'd say we have a pretty solid case. I wouldn't waste any more time if I were you."

Chapter 28

"DO YOU HAVE anything else for me?" Detective Nichols asked.

I thought over the conversation with Amy. It had filled in a lot of blanks for me, but it wasn't new information to the detective. "You're holding the wrong person," I finally said.

"I'll take that as a no. Good night, Ms. Tamblyn."

She hung up first. I set my phone down and laid Ebony's necklace on the sheet of paper marked MEDALLION. That left the money and the trench coat.

The trench coat equaled Grady. What else did I know about him? He lived close enough to Blitz's house that he could have gotten in to steal. He even could have used their friendship to gain entry without raising suspicion. I'd heard that both he and Blitz were big practical jokers. Had this started out as a joke? Steal a piece of jewelry and hock it—and then sit back and watch while the family freaks out?

I didn't understand the kind of games that these people would play, but as far as theories went, it felt thin.

And then there was the money. Dig had found it in an envelope in Ebony's car, and the envelope had blood on it. That meant the envelope had been on Blitz when he was killed and somebody took it and put it in Ebony's car. When? And was the plan all along to frame Ebony, or had her presence in the kitchen made her the easiest decoy?

Volunteering that Ebony had had $20,000 from Blitz after he was murdered would have raised a lot of questions. Some people might have claimed it was her motive. After Dig found it in her car, she must have moved the cash to a blank envelope. Maybe she was going to put it in the bank. Maybe she was going to hide it in her house. Maybe she was going to give it back to the Cannons. But she couldn't do any of those things. Not while under suspicion.

But the money still didn't make sense. Why had Blitz been carrying so much money at the costume party? His own costume party? Either it *was* the money he intended to pay Ebony with or he was planning on using it to pay someone off. But for what? Ransom?

Maybe Amy was lying about how she came to be in possession of the ring. Maybe she'd been the one to steal it all along. And maybe, just maybe, she demanded money in exchange for its return.

Blitz liked to play the joker, the leader of the pack of prep school pretty boys, but I'd learned enough about him to know that under that façade was a guy who had been forever changed the day his real dad died. Sure, he had money to spare, but the one thing he couldn't buy was the family he once had. That ring would have meant something to him, more than what it was worth. If someone stole it, he'd get it back, regardless of the price.

I thought it through. I had to follow the money. Blitz had the money at the party but it ended up in Ebony's car. There'd been blood on the envelope, which told me the killer had moved the envelope from Blitz to the Cadillac. Whatever Blitz had planned to do with that money didn't matter. Someone had used it as a diversion.

I picked up the phone and cued up redial. Would the detective believe me if I called her again so soon? Would she even take the call? I set the phone down. The last thing I needed was to annoy her while she was pushing to arrest Ebony. I didn't know what would happen if a judge signed off on the warrant, but if a warrant was issued, I'd annoy the detective plenty.

I pushed concerns about Ebony aside to focus on getting the place ready for my dad to come home. The combination of Soot and Ivory running loose was like having to clean up after a pair of five-year-olds who'd been allowed access to a playground. Pillows had been shoved from the sofa thanks to pushy paws, and the bedspreads had been tugged off center thanks to sharp kitty claws. Litter had been tracked a few feet from the litter box, and Ivory had left a little surprise on the kitchen floor. Toys were strewn about, like the discovery of a new one meant ignoring the last. I walked from room to room, peeking under chairs and tables, rounding them up. Both animals lay in the middle of my bed, two feet apart. Soot's head was propped on his paw. Ivory was upside down with his paws in the air. Neither had a care in the world.

I woke up Ivory with a gentle stroke of the fur and he rolled over and yipped.

"Outside," I said. "No more surprises in the kitchen." I clipped a leash onto his collar and we went downstairs and out back. He delivered both number one and number two almost immediately, and then hopped around my ankles like he was ten pounds lighter.

Back inside and upstairs, I dusted, ran the vacuum, Windexed mirrors, and mopped in the kitchen. Three bags of garbage and one overflowing bin of recycling were lined up by the stairs. I carried them downstairs one by one and dragged them to the curb. By the time the house was done, it was after midnight. My mind was losing focus and my body ached with exhaustion.

I went downstairs to the costume shop and found a note from Kirby taped to the register.

Day ended with rentals of Wizard of Oz *costumes for birthday party. Credit approved, sales slip under cash drawer in register. I unpacked, steamed, and restocked fringed dresses. Black Jack Cannon called about his next poker game. Hospital called and said Jerry will be released in the morning. I'll come after class to welcome him back.—Kirby*

It had been nice of Kirby to leave me a status report when I hadn't come back by closing time. He was a good employee. I'd have to talk to my dad about expanding his hours, especially while Dad was recovering. Kirby and I had been able to hold it together for the week, but when I went back to Las Vegas, there was no way Dad would be able to run the shop on his own.

I found the record of the rental deposit under the cash drawer like Kirby had said. Combined with Willow's order for the Conehead costumes, it had been a good day. Not just a good day, I realized, a good week. The murder hadn't affected our business at all. In fact, Blitz's party had introduced us to a whole group of people who might not have otherwise shopped with us. I had Black Jack to thank for that, I guessed. He'd rented *Maverick* costumes for his last poker game, and when Grady paid for the forty detective costumes, he said he'd square the bill with Black Jack.

Slowly, I felt a chill climb up my skin under the loose legs of the alien pajamas. Maybe Black Jack had offered to pick up the tab for the costumes since he had rented costumes from us in the past. Maybe Blitz had figured what the heck, let the old man do something nice for him for his birthday.

Or maybe everything Amy said really was true, and she had nothing to do with Blitz's murder. Maybe Black Jack did.

I closed my eyes and tried to think through my cloudy, tired brain. Black Jack had access to his wife's jewelry. Black Jack had known who wore which costume at the party. Black Jack had not benefited financially by marrying into the Manners fortune because Brody Manners had left his fortune to Blitz.

I picked up my phone and started to dial the police station. A sound from the stockroom startled me. I glanced at the door, open the width of either one cat or one dog. Or both.

"Soot? Ivory? Get out here," I said. Seconds later, the two of them streaked past me like Wile E. Coyote chasing Road Runner.

I set the phone down and crossed the store. When I reached for the doorknob to the stockroom, a hand shot out and grabbed my wrist and pulled me into the darkness.

Chapter 29

I STUMBLED FORWARD but kept my balance. My eyes were still adjusting to the lack of light. I blinked several times until I made out the stacks of boxes that had been opened earlier. They sat at odd angles in the middle of the room, blocking my view behind them.

"Who's there?" I called out. There was no answer. "I'm calling the police," I said.

"No, you're not," said Black Jack. He stepped away from the shadows and stood facing me. He wore a tall, black cowboy hat like the one we stocked for our Western costumes, a leather blazer over a collared shirt, jeans held up with a large belt buckle, and pointy cowboy boots.

And a gun. He held a silver gun.

I was so used to picking accessories for costumes that, at first, the gun didn't seem out of place with the rest of his outfit. When the threat of the revolver sank in, I realized how helpless I was.

"You're not calling anybody," he said. "Your phone is upstairs on your kitchen counter. Right next to your table of clues."

An ice-cold fear engulfed me. "You were in my house?"

"That was nice of you to give me some alone time when you took the dog out. By the way, you did a good job straightening the place up for Jerry's return tomorrow. Let's hope you don't make a mess of things down here by getting blood all over everything."

I stood rooted to the spot. My eyes had adjusted enough to make out the shelves surrounding the room and the costumes hanging below them. A few of the boxes had been labeled since Tak and I had worked in there. More of Kirby's helpfulness?

Black Jack stepped forward. "You've been nosing around too much," he said. "I can't risk anybody finding out what I did."

"You mean finding out that you killed your son?" I said boldly.

"My son. That's a joke."

"But you did kill him," I said.

"I killed him because he wouldn't play ball with me. All he had to do was let me hock his mom's jewelry. The engagement ring was just the beginning. Once we reported the robbery, the insurance would have paid out and I'd get the money I needed. But he wouldn't let it go. He actually thought the jewelry was more valuable than the money."

"Why do you need money? You have the most successful dealership in Proper City."

"They don't call me Black Jack for my health, hon. I've got deep debts and it's time to pay up. I thought I'd be sitting pretty after I married Linda."

"But killing him didn't solve anything. It just created more problems for you." I didn't know how long I could keep him talking, but I didn't know what else to do. While I talked, I stepped backward and touched the costume behind me. My hand connected with suede fringes. The Western costumes.

"Why did you kill him?"

"Brody Manners's will left all that money to his kid, but in the event of Blitz's death, it reverts to Linda. Twenty-five million dollars," he said.

His eyes glazed over. I fingered along the suede fringes until I found a leather belt with holsters like the one I'd worn last week. Slowly, I felt along the belt until I gripped a toy revolver. I tucked it into the waistband of my pj's by the small of my back. It was light and plastic—I was sure Black Jack Cannon's gun was neither.

"Reverts to *her*, not to you. What makes you think she'll give you half?"

"Nevada is a community property state, sweetheart. Once I divorce her, half of what she owns is mine. With Blitz dead, that half just got twelve-point-five mil richer. And there's nothing Linda Manners can do about it."

Black Jack's slip of Linda's surname told me one thing. He hadn't married her for her love and companionship. He married her because she was the widow of a very rich man.

"You won't get your hands on that money," I said.

"Oh yes, I will. It's just a matter of time."

Bobbie had told me about Blitz donating money to her charity, and about how he'd wanted to help people for the sheer good of it, not for the accolades that would come his way if his philanthropic gestures were known. If the public didn't know about his actions, I guessed Black Jack didn't know about them either.

"Blitz gave his money to charity," I said. "He's been doing it for years. Linda knows that he wants his money to help people. Brody's will says what happens to his money, but Blitz had his own plans for his inheritance. You killed him but you're not going to see a dime of his money."

Black Jack raised his hand and struck me.

Pops of light sparked behind my eyeballs. I fell to the side, grasping at the cardboard boxes for support. The fake revolver fell out of the back of my waistband and landed on the floor.

"Well, well. What have we here? The little lady's been armed all this time." He started toward the gun and my foot shot out and kicked it away from him. I knew it wouldn't do anybody any good, but if he thought it was real, I might have a chance at holding my own.

"I knew you were down here," I said. It was as big a lie as I'd ever told in my life. "I heard you when I carried the recycling down."

"You pay too much attention to what goes on around you, you know that?" He narrowed his eyes. "That's why you're here with a gun pointed at you. Poking around in other people's business isn't a good idea."

"This isn't other people's business. It's my business. This store is mine, and you sent Blitz here. You made him my business."

"*Your* store? I thought it was *Jerry's* store." He stepped forward again. I stood my ground. His gun was within a foot of my pajamas. If he pulled the trigger, no way he'd miss.

"I'm taking over the store so my dad can recover. He— he's due here tonight. That's why I'm cleaning so late. He'll be here any minute."

Black Jack's eyes cut to the door of the stockroom. It was the fraction of time I needed.

I pushed a cardboard box into him and he dropped his gun. I kicked it in the same direction as the plastic pistol. He grabbed my pajama top. I pulled away. He yanked me toward him. The fabric tore. I kicked at his shins but my alien slippers were no match for his cowboy boots. He twisted the fabric of my shirt in his fist and pulled me back toward him. I stumbled backward into his chest. His spicy-beef-stick breath puffed onto my cheek from behind. "You're too much trouble," he said.

"H-how'd you do it?" I said.

"Silly costumes made it easy. I threw on a trench coat and a fedora and nobody even noticed me."

"But the trench coat went with the Columbo costume," I said.

"You think there's only one trench coat in Proper? That worked out nicely, though. I always planned to set up that black woman but the trench coat spun you off on Grady's trail for a little bit. I wouldn't have minded him being taken down. Payback for his dad sticking it to me on my casino debts."

"What do you have against Ebony?"

"She made an easy suspect. My wife never liked her because of her history with Brody."

"So you framed her for murder because it was easy? You took the money from Blitz after you killed him. That money was intended for Ebony all along. If you were after money, why didn't you take it?"

"Twenty grand is pocket change compared to what I'm going after." He narrowed his eyes and watched me.

"How'd you get the pawnbroker to identify Ebony?"

"I'm one of Rudy's best customers. You think he's going to mess with me? Paid him off to ID your friend. Best money I ever spent. Even if the police never did see the word *Murderer* painted on her car, they found the knife I planted. Like I said—easy."

"You hired the crime scene cleanup crew, didn't you?"

"That's right." He let go of my pajama top and pushed me

into the boxes in front of me. They toppled over and I fell to the concrete floor. "Least I could do for the owners." He stepped past me into the dark corner of the stockroom. I knew he was looking for the guns. I had to keep him from finding them—or at least from finding his.

"You stashed the trench coat in the kitchen after the police were done with the crime scene. You wanted it to be found. You hired the cleaners and knew they'd incinerate it."

He laughed. "I waited until after the police released the crime scene and got the cleanup crew in there quick. Perfect opportunity to eliminate the evidence." His voice was muffled by the costumes hanging from the racks. I forced myself up, first to all fours, and then upright. I reached into the box next to me and pulled out a papier-mâché alien head. Swiftly, I ran up behind Black Jack and pushed the large hollow mask over his head. He twisted, too late. The head came down to his shoulders, swallowing his cowboy hat, his head, and his ability to see.

He cursed. His voice was muffled and dull from inside the mask. He bent down and felt around the floor for the gun. When he connected to it, he let go of me. He brought the gun around and pulled the trigger, firing it.

Click. Click. Click. Click. Click. Click. Click. A real gun would have exploded. A real gun would have fired seven bullets into me.

A real gun would have killed me.

He tossed the plastic revolver aside and tried to stand. I pressed down on the papier-mâché head with all of my weight. I saw Black Jack's cell phone jutting out of his pocket. I grabbed it and dialed 911 with my thumb while he swung at my legs.

"Help!" I said. "Costume shop on Main Line Road. Black Jack Cannon is trying to kill me. You have to break in. Hurry!"

Black Jack swung out with a wide punch that caught me in my midsection. He knocked me back a few steps and the phone fell from my hand. Before I could change my momentum, he lifted the alien head from his body and tossed it to the side. One of the antennae bent at an odd angle. He came at me, fists balled up, anger on his face.

And then, before he reached me, keys sounded in the front door of Disguise DeLimit, followed by the squeaky sound of a wheelchair rolling in.

Chapter 30

"MARGO? ARE YOU here? Don, the stockroom's open. Wheel me over there. Something doesn't seem right." My dad's voice both comforted me and scared me to death. He'd come home early. I bet he'd wanted it to be a surprise when I woke up. Only now I couldn't warn him. I couldn't save us both.

Black Jack took advantage of my surprise. He leapt forward and clamped a hand over my mouth. With his other hand he grabbed the gun and then turned me around and held me back against his chest. "You or your dad," he hissed in my ear. "Do you understand?"

I stifled sobs and nodded. I wouldn't put my dad's life at risk. Black Jack moved us to the side of the stockroom to a space between costumes. If my dad or Don looked in, they wouldn't see us. Not unless they passed the knocked-over stacks of boxes, and by then it would be too late.

Tears stung my eyes and salted my already-bruised cheek.

Had the 911 operator sent someone to check on me? Or had she written the call off as that of a crackpot? Would anybody come here to help us, or would the Tamblyn family line die tonight in the stockroom, surrounded by costumes?

Faint light shone into the stockroom. I saw the chair roll in. My dad's legs were loosely covered in a light blanket. Don was behind him. He whistled. "This place is a mess!" Don said.

· My dad scanned the interior from right to left. His eyes flitted over the hanging costumes and the newly labeled boxes. His scan stopped at the dented alien head on the ground. "Looks like Margo was doing a little reorganization," he said. "Probably wanted to surprise me. No use making her feel bad because we caught her mid-project." He put his hands on the wheels of the chair and rolled backward. "Roll me out, Don. It's late and you probably want to get home."

Anybody else might have thought I'd missed my window for help, but not me. My dad had seen something in the stockroom that let him know there was trouble. He was going to get help. I relaxed the slightest bit, until I felt the barrel of Black Jack's gun jab into my ribs.

Don apparently hadn't gotten the hint. He left his helm at the chair and came farther inside the room. He picked up the damaged alien head and tried to unbend the broken antennae.

"You better tell your daughter to take better care of the inventory," he said. "This can probably be fixed, but it'll never be the same." He looked up from the head and looked directly at me. I stood as still as I could. "Margo? Why are you hiding in the stockroom?"

Everything happened in slow motion. Black Jack released his grip on me and pointed his gun at my dad. I couldn't stand seeing a killer aim a gun at someone I loved. I grabbed his arm with both hands and brought it down on my knee. He wailed in pain. I ran forward and pushed my dad's wheelchair backward. He rolled out of the stockroom.

Right into Detective Nichols and a team of police officers.

I woke up sometime the next day. The only thing I knew was that the sun was shining brightly through my bedroom windows. Soot was on the foot of the bed, licking his paw and washing his head as if nothing particularly exciting had happened. I sat up and felt pain throughout my body. That's how I knew not to believe Soot's innocent act.

"You're awake," my dad said. He walked into the room, using a cane. He picked up a pillow and pushed it under my head so I was half sitting up. "You really surprised me last night," he said.

"I needed help last night. I don't know what would have happened if you and Don didn't show up when you did."

"Detective Nichols showed up a few minutes after we did, thanks to some information you told her earlier in the night and a call you made to 911. You kept your head on straight in the middle of a very scary situation. I'm proud of you."

I put my hand on top of his. "Everybody needs a little help taking care of themselves. But there's one thing I don't understand. I saw the look on your face when you came into the stockroom. You knew there was trouble. What was it?"

"I could tell the place had been reorganized. The shelves, the signs, the hanging costumes. If you took the time to organize it, you wouldn't have left the new costumes broken in the middle of the floor."

"That's it?"

"That and the plastic pistol you like to wear in your holster. It was lying on the ground."

"But what did that tell you?"

"It was dark and I saw a gun on the ground. I didn't know it was a toy. It was enough to tell me to get out of there and get help. What I don't understand is, why didn't you call out to us?"

"Black Jack told me it was me or you." The tears from last night returned, filling my eyes and overflowing down my cheeks. "Where is he now?"

"In jail. Where he'll be for a long time, thanks to you."

I leaned back against the pillows and thought about what had happened in the past twenty-four hours. Detective Nichols and company had taken Black Jack into custody. I'd given my statement before the police cleared out. The last of my energy had been spent scaling the steps, showering, and falling into bed.

"Do you think your job will understand if you stay away for a few more days while we wrap everything up here?" my dad asked.

"About my job," I started. He patted my hand, and I said what had been on my mind for the past few days. "When you were in the hospital in Moxie, you said you were willing to give up the store. And everybody keeps telling me how you want to go out around the country and scope out costumes for the shop. It's what makes you feel alive." I turned my hand over and squeezed his fingertips.

"Margo," he said, "the heart attack changed my priorities."

"It changed mine too. I want you to live the life you want to live, but I'm not ready to let the costume shop go. Not for a long time. I want to stay here and run the store."

"This isn't what I wanted for you."

"You always said you wanted me to find out what I wanted for myself. This is it." I leaned forward and told him about my ideas for displays and marketing, about how Kirby had approached the set designer of his school's drama club about painting backdrops for our windows, and how we could create themed party packs for people who didn't have their own ideas. I told him about Willow and the Conehead costumes and the medical uniforms that I'd learned about from the crime scene cleanup crew.

"You've really been thinking about this a lot, haven't you?"

"I'm a thirty-two-year-old woman who likes to dress in costume. I think running Disguise DeLimit just might be the perfect job for me." Soot walked across the bed and butted his head into my dad's hand. I looked around the room, confused. "Where's Ivory?"

"Ivory is out front with his owner."

"Ebony's here?" I asked. I threw the covers back and winced at the pain that shot through me.

"Join us when you're ready. She's not going anywhere."

I climbed out of bed and glanced in the mirror. I had a black eye—or rather, a purple, green, and yellow eye. There was pretty much only one costume that would hide it. I dressed in a pair of black leggings and a loose white puffy shirt, and then, after brushing my hair, slipped a black leather pirate's patch over my head.

Ebony was in the kitchen with my dad. I threw my arms around her and she squeezed back tightly, as though she thought she'd never have the chance to hug me again.

"Now things can get back to normal." She looked around and knocked on a wooden spatula. Today her Afro was pulled back into a puff on top of her head. She wore large gold hoop earrings, a latte-colored silk dress, and strappy gold sandals that laced up her calves.

"You're still missing something," I said. I picked the medallion from the table and hung it around her neck. "*Now* things are back to normal."

Immediately her fingers rubbed the metal. I thought about Willow's theory and knew, no matter how confident Ebony appeared to be, her medallion gave her strength.

"You never told me where you got that necklace," I said.

"My mother gave it to me before she died," she said. She looked at the metal, raised it to her lips, and tucked it into the neckline of her dress. "Now before you go hammering me with a hundred questions, sit down and relax."

"Why are you both up here? Shouldn't someone be downstairs running the store?"

"Kirby's down there. He said he didn't mind watching over things as long as you were up here."

Since everything ended last night, I couldn't stop thinking about giving up my job in Las Vegas and moving back to help run the store, but it bothered me that I hadn't bonded with Kirby the way everybody else had.

"You guys wait here. There's something I have to do," I said.

I found Kirby by the accessory wall, restocking neon fishnets and brightly colored plastic earrings. "Can we talk for a second?" I asked.

"Sure." He set the box down and looked at me. "Your dad told me what happened here last night. I can't believe Black Jack was holding you at gunpoint." He looked down at the toe of his black Converse sneaker. "I wish I'd had more of a chance to get to know you."

"You'll get that chance. I'm leaving my magician's assistant job and moving back to Proper. I'm going to work right here."

"That's why I'm looking for another job."

"Kirby, I know I don't have a lot of experience being the boss, but did I do something to offend you?" I asked.

"Offend me?" He seemed confused. "No."

"Then why do you want to quit?"

"I don't. But I know there's only enough work here for two people, and I figured it would be you and Jerry."

I couldn't believe how badly our signals had crossed. "My dad's not healthy enough to work, not yet. But when he does make a full recovery, he's going to head out around the country and look for new costumes for the store, like he did with the alien costumes from Area 51. I'm going to need somebody to help me run things here, and I was hoping that somebody could be you."

"Really? I could use the money," he said. His eyes lit up.

"Not just a few hours here and there, but something more regular. A permanent schedule. Do you think you could do that?"

"That would be awesome!" he said, and then, as if embarrassed by his enthusiasm, he thrust his fists into the front pockets of his baggy jeans. "Thanks, Margo. You're pretty cool," he added.

High praise coming from a seventeen-year-old. We shook on the deal, and then he handed me a package wrapped in plain brown paper. "I almost forgot. This came in the store's mail, but it's addressed to you so I didn't open it."

In lieu of a return address, the package said $+\Delta=?$ Money plus change equals possibility. Money Changes Everything.

"Anything important?" Kirby asked.

"Yes, I think it probably is." I started back up the stairs. Halfway up I stopped and watched Kirby pick the dune buggy magazine out of the trash bin, dust it off, and open it to a dog-eared page.

I carried the package to my bedroom and shut the door behind me. I pressed my ear to the door for a few seconds to make sure I was completely alone before I tore into the paper.

Inside the wrapping was a plain white shoe box. I opened

the lid and found a furry brown teddy bear with a note pinned
to his chest.

Dear Margo,

This bear needs a home.
(He also needs a costume.)
Welcome back to Proper City!

Love,
Bobbie Kay

I thought about Bobbie and her teddy bears, Tak Hoshiyama and his family's restaurant, and Ebony and Shindig.
All over Proper City were people who had decided that a little
desert town inspired by fairy tales and designed by city planners was the place they wanted to call home. Even the wealthy
families had put down roots in Christopher Robin Crossing
instead of moving to a more status-conscious city.

The people who lived here were a lot like me: friends,
neighbors, people who wanted to dress up for the sheer fun
of it. As long as people lived in Proper City, Disguise DeLimit
would be A-OK. And maybe, with a store full of costumes at
my disposal, I'd be okay too.

Disguise DeLimit Costume List:
Blitz Manners's Detective Party

Columbo
Rockford
Kojak
Nancy Drew (1930s)
Nancy Drew (1950s)
Mr. Moto
Nick Charles (*The Thin Man* movies)
Nora Charles (*The Thin Man* movies)
Ironside
Remington Steele
Cannon
Magnum, P.I.
Bob-Whites: Trixie Belden
Bob-Whites: Honey Wheeler
Bob-Whites: Jim Frayne
Bob-Whites: Mart Belden
Bob-Whites: Brian Belden
Judy Bolton
Tom Swift
Cherry Ames, school nurse
Three Investigators: Jupiter Jones
Three Investigators: Pete Crenshaw

Three Investigators: Bob Andrews
Philip Marlowe
Sam Spade
Hardy Boys: Frank
Hardy Boys: Joe
Miss Marple
Veronica Mars
Hercule Poirot
Shaft
Inspector Clouseau
Sherlock Holmes (classic)
Sherlock Holmes (BBC/Benedict Cumberbatch)
Sherlock Holmes (CBS/Jonny Lee Miller)
Sherlock Holmes (steampunk/Robert Downey Jr.)
Encyclopedia Brown
Mike Hammer
Perry Mason
Ace Ventura, pet detective

Recipes

———

*

HOSHIYAMA FRIED RICE

(serves 2–4, depending on hunger)

2 tbsp. sesame oil
2 tbsp. butter
2 cloves garlic, minced
2 scallions, sliced
2 cups cooked rice
½ carrot, diced
1 stalk of celery, diced
1 cup bean sprouts
Soy sauce
1 egg
Sesame seeds

1. Heat sesame oil and butter in skillet. Add minced garlic and scallions and raise temperature to medium. Cook for about 2 minutes. Push mixture to side of skillet.

2. Raise temperature to high. Add rice, stir-fry for 1 minute. Add vegetables. Add 1 tbsp. of soy sauce. Mix well and cook

for additional 1–2 minutes. Push everything to sides of skillet, leaving room in center of pan.

3. Beat egg slightly and pour into center of skillet. When egg begins to set, scramble and combine with rice mixture.

4. Add additional splash of soy sauce.

5. Sprinkle with sesame seeds and serve.

———

CATCH-22 SALVADORIAN SHRIMP SALAD

(makes 2 big salads or 4 smaller salads)

1 lb. uncooked, peeled shrimp
2 tbsp. butter
1 packet Goya Sazón seasoning (for lower sodium, use
1 tsp. achiote/annatto)
1 head lettuce (romaine, red leaf, green leaf, or iceberg)
½ carrot, sliced
1 Roma tomato, diced
1 cup jicama, sliced
1 avocado, sliced
½ cup white onion, diced
1 bunch cilantro

1. Cook shrimp in saucepan with butter and Sazón for 3 minutes. Remove from heat and let cool.

2. Tear lettuce onto plate.

3. Add: carrot, tomato, jicama, avocado, white onion. Add cooked shrimp and drizzle any juices from pan on top.

4. Garnish with cilantro leaves.

DRESSING: FRESH SALSA ROJA (RED SALSA)

Olive oil
¼ cup white onion, chopped
1 clove garlic, chopped
1 jalapeño, chopped
2–3 Roma tomatoes
1 tsp. dried oregano
Salt
Pepper
¼ cup cilantro

1. Place all ingredients in blender.

2. Puree until smooth. Add water if necessary.

———

MARGO'S EASY FRUITY PEBBLES DINNER

Fruity Pebbles cereal
Milk

1. Pour Fruity Pebbles into bowl.

2. Add milk.

Costume Ideas

A creative costume lies less in the construction and more in the imagination. The best way to determine a good costume is to choose a recognizable character and then identify 3–4 elements that are unique to him or her. Often it's not only the clothes that make a costume work, but it's the additional props that sell the concept. Here are a few examples pulled from Blitz Manners's birthday party:

SHERLOCK HOLMES

1. Deerstalker hat
2. Men's plaid suit
3. Tweed cape*
4. Prop: pipe
5. Prop: magnifying glass

*Instructions for making an easy, no-sew, costume-appropriate cape:

1. Buy 2 yards of fabric
2. Fold in half (cut edge to cut edge)

3. Fold in half again (side to side)
4. Lay flat
5. On the folded corner, cut a small quarter circle out of all layers
6. Cut a large quarter circle out of all layers of the unfolded edges
7. Unfold one time. Fabric will still be folded in half, but will now resemble a semicircle with a smaller semicircle where the head will go
8. Cut a straight line down the center of the fabric from the neck hole to the hem
9. Cape is complete!

For enhanced instructions and photos, visit dianevallere.com.

COLUMBO

1. Men's rumpled trench coat (suggestion: purchase from thrift store)
2. Men's rumpled suit in neutral color, white shirt, and black skinny tie (thrift store)
3. Wedding ring
4. Wet all clothes and garments, ball up, and run through dryer for extra wrinkles
5. Prop: cigar
6. Prop: police badge

CLASSIC NANCY DREW

1. Sweater set
2. Plaid skirt (below the knee)

3. Blond wig that falls to shoulders
4. Cloche hat
5. Prop: magnifying glass
6. Prop: invitation from Ned Nickerson
7. Prop: set of car keys labeled ROADSTER

MISS MARPLE

1. Turtleneck
2. String of pearls
3. Wool blazer
4. Wool skirt (below the knee)
5. Thick tights
6. Sensible shoes
7. Wool hat with brim
8. Prop: magnifying glass
9. Prop: teacup

KEEP READING FOR A SPECIAL PREVIEW OF
DIANE VALLERE'S NEXT COSTUME SHOP MYSTERY . . .

Masking for Trouble

COMING SOON FROM BERKLEY PRIME CRIME!

THE LAST TIME I had been this close to an angry lab rat was high school. That time, I'd understood the rat's anger. He'd been forced to live in close quarters with four others, and, having once shared an apartment with four girls myself, I recognized the universal crankiness that comes from the invasion of personal space.

Today, the angry lab rat in front of me had a different reason to be upset. I'd just accidentally jabbed him in the head with a fistful of pipe cleaners.

"Hold still," I said. "If I don't get these pipe cleaners in at the right angle, the ears will never stand up." The lab rat mumbled something unintelligible. "You have to stop talking! I can't understand you."

The rat reached up his arms—two furry white appendages that ended in pink oven mitts—and lifted the carefully crafted mask from his head. "You're going to have to put more ventilation in there," Kirby said. "I could barely breathe."

Kirby Grizwitz was a part-time employee of Disguise DeLimit, my family's costume shop. After my dad's heart attack six months ago, Kirby's hours had become more regular, filling in his spare time between swim team practices. Usually his job responsibilities included keeping the racks straight, handling rentals, and cataloging new inventory, but October was to our costume shop what April was to tax accountants, and our individual job responsibilities flexed to fit the needs of the business. Today's need was to put the finishing touches on a giant lab rat costume for Kirby's chemistry teacher. He'd allowed his honors class to choose his costume for this year's Halloween, and they'd decided to go ironic. Enter Disguise DeLimit.

"More ventilation. I can do that. But look, the ears are perfect." I took the head from Kirby and turned it around so it faced him. He seemed unimpressed. The cowbell over the front door rang, and Ebony Welles walked in. I quickly pulled the rat head over my jet-black hair and stepped behind the register.

Ebony was a strong black fifty-six-year-old woman in a 1970s wardrobe. She had a brushed-out Afro, a collection of bell-bottoms to rival J. J. Walker, and a white bichon frise named Ivory. I'd never known my own mother because she died in childbirth, but Ebony was like a mom to me—having stepped into the surrogate role sometime around when I was five. She and my dad had never been more than friends, though they often acted like an old married couple, especially when it came to raising me. Somewhere along the last fifteen years, her concerns had shifted from convincing my dad to raise my allowance to helping me find a nice single man and settle down.

Ebony had enough superstitions to challenge the most powerful rabbit's foot, and this time of year she preferred not to venture far from Shindig, her party planning business. When she did, she added what we called her "October Accessories": a garlic necklace, silver-bullet earrings, and a rubber mallet that no one could explain except that it might help her destroy zombie brains.

I watched her scan the interior of the store. When her eyes alighted on me, I stood straight up. She pointed a shiny black talon at me. "See, that right there is what's wrong with this holiday. There ain't no good reason for a giant lab rat to be running around our city."

I dropped down behind the counter, knocking a tray of vampire teeth into a plastic tub filled with foam clown noses. The tub spilled and round foam balls rolled across the floor. The mask shifted so I could no longer see, and, even more than before, I had trouble breathing.

As it turned out, Kirby was right. The mask needed more ventilation.

Muffled sounds from the costume shop blended in with indiscernible noises around me. I put my hands on the head and lined up the mesh that I'd inserted for vision and watched a group of teenage boys flip through a rack of motorcycle jackets.

"She's coming this way," Kirby warned.

I put my hands on the back of the counter and pulled myself up enough to peek over the top. Sure enough, Ebony was steps away from where I crouched.

"It's no use, Margo. I know it's you."

Slowly I stood and pulled the rat head off. From the corners of my eyes I could see my hair defying gravity thanks to static electricity. I set the head on the counter and smoothed the ends of my flip with my fingers.

"It doesn't matter. I was just trying it on to show Kirby that the ears were straight. That's not my costume for tonight."

"I certainly hope not. No way you're going to meet a man dressed as a giant rat."

"What about you? What are you wearing tonight?"

"Ebony doesn't need a costume. You know why? Ebony is going to be safely locked away inside of her apartment." When she was worked up, she liked to refer to herself in the third person. The idea of spending time at an old, run-down hotel that she not-so-secretly believed was haunted definitely got her worked up.

"Best costume has come from Disguise DeLimit for the past twelve years. You don't want to help our odds? We're not about to let it fall into the hands of an amateur," I said.

"You'll win. You always do." She looked down at the rat head and tugged on the pointy, blood-tipped teeth that jutted out from under the nose. "He is kinda cute," she said. She adjusted his blood-tipped fangs, smiled, and left.

Kirby pulled the pink mitts off his hands and threw them down on the floor next to me. "I thought she'd never leave. That garlic was making me hungry for pizza." He reached around behind himself until he found the ties that kept the rat suit closed in the back, undid them, and shrugged out of the body of the costume. It fell to the floor in a mound of shaggy white fur, and Kirby was left wearing his Proper City Prawns swim team T-shirt and jeans. He kicked the costume to the side by the plastic tub of colorful clown noses and stormed off.

Halloween was just shy of a week away, but tonight was the big kickoff costume party at the long-vacant Alexandria Hotel. The tall brick building had been abandoned decades ago, and was sorely in need of some TLC. A wealthy developer had purchased it, but agreed to allow the residents of Proper City to hold our annual party inside. Ebony had turned down the job of converting the interior into a suitably haunted but not dangerous reception hall. Something about not wanting to stir up the ghosts and goblins who had taken to the hotel after it had been boarded up. Candy Girls, the tacky ready-made costume/theme party supplier—who, much to our chagrin, occasionally gave both Ebony and Disguise DeLimit a run for our money—had ended up with the job.

The party started at six so even the youngsters could go and was the first chance the residents of Proper had to show off their costumes for the Halloween season. Ebony might have planned to stay away, but not me. In a couple of hours, I'd be in my own costume, meeting up with a friend in the parking lot, ready to see how everything would turn out.

The cowbell over the door chimed and I looked up. A fiftyish man in a black business suit walked in. His shirt and tie were impeccable, and his briefcase was practically brand new. His white hair was parted on the side and smoothed into place, and contrasted sharply with the black frames on his glasses. I came out from behind the counter and met him halfway in the store.

"Nice costume," I said. "Government agent? We carry clip-on IDs if you'd like to accessorize."

He looked down at his suit and then up at me, confused. "I'm looking for Jerry Tamblyn, owner of Disguise DeLimit. Is he here?"

"No, he's not. I'm Margo Tamblyn, his daughter. I run the store these days. Can I help you with something?"

The man's expression told me he wasn't here to rent a costume. He reached down to a bookcase filled with brightly colored clown feet and pushed the feet to the side, knocking a few pair onto the floor. I stooped to pick them up. He set his briefcase on the top of the shelf, popped open the locks, and pulled out a white envelope.

I glanced around the store. Kirby was busy with the teenagers by the rack of black leather jackets. One of the girls held a pink satin jacket with PINK LADIES embroidered on the back. Two teenage girls held up shapeless red-and-white striped all-in-one jumpsuits that we rented with blue wigs. Thing One and Thing Two from *The Cat in the Hat*. Always a good choice.

"If you're selling something, I'm not interested," I said. "We're pretty busy right now, so I can't spare any more time."

"I'll only take a moment of your time. I've tried at length to contact you by mail. I can only assume from your lack of response and your continued focus on renting costumes that you've chosen to ignore the issue."

"What issue?"

"The issue of Halloween. As you know, this year's festivities are scheduled to take place at the Alexandria Hotel in West Proper."

"I know all that. What's the problem?"

"The problem is that I now own the Alexandria Hotel, and I've restricted access to the party to those in my employ." His mouth pulled into a line that must have been what passed for his smile. "Read the letter inside. The situation is self-explanatory." He checked his watch again, and then closed up his briefcase and lifted it from the now-empty shelf. "Good day, Ms. Tamblyn," he said. He turned and left without waiting for me to look inside the envelope.

Kirby joined me. "What was that all about? Government agent needs Jerry's testimony about some aliens?"

"No. That man said he bought the Alexandria Hotel. He said now that it's under private ownership, we're being banned from entering a costume in the contest!"